contents

PROLOGUE	1	AT RIVER NUMBER 50 — Crisis_of_Blue_Ocean.
CHAPTER 1	7	WHO WILL MAKE THE PREEMPTIVE STRIKE? — First_Contact.
CHAPTER 2	39	DETONATOR — Natural_Bomb.
CHAPTER 3	87	THE SCORCHING LAVA'S AIM — Case_to_War.
CHAPTER 4	127	COLLAPSE OF RULES AND ISOLATION — Trident.
CHAPTER 5	167	WHAT SHOULD YOUR STRENGTH BE USED FOR? — The_Old_Glory.
EPILOGUE	229	THE EVER-RELIABLE BIRDWAY — Queen_Period.

"You're up, widdle Mister Cheat Code."

Sorcerer of Gremlin, an organization fusing science and sorcery

Salonya A. Irivika

VOLUME 3

KAZUMA KAMACHI
ILLUSTRATION BY: KIYOTAKA HAIMURA

New York

VOLUME 3

KAZUMA KAMACHI

Translation by Alice Prowse
Cover art by Kiyotaka Haimura

This book is a work of fiction. Names, characters, places, and incidents are the product of the author's imagination or are used fictitiously. Any resemblance to actual events, locales, or persons, living or dead, is coincidental.

SHINYAKU TOARU MAJUTSU NO INDEX Vol.3
©Kazuma Kamachi 2011
Edited By Dengeki Bunko
First published in Japan in 2011 by KADOKAWA CORPORATION, Tokyo.
English translation rights arranged with KADOKAWA CORPORATION, Tokyo,
through Tuttle-Mori Agency, Inc., Tokyo.

English translation © 2024 by Yen Press, LLC

Yen Press, LLC supports the right to free expression and the value of copyright. The purpose of copyright is to encourage writers and artists to produce the creative works that enrich our culture.

The scanning, uploading, and distribution of this book without permission is a theft of the author's intellectual property. If you would like permission to use material from the book (other than for review purposes), please contact the publisher. Thank you for your support of the author's rights.

Yen On
150 West 30th Street, 19th Floor
New York, NY 10001

Visit us at yenpress.com
facebook.com/yenpress
twitter.com/yenpress
yenpress.tumblr.com
instagram.com/yenpress

First Yen On Edition: September 2024
Edited by Yen On Editorial: Maya Deutsch, Ivan Liang
Designed by Yen Press Design: Andy Swist

Yen On is an imprint of Yen Press, LLC.
The Yen On name and logo are trademarks of Yen Press, LLC.

The publisher is not responsible for websites (or their content) that are not owned by the publisher.

Library of Congress Cataloging-in-Publication Data
Names: Kamachi, Kazuma, author. | Haimura, Kiyotaka, 1973– illustrator. | Prowse, Alice, translator.
Title: A certain magical index new testament / Kazuma Kamachi ;
illustration by Kiyotaka Haimura ; translation by Alice Prowse.
Other titles: Toaru majutsu no index NT. English
Description: First Yen On edition. | New York : Yen On, 2023.
Identifiers: LCCN 2023042206 | ISBN 9781975380656 (v. 1 ; trade paperback) |
ISBN 9781975388355 (v. 2 ; trade paperback) | ISBN 9781975388379 (v. 3 ; trade paperback) |
ISBN 9781975388393 (v. 4 ; trade paperback) | ISBN 9781975388416 (v. 5 ; trade paperback) |
ISBN 9781975388430 (v. 6 ; trade paperback)
Subjects: LCGFT: Light novels.
Classification: LCC PZ7.1.K215 Cem 2023 | DDC [Fic]—dc23
LC record available at https://lccn.loc.gov/2023042206

ISBNs: 978-1-9753-8837-9 (paperback)
978-1-9753-8838-6 (ebook)

10 9 8 7 6 5 4 3 2 1

LSC-C

Printed in the United States of America

PROLOGUE
At River Number 50
Crisis_of_Blue_Ocean.

[Nov. 10 / Source: Oahu, EAC News relay camera in a press conference room]

"Time is of the essence, so let's keep introductions short. I doubt you fine ladies and gentlemen want the recording to be buried in flowery words. And the masses on the other side of the cameras are always looking for a thrill."

A man in his forties was speaking. He had pronounced Latino facial features and a level of intimidation and wildness your average teen punks couldn't hope to match. His dark skin hid muscles rivaling average athletes. Somewhat unfortunately, one didn't get a particularly *intelligent* impression from him, but the citizens bore the responsibility for choosing him anyway.

Roberto Catze.

He was the president of the United States of America and the third Latino person to ever hold the office. Tell him that, though, and he wouldn't be proud—because he wasn't the *first*. Instead, with a perfectly straight face, he would implore you to call him the first president ever to have dropped out of high school.

The suit, necktie, and leather shoes he was wearing had all been provided to him by benefactor groups; the outfit looked less like something he'd chosen to wear and more like something they'd forced on him. But nobody mistook his absent-mindedness for sloppiness—one of the man's rare talents was his ability to make himself approachable.

"So time for questions! We explained the gist of it at the ceremony two hours ago, so don't go asking anything you already know the answer to. Waste this precious time, and you'll just be laughingstocks for the viewers."

"Mr. President," said one of the reporters gathered there, raising his hand. "You mentioned the giant golden rings and bones that appeared during World War III being discarded in the seas near Hawaii. *Why did you accept that worthless debris?*"

"A mediocre question. We're already in a publishing recession—the good folks at the *Condor* must have their work cut out for them."

"Why bring it into U.S. territory instead of leaving it in international waters? Was there a political motive for the decision?"

"No, it's simpler than that." The president waggled his index finger. "If you just drop a bunch of those things in the middle of nowhere—and they're dozens of meters long each, let me remind you—you'll alter the ocean currents. Naturally, that could eliminate sources of plankton and oxygen, which could disrupt the entire ocean ecosystem. *We* investigated waters around the world to find a place to dispose of them, and the zone we settled on just so happened to be close to Hawaii. Make sense?"

"Mr. President, local fishers and surfers have voiced their concerns as well. What would you say to them?"

"I've shown them the results of Glamorous Devil's simulation. If you're unfamiliar with it, that's what they call the supercomputer in Florida. But for some reason, every single one of them fell asleep twenty minutes into our explanation. They must really trust us!"

"Some are of the opinion that we brought these objects into U.S. waters for the purposes of surveying them behind closed doors."

"You have to pick your words better, Mr. Journalist. That isn't an opinion, it's speculation—and if you really want to get precise, it's anti-American propaganda from the German Intelligence Service…

Whoops! Look at me, calling them out like that. I shouldn't have announced our disagreement with the EU this early…"

The president actually stuck his tongue out bashfully in front of all the cameras as the young newspaper reporter looked down and trembled, trying to hold in his rage. One of the journalist's duties was to get the president to mess up during press conferences and say things he shouldn't—but now, it was like the president was just *giving* everything to him. Catze didn't even seem to think he was in conflict with the press. Moments like these were why *London in God Magazine* had described the president as "a strange politician who likes to let things slip to raise his approval ratings."

A different reporter raised her hand. "Mr. President, it seems like the EU is trying to dump the golden rings and bones by going through the Atlantic Ocean, but they don't appear to be financially compensating us enough for it. Could I get your thoughts on this?"

"Hey, come on now! I'm the president of the USA, so keep your questions domestic. It's like you're asking me to talk about another woman during a dinner date."

"May I put that on the record as sexual harassment?"

"Oh, when I pursue a woman, I give her enough memories to make her forget all her complaints."

A middle-aged male reporter cut in. "Is that why you're the first single U.S. president, Mr. Scandal? Because women also forget you proposed to them at all?"

"I can't help not being used to it, Nick. Or do you want me to be the first president to go bankrupt over alimony payments instead? 'Cause I might rack up as many divorces as the U.S. has rivers."

[Nov. 10 / Source: Oahu, tourist video camera near a press conference room]

"Mommy, where's the president?"

"You might be able to get a little peek at him."

In the center of the frame was a five-year-old girl with blond hair, with the voice coming from off-screen belonging to her mother. The girl waved her little U.S. flag around. "If I wait here, will he shake my hand?"

"I'm not sure about that, honey. They're a lot stricter now with all the terrorist things happening. We might not even be able to get close to the row of black cars."

While the mother was being extremely blunt about it, facts were facts. If she didn't tell her daughter the truth, the girl would be liable to let go of her hand and charge toward the cars.

The security measures recently put in place due to the war were so outlandish they beggared all description. The president's escorts would show no mercy to anyone who approached him, even a five-year-old girl.

…And because of that, their recording would be worth a whole lot more if they could just get a glimpse of the president's face on camera—at least something they could brag about to the neighborhood. Unfortunately…

"Huh?"

"What is it, Jenny?"

"It's the president. The president's coming this way. Hellooo!"

The video image shook suspiciously.

Young as the girl was, she saw the president's face on the news every morning, so she'd never mistake him. But…

Then it happened. The camera shook violently. The video lost its meaning. It was snatched away.

Someone had plucked the video camera from the mother's hand as she tried to aim it where her daughter was pointing.

Outside the frame, which now showed a tilted picture of the young mother's abdomen, an exchange could be heard.

"Eek! What did you do that—? HUH?! M-Mr. President?!"

"Sorry about this, miss! I need to borrow this for a moment," said Roberto Catze, his tone completely different from how it sounded on TV. "Unfortunately, I'm not indiscriminate enough to go after someone who already has a kid, so let me be quick!"

"H-hey, what are you even doing here?!"

"Mr. President, can I have a handshake?"

In the wobbling camera image, the tall Hispanic man politely did as the little girl asked, then ran a large hand through her hair before getting his own face fully into the frame of the camera.

His eyes darting every which way, he said, "You may not believe me, but something has gone terribly wrong at the core of our government. We don't know the details yet, but external factors are at play. People who were sane just yesterday are now enemies of the USA, and they're trying to take it over from the inside. Who they were before all this doesn't seem to matter. Ultimately, I run the risk of having the same thing happen to me if I go to the White House. So I'm going to erase all information related to my whereabouts for a time."

With irregular noises mixed in—his ragged breath was probably hitting the mic—he continued:

"I repeat. I am voluntarily erasing all information on my whereabouts. My disappearance is *not* the result of a kidnapping. Whoever sees this, please stay calm. As the commander in chief of the United States of America, I'll confront the threat taking hold of our nation."

After Catze said his piece, the image tilted dramatically. He must have given the video camera back to the mother. It wobbled more, showing the president's full body.

Clutching his small attaché case in one hand as he gently moved the woman away from him with the other, he said, "Don't bother tellin' the police about this. Probably won't matter anyway. As long as my comments are available somewhere in the U.S., that's all that matters. You and your little one should enjoy Hawaii like nothing ever happened."

Ignoring the still-baffled mother, the president walked straight across the crowded highway. The back door of the press conference room was already open, and several men in black suits ran across the frame.

"Wow... We got more than a little peek, huh?" said the woman, cradling the treasure she now held in her hands in excitement.

"Mom, do you think I can marry the president...?"

Her daughter's disturbing words, however, brought her back to reality.

CHAPTER 1
Who Will Make the Preemptive Strike?
First_Contact.

[Nov. 10 / Source: Oahu, surveillance camera at New Honolulu International Airport customs]

Even though it wasn't the height of the summer or winter tourist seasons, people were still packed like sardines in the gates of the airport. Hawaii's main industry was tourism, though, so if people stopped coming, the entire archipelago's economy would come crashing down.

Sightseers, businesspeople, carriers, and a guy with a card hanging from his neck—a researcher of volcanoes, perhaps, or of tropical fish. The crowd could be separated into a few general groups, but among them were a few particularly strange people.

That Asian with the spiky hair, for example. Or the third-ranked Level Five walking next to him.

...You *could* slot them into the sightseeing group, of course. But it was still strange that a boy and a girl, both minors, were loitering in the international airport without parents or adults to assist them.

"...Birdway's group isn't here yet? She said we'd meet around here."

That was the boy speaking—Touma Kamijou. Despite knowing zero foreign languages, he was acting oddly accustomed to being overseas. However, he'd been shaking madly just twenty or so minutes ago on the passenger plane, incoherently muttering words like *parachute* and *seven thousand kph* under his breath. Evidently, his time on the plane hadn't been great.

Meanwhile, the girl—Mikoto Misaka—was having issues of her own.

Ah, crap, crap, crap! I know I went full-on theater kid and told him he wouldn't be alone next time, but now I'm overseas all of a sudden, and there's no dorm parent or Kuroko or anyone watching me! What should I do?! This definitely can't be a one-day trip, right? We're gonna be staying the night at least, right? What do I do? What the heck is the right move here?!

The big sister to end all big sisters (according to middle schoolers, at least) was completely red in the face, too flustered to notice that Kamijou was sitting on his suitcase and fanning himself.

She had her hands full just processing the situation in her own tiny corner of reality. She couldn't even spare the energy to figure out who was coming on which of the several flights they'd all taken here.

Ding came an electronic noise. It was from the announcement speakers set up all over the airport.

Kamijou glanced up, but when he heard a woman start speaking in fluent English, he frowned.

"...What's she saying?" he wondered aloud.

"You came overseas without knowing English?" replied Mikoto, wondering how on earth he'd answered the officer's questions at customs.

Inside, however, she was thinking something different.

Wait, does this mean he'll be totally reliant on my English abilities? Whoa! For the first time since coming here, I think I finally have the advantage over him!

And for some reason, she was trembling.

[Nov. 10 / Source: Oahu, in-store pet robot camera at Café Simple Coconuts near New Honolulu International Airport Terminal 3]

* * *

In an airport café so expensive that four-fifths of the prices might as well have been a venue fee, Leivinia Birdway put her cup of coffee to her lips.

Then she frowned.

"...Disgustingly sweet," she decided. "Can't say I didn't expect it, though. There's so many calories in here you could use this to fuel up during a marathon."

"You color-blind or something? That stuff's literally white. Also, you might want to take another look at the name of this place."

The snark had come from Academy City's number one Level Five, Accelerator.

Birdway dropped a bunch of tapioca in her drink; it was evidently free. "The way you're talking right now—it's soft."

"Eh?"

"I'm gonna assume it's because of how used to dealing with little brats you are by now, but you don't need to switch things up just for me."

"......"

"If you want to escort me, I'd much rather you treat me like a proper, *grown* lady. Mostly to protect my pride."

Accelerator clicked his teeth, then took a sip of his weakly colored coffee. He hadn't even noticed his tone until she pointed it out. He figured it was better not to make a show of taking his phone out and fiddling with it—he didn't want her to know he was wondering if he should get in contact with one such "little brat."

The enemy was already on the island. There was no guarantee they weren't listening in on this conversation somehow to get an advantage over them.

"So when are we gonna meet up with the others?" he asked.

"No way to predict when they'll arrive—or how crowded the gates will be," Birdway replied simply, choking down the contents of her cup like a rich dessert. "Aleister has less influence now, but it would have been really rough getting this many people out of the city even before. Put us all on the same flight, and they'd pinpoint us in a flash. That's why we split up into little groups—to mitigate risk. They bought our safety with money and time so no complaining."

That must have been why Birdway's usual men in black were nowhere to be found. She didn't seem too bothered by it, though.

"Gremlin, the group that put Radiosonde Castle in the air, knows Imagine Breaker is alive. And now they're plotting something wicked in Hawaii. He's every sorcerer's natural enemy, and they're prepared for that—their plans will have him covered. So we chased them here to stop them. But we're not exactly international police; we're not allowed to just sneak on through here. We'll need to prepare before we go riding off into battle."

"...No way to trick their sorcery or whatever?"

"Oh, I could work something out if I wanted to. But it's the phantom thief's dilemma. Use a trick once, and they'll figure it out. We're better off finding another way to bring them down, not blindly bringing out the big guns."

"So all of it's just based on *your* needs," said Accelerator in exasperation, then asked, "You said these Gremlin guys already infiltrated Hawaii, right?"

"More than likely, yeah."

"Then how do we narrow 'em down? There's eight islands to go through. Almost 130 if you count all the small ones. And more than 1.4 million people live here, with another 3 million staying here on vacation or whatever. If we just run around without any hints, we ain't finding anyone who wants to stay hidden."

"Good thing I thought of that before."

Just then, they heard an electronic *ding*.

Birdway looked up at the ceiling. "It's about time."

[Nov. 10 / Source: Oahu, automatic information kioski camera near New Honolulu International Airport Terminal 2]

* * *

Shiage Hamazura was standing in front of a big signboard in the airport, confused.

To be more accurate, it was an electronic directions board. Not only did it have a simple map, but you could also use an on-screen keyboard to type in your destination, and it would show you how to get there. There were also voice recognition functions for connecting with an operator, but that wasn't any help to someone who couldn't speak a word of English.

Additionally, there was one thing impeding his already unfortunate level of intellect—that being the girl standing next to him.

Umidori Kuroyoru looked about twelve years old. She was the core of the Freshmen, an underworld Academy City group—and a cyborg, whose very body was an agglomerate of closely guarded engineering secrets.

"…Why? There were a million ways they could've grouped us up. So why'd I have to get put with her?! They had so many options! Like, they could have paired her up with someone who she wasn't trying to kill just the other day! Or at least someone who could restrain her if she gets out of hand!"

"Get it through that boulder you call a brain, Hammyyyyyy! They freakin' *kidnapped* me for this!"

"No! No, no, no! Now she's got a nickname for me, and I hate it!"

"I swear to God. They dare rob me of *my* freedom? *Just* because I might try and kill Fremea again if they leave me alone in the city? Oh, sure, that's a good reason to let you assholes drag me into this! Well, they don't know what's coming to 'em. They're underestimating me! They have no idea when they'll find my teeth in their jugulars!"

"Come on! I'm in Hawaii! The only thing I should be worrying about is what to get my dear, sweet Takitsubo as a souvenir! Macadamia nuts maybe? That's pretty cliché, though. She might not like it. But hey, if I go with the tried-and-true, she's guaranteed to be happy! Anyway, why am I already fighting for my life right in the airport?!"

Hamazura was already in a mortal crisis. He was sure that Kuroyoru had been waiting until they got out of Japan to spring something. Even if all she wanted to do was run, it would be much easier to do once she was overseas.

But before the villainous cyborg could get a chance to launch a terrorist attack with her Bomber Lance ability, someone crept up behind her.

Misaka Worst—a mean-eyed girl with one arm in a sling wearing an ao dai. She looped her free arm around the cyborg's neck.

"Oh, Kuuuro…"

"?!"

"Do whatever you like, all right? But do you *really* think the Misakas would have set the plan up like this if it stood no chance of success?"

"Ga-ga-ga-ga-ga?!"

Kuroyoru screamed abruptly when Misaka Worst used her power to manipulate electricity on the cyborg's control unit.

That was why the normally coolheaded Kuroyoru suddenly posed as if she were about to transform into some kind of superhero. It did *not* mean this was the perfect time for a school counselor to rake in a profit.

"Nya, nya… Gah recently."

"Ha-ha-ha! Fiddled with your organs to hang on for dear life again, eh? Lemme guess, you didn't do your research before trying to fight back, did you? Otherwise, you'd have known that machines are a bad matchup for electric espers."

"Argh, damn it. That General Board asshole…"

"Oh? Hmm? You thinking they put cyborg research back on the table to help out the Third Season project? Misaka supposes it's possible, but without any proof, Misaka doesn't think your resentment is very justified. That wasn't much of a security hole just now. They could probably patch it up in two weeks if they really tried. Even Misaka had a selector embedded in her, after all."

But even the simplest holes were weaknesses until they were filled in. And naturally, there weren't any Academy City research facilities to do the job on Hawaii.

"Phew… I'm saved…" Hamazura groaned, bringing his arm to his face to wipe off his sweat.

But Misaka Worst wouldn't let that go. "Hmm? Oh, Misaka wasn't taking your side or anything, you know."

"I knew it!" he yelled. "There must have been some huge mistake when they set up this group!"

The two girls steeped in darkness didn't react to his outburst. Like some kind of street punk, Misaka Worst cozied up to Kuroyoru, whose arms were still spasming. Maybe she felt superior because she was in control of the situation.

"Now, how on earth are we going to find these suspicious people in Hawaii's crowds of tourists?" she mused. "Asking people questions won't do much good. Locals are used to seeing tons of unfamiliar outsiders. Not much point there."

"…Then what *would* you do?" grumbled the cyborg.

"Not even gonna try to figure it out? I'm surprised. I thought they put some of *his* thought patterns in you." Misaka Worst cackled. "Anyway, Gremlin's one of those ideologically motivated criminal groups, right?"

"You mean they're sensitive?"

"Could be a decent angle of attack."

As the pair tried to figure things out, they heard an electronic tone. Then a woman began giving a message in fluent English.

Hamazura looked up. "Maybe it's one of those missing child notifications."

"Oh, it's way worse than that," said Kuroyoru bitterly. "Here we go."

[Nov. 10 / Source: Oahu, in-store pet robot camera at Café Simple Coconuts near New Honolulu International Airport Terminal 3]

Accelerator was the first to notice something wrong as he put his cup of coffee back on the table.

"Figure out the announcement?" asked Birdway, who still hadn't finished her sweet drink. "It sounded like they were just telling everyone to keep clear of a part of the airport where the floors are getting waxed, but the place is three blocks away. No reason they'd need to broadcast it here. That's an anti-terrorist warning. They're trying to keep everyone away while keeping them from panicking and hurting anyone."

"If some idiot was spraying bullets everywhere, they wouldn't have been able to use this trick," replied Accelerator. "They must have found an *unattended bag somewhere it shouldn't have been*."

Birdway took a tiny sip of her too-sweet drink. "Yep, probably… But we don't know for certain that Gremlin left it there."

For a moment, Accelerator thought she was telling him to consider the chance that this was the work of a separate terrorist group. But an instant later, he changed his mind.

There was one other possibility.

"…You…"

"I asked you the question already. Figure it out?"

"A normal search would never turn up Gremlin with so many people around. They knew that—so they're *coming at us* instead?!"

"It's a matter of efficiency." Birdway's posture was still relaxed. "Leave Gremlin alone, and they're sure to do *something*. Make a lot of people suffer. So we smoke them out first. Gremlin is based on ideology, and we didn't know if a common sense approach would work. In other words…"

"…they're very sensitive when it comes to their own ideals," finished Accelerator, thinking about his electrode choker. Birdway must have gotten one of her men in black to plant the suitcase. "A group like that would jump at the chance. Once they discover that their name is being used for someone else's benefit in a copycat crime, they'll intervene, even if it puts them at a disadvantage…"

"Gremlin's trying to do something here in Hawaii," declared Birdway with a grin. "But that doesn't mean we have to wait for them to make the first move, right?"

In all likelihood, the commotion would trick someone with Gremlin into acting. If Birdway and company could capture the person, it would give them an opportunity to home in on the group's hideouts or plans.

Birdway was right. From an efficiency standpoint, this was the optimal choice.

But still...

"Just one question," said Accelerator.

"Yeah?"

"What did you put in the suitcase you used as bait?"

Birdway shrugged. *"You've got to keep these things realistic.* If it doesn't make local police antsy, even Gremlin would think twice before intervening."

Accelerator stopped himself before he unconsciously split the table in half. He was proud of himself for that—in his opinion, that was real growth.

[Nov. 10 / Source: Oahu, surveillance camera in the central lobby of New Honolulu International Airport]

Kamijou and Mikoto hadn't taken a single step out of the airport—they were looking around at the souvenirs in the duty-free shops. Just then, however, Kamijou got a text on his phone. When he read it, he cried out abruptly and started to run. Did he not understand how dangerous this nation of guns was?

"Aaaaaaaah! My rotten luck just entered a new dimension!"

"Wait! Hey, wait up! Are you really just gonna run through here?! That announcement about the wax or whatever was a coded message about a terrorist threat!"

"I just got a text saying Birdway planted a bomb!"

Naturally, nobody else there wanted to get close to an area being treated with awful-smelling wax by lawn mower machines. Upon calmer observation, there were airport employees just outside the area keeping a watchful eye out, but those who believed the announcement didn't seem to think of it as dangerous. They willingly moved away from the cautionary signs and the bad smell of liquid wax.

Meanwhile...

Kamijou sprinted straight across the floor covered in half-dried wax.

Mikoto scrunched up her face at the odor and glanced at her clothes before she resigned herself to following him.

An employee right outside the wax-treated area tried to stop them only to be ignored.

"Seriously, who's the terrorist here...?" said the boy as they ran. "Do we stop Gremlin now or do something about the suitcase?"

"Is that it right there? The bag?" asked the girl.

Several members of airport security were standing around a large suitcase. The police must not have arrived yet.

Kamijou didn't head straight for it; instead, he hid himself behind a nearby column. Mikoto followed suit.

"Are these Gremlin people the masterminds?" she asked. "Could they have infiltrated security?"

"...Unfortunately, I never got immersed enough in sorcery stuff to know if someone's a sorcerer at a glance."

Kamijou looked around, then spotted Hamazura and Misaka Worst peeking out from around a corner about seventy meters ahead. If they were here, then Accelerator must actually be pretty close by, too.

He took out his cell phone, his thumb moving across the buttons.

"Who are you calling?" asked Mikoto.

"Birdway," he replied. After a couple of tries, the call went through. "Hey, I found the suitcase you planted. There's a bunch of airport security guys nearby, too. Is Gremlin really coming?"

"They're already here."

"?" Kamijou frowned.

Birdway put it simply. *"They're dealing with the unexpected emergency in their own way, trying to punch through security with a jerry-rigged spell. I can easily reverse engineer and eliminate it."*

"...Did they change how they look? Are some of those guys actually from Gremlin...?"

"No, not that."

He heard someone clap their hands over the phone. A moment later...

Shudder!!!!!!
With a chilling sensation, almost twenty people appeared out of thin air.

They were all western European men in formal attire—Birdway's subordinates.

"We're not the main dish," said one of the men named Mark Space to Kamijou, pointing toward nothing. *"Pay attention to her instead."*

"?!"

There wasn't anything there. There was nowhere to hide.

And yet.

There she was.

A woman.

With blond hair and pale skin, a slender figure, and beautiful features, she looked less like a real person and more like the platonic ideal of a woman plucked straight from a picture book. In a word, a princess. This impression was made all the stronger by her outfit, a strange dress that appeared to be composed of several thin layers of cloth woven on top of one another.

But she didn't look like just any old fairy-tale girl—beneath her elegant dress was an article of tight posture-correcting underwear resembling a diving suit. A modern corset, the kind that infomercials had launched into popularity recently.

She was a sorcerer.

And she belonged to Gremlin.

That wasn't some hearsay through the grapevine nor was it a first-hand account. For the first time, Kamijou saw, with his own two eyes, a true antagonist.

She wasn't intimidating in a clear, easy-to-understand way. No, her presence was altogether different—something almost *alien*.

The unpleasantness of seeing something in front of you that wasn't supposed to be there. The panic from the hunch that leaving her alone would invite tragedy. Fear and terror were supposed to be signals your brain used to warn you of mortal threats, but the feeling this woman evoked was purer than that. It wasn't the powerful emotion of fear but rather those vivid danger signals that caused Kamijou's mind to sharpen.

The fact that this woman, who felt instinctively anomalous, was part of a group who had tried to drop Radiosonde Castle on Academy City instilled in him a rational loathing.

Did Birdway seriously just disengage the spells everyone *was using to hide?* Whatever she'd done, it had encompassed the entire central lobby. That was why all the men in black who'd planted the suitcase had popped into existence and also why Gremlin's sorcerer had appeared at the same time.

The Gremlin sorcerer glanced down at herself, as if to confirm that others were able to see her. She didn't seem particularly flustered, though.

She then spoke in French.

"Godmother of the pumpkin carriage."

It sounded like a song. Her voice was innocent, like that of a fairy-tale princess.

"Please give me the test of the glass slipper. The test that flung my selfish, unfaithful mother and sister deep into the pit of despair. That impartial, heartless test."

A moment later.

Something happened that transcended the laws of physics.

[Nov. 10 / Source: Oahu, a vending machine surveillance camera in New Honolulu International Airport]

As he watched the situation develop from around the corner, Hamazura widened his eyes.

The first thing he heard was an awful *bkkk-rkkk*, like cracks running through glass.

"What? They're…," murmured Kuroyoru dubiously, Misaka Worst's hand still on the back of her neck.

Ignoring the airport staff, who were flabbergasted at the sudden appearances, the black-suits—numbering close to twenty—all converged on the woman in the dress.

And then every single one of them tripped and fell on the freshly waxed floor. It was like their legs had gotten caught in a trap—an invisible wire or something.

That's what it looked like.

But that wasn't the case.

Hamazura heard several different groans, and those who couldn't hold it in let out screams. The black-suits were all clutching their feet—specifically the ends of them.

It was as if…

As if every single one of them had broken all their toes.

As if an invisible explosion had gone off around the woman in the dress, crushing the feet of everyone in range.

"What?" said Hamazura, his voice unsteady. "The hell's going on?"

"*Shhh.* She's muttering something in French."

The woman was the only one standing among the fallen men, and she was murmuring something under her breath.

"…Godmother of the pumpkin carriage. Please lend poor Cendrillon your strength. One further test of the glass slipper—until all the arrogant, lying challengers lay at my feet."

"It's 'Aschenputtel.' Is she an Uncut Gem? An auto-suggestion type?"

Misaka Worst seemed convinced about the whole thing, but Hamazura felt like there was something off.

The woman didn't appear to be an Academy City esper. At the same time, he could make out that she was following some sort of rule set.

She was a sorcerer.

Gremlin.

A woman calling herself Cendrillon and wielding the laws of another world.

One who had summoned Radiosonde Castle for her own ends.

As Hamazura sucked in his breath, Misaka Worst asked in a casual tone, "What now?"

"We don't know what she's doing," answered Kuroyoru. "Which means we don't know where's safe. Which then means getting close to her right now is a bad idea… Best to find a way to attack her from a distance."

"Oh, Misaka knows one person in particular you're *never* safe from, even at a distance."

[Nov. 10 / Source: Oahu, a novelty pen–shaped camera dropped by someone evacuating from New Honolulu International Airport]

Accelerator was near the ceiling of the central lobby, hugging the point where several metal beams converged.

From there, he observed the situation.

…Is she targeting anyone standing on the floor? No, because then the Level Zero and Number Three hiding behind that column would have been affected. It must just come down to distance.

In terms of horizontal distance alone, Accelerator was closer to Cendrillon than those two were. But the central lobby was just as tall as it was wide; he was up about three stories, which put him pretty far away in reality.

Just one spell cast.

Cendrillon had attacked in every direction, immediately making everyone's positions clear.

All the men in black were on the floor, clutching their feet. He couldn't figure out what exactly the spell had done to them.

But then Cendrillon opened her mouth to speak.

"Warning."

Her words seem to be for Kamijou, but he didn't appear to understand them.

"This spell accepts nothing except my shoe size—22.5 centimeters.

If your size is smaller, the bones in your feet will stretch to match mine; bigger, and your toes will be cut off."

"......"

Accelerator didn't need to guess what had happened to the men in black.

"However, this is but a warning. I have merely dislocated the joints in your toes. I can go further. So what'll it be? Will you wash your hands of Gremlin or lose your collateral?"

With Number Three interpreting for him, Kamijou eventually understood—and when he did, he paled. *"Collateral"?* That had to mean she'd go after the toes of anyone who stood up to Gremlin.

The issue is what the conditions for her glass slipper are, thought Accelerator. *If it travels along the floor or radiates out like an explosion, it'll be simple to nullify. But she's a sorcerer. If she can ignore distance and vectors like a voodoo doll, she could be able to attack anyone with feet. Which would be a problem.*

Not long ago, he would have scoffed at this line of thinking, but he wasn't laughing now.

And there was no guarantee his vector manipulation, which relied on distinct values, would affect that unknown means of attack.

[Nov. 10 / Source: Oahu, a wild bird observation camera for bird-strike prevention near Runway 3 of New Honolulu International Airport]

It was grass all around punctuated by gray runways, as though patches of it had been peeled off with duct tape. On one of the countless crisscrossing paths of asphalt stood a girl of about twelve. Naturally, this was not somewhere civilians were allowed to set foot.

She contacted someone on her cell phone.

"Mm. Yep. Nah, it won't work. Just pretend you don't know French or something and stall for time. That was the whole point of those morons lying all over the floor. And I'm certainly not expecting you to *win*. You and the middle schooler interpreting for you should act panicked. Make it seem like you can't communicate."

Noting her surprise at all her men going down in one fell swoop, the girl headed for one end of the runway. She wasn't after a big passenger plane.

"I'm telling you, don't bother. Huh? Hamazura's group started shooting compressed gas out of modified fire extinguishers? That *definitely* won't work. The sorcerer must be dodging everything with unnatural speed. She overwrote Cinderella with a religious motif to convert it into a weapon. You know, that fairy tale embedded with *dance techniques* so good they allowed an amateurish girl to floor a prince accustomed to balls. That woman could hop and skip her way through a cluster bombing."

From the terminal, this distance had looked easy to cover by walking. But now that she was actually trying, she realized that it was actually much farther than it seemed. She kept her frustration to herself as she continued.

"Of course, it was probably meant to deal with Imagine Breaker originally. After all, she's busting people's feet up in high-speed combat. It's really obvious. They know you're alive from the Radiosonde Castle incident the other day; Gremlin must see you as a natural enemy. Your right fist is a powerful weapon, but that won't matter if you can't hit her. If she's got the physical ability to dodge a bullet after seeing it coming at her, I suppose it's not a half-bad plan."

Finally, Birdway stopped.

"That's right. So just buy me some time. Don't try to beat her. Step in, and she'll counter. Either your toes will be done for, or your jaw will be shattered by a straight right with all her weight behind it. I doubt you'd want to experience either outcome."

She looked up at what was parked at the edge of the airport.

There it was…

"I started this game. And don't you worry—I've got a plan to finish it."

* * *

[Nov. 10 / Source: Oahu, a surveillance camera in the central lobby of New Honolulu International Airport]

Thunk! Thunk! Kamijou's ears were rattled by a series of sounds resembling a drum being struck. They were coming about once every five to ten seconds.

The source of the noise was Hamazura's group, who were around the corner about seventy meters up the passage. They were using improvised gas-powered guns to shoot at Cendrillon from a distance. Though "guns" was putting it generously—their weapons were nothing more than four large fire extinguishers bundled together, the ends of their hoses hooked into steel pipes. They would load corks stabbed through with nails into the pipe, then fire. This sent their ammunition flying through the air at 230 kph; a direct hit meant the tip of the nail would stab into your limb and shatter the bone like glass. Essentially, they were using their improvised firearms like disposable bazookas.

And despite all that.

"I give you my thanks, godmother."

Cendrillon's pure singsong voice went on.

Not one shot had hit.

"Thank you for granting me this wonderful dance with the prince. The sparkling dress, the glass slippers—these wonderful gifts have encouraged my weak heart. Tonight, I am made a beautiful, perfect princess."

Klak-klak-klak-klak-klak!!

She tapped her high-heeled shoes with the speed of a sewing machine.

Her eyes met Kamijou's.

But she didn't just look at him. Cendrillon flowed toward him, continuing to avoid the projectiles.

The situation had changed.

It was no longer possible to stall for time by negotiating.

"Ugh!"

He quickly readied his right fist, but he had nowhere near enough time.

Two slender arms wrapped around his right arm, and a high heel buried itself between his legs. Kamijou's body moved on its own to escape the intense pain. He whirled around—almost like the follow in a social dance.

And that placed him directly in the firing line of Hamazura's group.

"Godmother of the pumpkin carriage."

Cendrillon shoved a hand through Kamijou's armpit, then aimed her palm at Hamazura, who had stopped dead.

"Please give me the carriage quickly. Before tonight's dream ends. Quickly. Have the carriage set off."

Bwoooom!!!!!! A shock wave blasted through.

It was like an invisible passenger car had just flown by, leaving a line of destruction along the floor in its wake. Likely feeling vulnerable, Hamazura's group ducked back around behind a corner—and then the entire corner section of the wall blew to smithereens.

"Why, you!"

Sparks danced across Mikoto's bangs right next to Kamijou.

But Cendrillon didn't release him from her entanglement; she squeezed his arm, swung him around, and positioned him as a shield again—a shield blocking everything Mikoto was capable of.

"Godmother of the pumpkin carriage."

Cendrillon swept at Kamijou's legs, sending him careening into Mikoto, pushing her down to the floor.

As the sorcerer leaned over them, the only thing they could hear was her beautiful singing voice.

To deliver a single strike to crush the feet.

To cause a new explosion with her sorcery.

"Please give me the glass slipper. Distance, five hundred. Number of targets, unlimited. Grant these insincere liars the impartial and cruel test of the glass slipper, so that they may all hang low their heads."

"Wait, is that the same sorcery as before…?!"

That was when Kamijou, laying on his back, saw it.

Accelerator was clinging to one of the steel beams near the ceiling.

…Damn it, she knows he's waiting up there! he thought. *That's why she's using such a wide-range attack…!*

Even Accelerator's reflection wasn't guaranteed to work on this opponent.

She was an unknown quantity.

And Kamijou, who had nothing to defend himself with except his right hand, was hopeless.

He'd been naive.

They hadn't been the only ones trying to draw enemies to them. Cendrillon had seen through their trap, then gone right into the middle of it to eliminate everyone resisting her at once.

That was what he'd thought anyway.

However.

"Still in the central lobby, right?"

He heard Birdway's voice.

Still pinned down, Kamijou searched for the source until his eyes fell on his cell phone a short distance away.

"Stay away!" he yelled. "You'll get another chan—"

"That's all I needed to know," she interrupted.

And then a moment later…

Craaasssh!!!!!!

The windowpanes along the wall shattered all at once.

All of them—every last one of the reinforced glass windows, stretching three stories up and over three hundred meters across.

And the cause of this was clear.

A supermassive tanker loaded with five tons of jet fuel had busted through the windows at full speed and plunged into the central lobby.

Birdway was there.

Not in the driver's seat but on the roof.

She stood there firmly, her feet set apart, as a shower of glass fragments harmlessly rained down on her, perhaps because of a spell she'd used.

"What…?"

Still straddling Kamijou and Mikoto, Cendrillon cocked her head in puzzlement, then froze.

Birdway ignored her and said into her cell phone, "Hold her foot down for me."

Like a drowning man grasping at straws, Kamijou reached for her foot.

This delayed Cendrillon's response by a few seconds.

Which was more than enough time for a decisive maneuver.

A direct hit.

Whump!! Something roared right past Kamijou's nose. The cars in the U.S. weren't just bigger—they were taller, too. He and Misaka crawled underneath the chassis, leaving only Cendrillon, who had been straddling them, to be knocked far in front.

"Guh, gh, gah…?!"

She tried to shout something, but the tanker was going at two hundred kph and wouldn't give her the chance.

The truck smashed into a wall of the central lobby.

The camera recorded yet another thunderous sound. This time, the noise clapped even harder against Kamijou's eardrums. Huge cracks appeared in the wall, shards went flying, and something like dust burst into the air. The tanker's passenger seat was crushed like a tin can.

Birdway, who had been standing on the roof, shouldn't have gotten through that unscathed, but for some reason, she was cool and collected. She let herself drift down to the floor of the central lobby.

"That's all, huh?" the young girl said, twirling her hair with a finger. "Why's everyone gotta go down so easy? They sure made it hard to plot a course for the tires."

"Y-you're a monster…," said Kamijou, his voice trembling as he slowly got up.

The men in black had stopped groaning and screaming, too; maybe the crash had forced Cendrillon's spell to deactivate.

"Didn't we need that Cendrillon lady to find out where Gremlin's hiding and what their plans are?!" he continued. "If you were trying to show mercy, it really doesn't seem like it worked! She's gonna need a little more than an ambulance after that!"

"Incorrect." Birdway waved her hand at him dismissively.

At some point, a staff had appeared there.

"Check it out. Looks like Gremlin's got a bunch of tricks up their sleeve."

"?"

Just as Kamijou tried to ask what she meant, it happened.

He heard a *krsheeee*.

It sounded like a metal plate bending. And it happened again. *Shree, kshee...* Little by little, the noises grew louder, and the intervals between them shrank.

In between the tanker's crushed passenger seat and the destroyed wall, something writhed as if to overcome the pressure that could smash metal plates flat as paper.

Then fingers.

Fingers, slender and feminine, leaped out—as if to block a train or elevator door from closing, as if trying to pull it open again.

"Cend…rillon…?!"

"Well, yeah. Aschenputtel was a perfect, flawless princess in front of the prince. Failure would be impossible. She's readjusting all the factors around her to *make* it impossible. A very convenient plot tool to let her win—it must be the 'ball.' It'll take more than a huge, massive object to cut short the longings of a maiden, I suppose."

A *grrr-chee* rang out clearly from the gap between the tanker and the wall.

And from that gap, a blood-soaked eye gazed at them.

"However," said Birdway, twirling her staff around in front of her, "there's a limit to the functions of her dress. A time limit, to be precise—midnight. Maybe the significance is in the boundary between days, but speaking of a night's dream ending, there's another symbol she could apply—one that's easier to understand."

She stopped twirling her staff.

Its tip was pointed at the tanker.

At some point, a golden pocket watch with a slender chain had coiled around the staff.

Not to mention the positions of the long and short hands.

But true to her word, she further reinforced the symbol and the role.

"Dawn."

A moment later…

Five tons of jet fuel ignited all at once, causing a huge explosion of heat and light that filled the central lobby.

Though it didn't disperse into the air or vaporize, jet fuel was of a fundamentally different structure than gasoline.

Kamijou immediately scooped Mikoto up and ran behind a nearby pillar.

Even as her face reddened, Mikoto stuck out her right hand and manipulated magnetic forces to assemble a wall out of a bunch of metal objects to protect the baffled airport staff. The men in black, who knew Birdway's character much better than Kamijou and the others, hastily sprinted behind the wall.

Kamijou didn't even have the time to check what Accelerator and Hamazura had done.

Ignition.

His five senses were flooded.

Not knowing if this was the proper countermeasure, he just watched as the incredible burst of light filled the entire central lobby.

He only got his vision back thirty seconds later.

It took another ten for him to realize that meant he was still alive.

There was flame.

Closer to white than scarlet, it was like an unnatural ocean on the floor. And in the middle of it stood a girl twirling a staff.

She shoved her free hand into the blown-up tanker wreckage and then pulled.

Out came a very beaten-up Cendrillon. Birdway had grabbed her by the hair. Parts of Cendrillon's dress had melted, and she had burns on her skin, but the fact that she still had all her limbs intact after taking a point-blank explosion was abnormal in itself.

Only one remained.

Leivinia Birdway, standing tall amid the flames, her target's hair in her hand, seemed almost bored as she spoke her next words.

"That's it for the prelims. One win for us."

[Nov. 10 / Source: Oahu, an ATM security camera]

"*Huff! Huff!*"

Shiage Hamazura put a hand on a guidepost in front of the now-smoking international airport and tried to catch his frantic breath. He'd just escaped the building. Fortunately, all the guests and staff—numbering almost twenty thousand—had evacuated outside after the explosion. Things were so chaotic that nobody criticized him for running around like crazy. Perhaps they'd also cut him some slack because they thought of Japanese people as pacifists who wouldn't know what to do during an emergency; whatever the case, it had saved him trouble.

He saw people in suits and ties here and there—subordinates of the girl who had caused the explosion, perhaps.

They were supposed to all flee separately, but unlike Hamazura, they were unbelievably adept at blending in with the crowd, even in a situation like this.

"Damn it, damn it! Now you can't even tell which side's the terrorists! Some of our people actually got hurt, after all! I bet that suitcase is gone, too!"

"I've been telling you very calmly that she's not on the government's side, you know. I smell a different kind of darkness from mine on that woman," said Umidori Kuroyoru, exasperated, before turning back to look at the international airport. "Anyway, how far are you planning to run exactly?"

"Far enough that the police don't get suspicious," said Hamazura between breaths. "We're finally through the first gate, right? Gremlin hasn't even made a move yet. I don't want to get in trouble with the cops until we stop them. I mean, the police would be on the side of arresting them, wouldn't they?"

"If there's one thing I hate hearing more than someone giving themselves a pat on the back, it's someone giving themselves an excuse," said Kuroyoru mockingly.

Hamazura ignored her and wiped the sweat off his face. "Anyway, if Birdway gets any info from Cendrillon, she'll call us. We should probably hide somewhere and lay low."

"Ah. Gotcha. Oh, and by the way…"

"What do you want?"

"…haven't seen Misaka Worst for a while. It would be pretty funny if she got separated from us in the crowds, huh? Mainly talking about my dramatic turnabout here."

"Eeeeeeeeeeeeeeeeeeeeeeeeeeek!"

Then a moment after Hamazura yelled like a girl and made the pose from *The Scream*…

"…What on earth are you doing out here?"

…there came a very reasonable comment—in Japanese. It was from Touma Kamijou, the spiky-haired boy.

[Nov. 10 / Source: Oahu, a tourist's cell phone camera]

"Now how in the world did this happen…?" asked Mikoto Misaka, brushing her bangs out of her face.

Next to her stood a girl in an ao dai with the exact same features and body type, save for the evil look in her eyes (and the size of her chest): Misaka Worst.

Both girls had gotten separated from their friends (?) while fleeing and had bumped into each other while looking for them.

"Misaka's fresh out of the Third Season ovens herself, so she doesn't have many Earth acquaintances. And without that person, her desire for battle goes ninety percent away."

"Third...Season...?"

"Don't raise your eyebrows like that, Sistie. It was canceled. You never knew about it."

"?"

"Just saying there's actually a lot of heroes scattered around the world," said Misaka Worst. "Anyway... What is Number Three doing in such an emergency?"

"What are you trying to say?"

Mikoto was busy thinking about how to meet up with the others, tapping away on her cell phone to call up a map application.

"You've got a totally unrelated location pinned in your map," pointed out Misaka Worst. "What is it? Checking the main store branch of Cupid's Arrow?"

"Fwoh?!"

Mikoto immediately turned her phone off, but Misaka Worst kept smirking at her.

"That's a long-standing wedding ring shop, isn't it? I heard profits have been down lately, so they've been expanding the scope of their business."

"...How do you know all that when you were just born recently?"

"If you're fine with something quicker, you can get plenty of info all over the internet. Anyway, the story goes you can only get engagement rings and wedding rings from there after a background check from an external detective agency. I seriously doubt they'd respond to orders from a middle schooler."

"Urk."

"Which means, smirk, you're after their new service, heh, a tag ring that less serious lovers can wear, smile."

"Argh! Fine! Sorry or whatever! When I heard we were going to

Hawaii, I figured I'd find some free time and go get a tag ring from Cupid's Arrow!"

"...Those are titanium rings, right? They're cheap, sure, but kinda rugged, huh?"

"They can color titanium with electrolysis in a solution. If they use the same device for a pair of rings, the pattern will make them look connected... That's why people say unscientific things about them, like that they're charms that can stop your boyfriend from cheating."

"Right, so you want to use the store's device with your sparks to color it? ...Hate to break this to you, but that's like getting hair in your valentine's chocolate. The girl is the only one who would think that was romantic."

"What?!"

"Also, you're not even dating, and also, the woman giving the guy the ring is really serious, yeah? He might wonder why the heck you even know his finger size."

As Mikoto froze, Misaka Worst heaved a sigh. She wasn't even a year old, and she already felt too sorry for Mikoto to keep teasing her.

"Tag rings from Cupid's Arrow don't matter right now," said Misaka Worst. "Anyway, like, I knew my appearance wasn't going to be any different from the ones in the old projects, but..."

"Wh-what are you trying to say?"

"It's just, why does the clone beat the original? In more ways than one? Is there even a point to you being around?"

"...Are you talking about breasts right now...?" asked the fourteen-year-old, head still cocked in confusion as sparks burst from her bangs.

Misaka Worst ignored them. "Was I? I didn't say anything about that. Maybe I was just talking about our roles in the mission. Who's to say?"

"You just crossed a line, you little runt!"

[Nov. 10 / Source: Oahu, a security camera in a warehouse in New Honolulu International Airport Terminal 3]

* * *

"You're the only one left who hasn't run away."

Accelerator clicked his tongue at Birdway's casual tone.

She ignored him. Instead, she prodded the woman lying in front of her with her foot.

Cendrillon.

They'd stripped her of her very essence—her transparent dress. Now she was naked save for her underwear…which might have been sexy in another situation, but her underwear was actually a contour-correcting bodysuit that looked like something you'd wear to go diving. From her collarbone down to just past her knees, everything was covered in synthetic fiber. She could have walked straight past a policeman like that if she were carrying a surfboard.

"Retaliating?" asked Accelerator bluntly.

"Stripping another girl doesn't do anything for me," said Birdway flatly. "She constructs her spell by combining her body with her dress. It's different from how my staff operates. Clearly, she wants to make her entire body into a Soul Arm. Anyway, take off the dress, and she can't use the spell. Either she really wants to soak in a big ocean of sorcery, or she latently fears her own technique and wants a safety mechanism that is easy to see and understand. Now then…"

Cendrillon already had several wounds. They weren't from torture—they were burns from when all that jet fuel had exploded.

Accelerator narrowed his eyes. "Think she'll squeal?"

"Why would we make her talk? Sounds like a pain to me," said Birdway offhandedly, sticking several amulets made of papyrus to Cendrillon's face. Either the damage from the burns or the absence of her dress had turned her into a weak, squirming girl who was powerless to resist.

"*Reject it*," said Birdway with a grin. "I'll scan each thing you try to reject. So when I ask you a question, reject it with all your heart."

If she answered honestly, then fine. If she resisted with all her heart, she'd be marked.

The only real way out was via ultimate apathy, but the brain wasn't built to be perfectly apathetic when someone was yelling at you. Especially if they were enacting violence. Your defensive instincts would naturally kick in. From the time they're self-aware, people all try to get as much info as they can from the words of others.

Cendrillon slowly shook her head.

Birdway ignored her and asked, *"Where are your friends?"*

Cendrillon was trying not to move the muscles of her face, but her cheek trembled ever so slightly.

"What is your objective?"

An amulet lit up.

Birdway was intentionally instilling Cendrillon with the desire to reject her, rampaging through her mind in a place Cendrillon was trying to wall off and protect.

Cendrillon couldn't resist her.

Which was natural.

This wasn't like a puzzle or video game made to be beaten. Net traps set up by professionals didn't have "goals" to begin with. The player's skills didn't affect anything.

"The computation is going well. Another thirty seconds, and we should have some good news," said Birdway casually, when just then...

"Oh, what's this? Widdle Cendrillon, they really got you good, d'dn't they?"

A new voice.

And it had come from Cendrillon's own mouth.

"......" Birdway immediately shoved the tip of her staff between Cendrillon's lips. There was an awful crunching noise as Cendrillon's front teeth broke, and dark red blood dripped from her open lips. But Cendrillon was smiling—being *made* to smile.

"Trying to hold me back like that won't work. I could just break your limbs, you know. But now that she's under an external influence, she's like a marionette waiting to be controlled. And of course, one with enough strength to tear through human limits—heh."

Crrrick-crack-crunck!! The sound of something breaking rang out.

It was Cendrillon crushing Birdway's Soul Arm with her teeth. Except her own front teeth were already broken. She was using the strength of her jaw alone—plus what little remained of those broken teeth. The pain must have been excruciating.

But someone was making her do it anyway. When Accelerator flipped his choker switch and kicked a piece of debris at her at an insane speed, she easily avoided it by jumping clear over five meters back. At last, she spoke to this "external influence."

"...I've been waiting."

"Sure, sure. No dress, so all your widdle fairy-tale stuff must have been wiped out, yeah? I'll trigger my spell through you. Could you use your sorcery-based unlock key to give me complete control for a bit?"

"Shit!" cursed Birdway, twirling what was left of her gnawed-away staff. At some point, it had changed into a small drinking dish.

But before she could cast an actual attack spell, Cendrillon intoned something.

"...Injecting total amount to red number 25..."

"There ya go. The battle's results go into black number 11. Approval granted."

Bang!! Something snapped inside Cendrillon's body. Her eye color drastically changed, and suddenly, it wasn't her standing there any longer.

And then...

"All right, widdle Cendrillon, I'll protect Gremlin's secrets for you."

She smiled sweetly, and...

Whump!

She took the sharp staff fragment out of her mouth and rammed its tip into her temple.

"What...?" somebody asked.

The question had come from Cendrillon's own mouth.

She slumped over to the side, a look of surprise on her face. It was so quick. She didn't catch her fall; her limbs, hair, and her red blood spilled out over the floor and spread.

And that was it.

No screams, no voice at all. Not even from the person controlling Cendrillon.

"They got us. The staff didn't go through her skull, but the blow probably shoved a piece of bone into her brain. She'll have subarachnoid bleeding, too. I see. This does make getting information rather difficult."

"……"

"Oh, don't look at me like that. I'll at least report this to a hospital."

"Now what? She was our only lead, wasn't she?"

"We caught the fish, actually," said Birdway, looking around in boredom. "Gremlin made contact with us to silence her. Now we just have to reel them in."

CHAPTER 2
Detonator
Natural_Bomb.

[Nov. 10 / Source: Oahu, congressional proceedings recording camera on forty-ninth floor of Hotel Firefly]

The hotel was a far cry from the luxury offerings on Oahu. While there were other superexpensive hotels more fitting for use by VIPs and several other facilities with suites not even known to the public, places like those could have instead been marked as used by high-risk individuals.

"What do you want at this hour? Is that thing still on?"

The unhappy voice belonged to a woman named Roselyne Crackhart, President Catze's aide. She was in her early thirties, and she gave the impression of a home tutor who was superbly talented (in *several* areas). She had once smashed the nose of a reporter who'd asked her, very rudely, to confirm the rumors claiming she knew every nook and cranny of Mr. Scandal's body—and on national television, no less. Fortunately, this led to her being seen as an advocate for victims of sexual harassment rather than anything else, and her actions seemed to make the president's approval rating climb even higher.

That anecdote, combined with how she perfectly wore a made-to-order suit from a gentlemen's formal wear company supporting the administration, should paint a good picture of her attitude and behavior.

One of the secretaries holding a video camera answered the question posed to her in a straightforward way. "It's my job to record all conversations during business hours, ma'am."

"I see. Thanks."

Lying across an entire three-person sofa herself, Roselyne picked up a financial magazine. The feature was titled "The USA's Most Important 100." Frack Kateman, the king of cars; Aurey Blueshake, the media queen; Douglas Hardbell, a rock star. The article listed name after name, and as she scanned them, she narrowed her eyes.

"...The literal president isn't on a list of the most important people of the country? Yeah, that's a problem."

"Ma'am, let's focus on the topic at hand."

"I always want to put off things I know are gonna be annoying."

Sinking deeper into the sofa, Roselyne tossed the magazine away. Then she turned her eyes to the wall of the room.

"Commander, has the president been found yet?"

"N-no, ma'am. But everyone we can muster is still searching for him."

"Even the Marines are having trouble, eh?"

"His GPS was found in a trash can near the press conference room—in a condom tied at the opening, for some reason. The decryption team thinks it could be a messa—"

"That's just his sense of humor."

Roselyne put a hand to her forehead. She was frustrated but not directly angry at being toyed with like this.

"That moron. A condom? If anyone found out the president was carrying that around, the Crossists would get all up in arms again."

"Um, ma'am, what about the Secret Service? We're doing everything we can, of course, but I feel like we'll need the experts to help us with this..."

"Commander? Commander of the Marine Corps? Complaining about a lack of human resources is one thing, but don't be afraid to single-handedly accept responsibility for unpredictable situations in times like these. Haven't I already explained why we overstepped our bounds to ask you for help?"

Roselyne reached for a bottle of wine on the table but then remembered the camera was still going and took the mint-flavored gum instead.

"They're suspicious."

"……"

Her voice was quiet but had a powerful implication behind it.

The commander fell silent.

Roselyne continued, "I know something's going on. But that's it. I don't know what. This isn't simple bribery or a threat. We can't just blacklist people to isolate them. Normal people are suddenly turning against the U.S., like they've been possessed by some kind of demon."

If the hostile group had simply been expanding around a mastermind, the government could have stopped that expansion by isolating each of the dangerous individuals one by one. But when some sort of unseen entity was choosing people to manipulate based on the whims of a mastermind, trying to isolate individuals was meaningless. Everyone would be fundamentally unsafe until they stopped the mastermind.

And how exactly they were controlling people was anyone's guess.

Roselyne and the others had speculated that the people who had turned possessed a quality that made them easier to control, and they were trying to distance those who showed even the slightest propensity for being controlled to secure their safety, but she couldn't be confident in that approach's effectiveness at this point.

"Of the Senate and the House of Representatives…I'd say about half are *suspicious*," she went on. "They seem to be expanding behind the scenes. Including into your organizations in the military."

"W-we've heard the story, ma'am, but it doesn't seem real…"

"Doesn't seem real to me, either. I saw it with my own eyes, and I still don't believe it. But it's happening. Thankfully, the only confirmed victims so far have been U.S. citizens. You and several other units managed to escape because you were working jointly with the Australian Defense Force on the war cleanup."

Despite that, Roselyne Crackhart didn't know much at all about the occult, as she'd mentioned before. Her only impression was that it was probably different from the supernatural ability development that Academy City did.

And on that point, their on-the-lam president was most likely the same.

They had several teams of analysts trying to make sense of all the unexplainable phenomena that had occurred during World War III, but none of them had come up with anything useful.

That was why Roselyne, despite having witnessed all the clearly strange things happening in the White House, could only discuss the issue in the broadest of terms.

"Th-then could it really be…?"

"We're only here now thanks to dumb luck. But we need to find out why this dumb luck is on our side. We're looking at a worst case of *we'll be possessed as soon as we take a step outside*. And if that happens, America's image as the police of the world will be in tatters. We also can't assume this phenomenon will stop with government functions—it could happen to some random children or old people walking around nearby, and they suddenly start firing into crowds. Any citizen in the nation could end up being an assailant or a victim. We need to figure out how this occult phenomenon works as soon as we can and stop the mastermind's invasion. Otherwise, we run the risk of them getting their hands on the nuclear launch codes."

"Is this why the president has struck out on his own…?"

"Probably. He's seen what's happening, and he's stupid enough to think he can stop a national crisis by himself. He would have been surrounded the moment he tried to pull anything on the mainland, so he made a show of being a puppet until we arrived here, where our influence is weaker. Maybe he assumed that influence wouldn't extend this far… And all this when nobody even knows the actual rules of the game."

"So then…" The commander wiped the sweat from his brow. "By trying to track the president down, aren't we just putting him in more danger? If there's any chance he can get us out of this, then…"

"Are you being serious right now?"

Roselyne automatically sent a piercing glare at the man, then noticed him shrink in his uniform and set about trying to placate him instead.

"Whatever his reasons, however dangerous this situation is, the president must always be in a position to access the public. Try telling someone that he's missing and see what happens. People will think he's not fit for office, and all powers will be transferred to the vice president… He has something that will put that off for a time, but that's no reason to feel safe.

"And," she continued, "*the vice president is already suspect.* He's committed no crime, and he's even acted like he wants to help us. But as long as there's a chance he has what the mastermind needs to control him, turning the Oval Office over to him would be extremely risky."

Nobody spoke of what would happen after that.

Because they all knew they couldn't afford to tell anyone that an unidentified individual had hijacked one of the world's superpowers—not even as a joke.

"…The only silver lining here," murmured Roselyne under her breath, "is the item in the president's possession I just mentioned." Then she continued in a normal tone, "Find him if it's the last thing you do, before the mastermind gnawing away at the other politicians—including the vice president—finds out about this."

Not bothering to watch the commander's rigid salute, she fell into thought, her face sour.

…The most concerning part is that a vanishing act isn't the only thing that would constitute the president being unfit for office. A bullet to the head would serve just as well.

[Nov. 10 / Source: Oahu, a dashcam outside My Dear Car's Oahu branch]

* * *

Roberto Catze.

Carrying a golden attaché case, the president of the United States of America headed into the car rental store.

He went up to the young clerk at the reception desk and said, "I'd like something cheap. Doesn't matter what it is. Hmm—electric cars make for better publicity, right? Roselyne won't shut up about that stuff. I don't care if it uses gasoline or deuterium or what but nothing coming right off a car sex incident, please. Doing the nasty leaves a smell even ethanol can't get rid of."

"Well, look who thinks he owns the place? Who do you think you are, old man?"

"I'm the God-damned president! As a citizen of this great nation, you could at least watch the morning news once in a while!"

"Oh, you're one of those impersonators. Do that thing he always says! You know—*'We'll save the world!'*"

"…You know what, I don't care. Just gimme a key, will ya?"

After throwing a bunch of crumpled-up bills on the counter and being thrown a key in return, Roberto walked past a row of two-seater cars, eventually laying eyes on an especially beaten-up convertible.

He almost thought he'd kick one of its tires, but since it was a model produced by a major lobbying group, he stopped himself and opened the door. As he put the key in, the young woman came up to him.

"Wait, shit," she said. "Almost forgot the paperwork! All right, you strapping young comedian, we've gotta get your license information. Hand it to me for a sec."

"You can't just use my Social Security number?"

"Nope. Your driver's license, sir."

"…Ugh, what a pain. I'll have to draft a bill for Congress later," muttered Roberto, taking a card out of his wallet. The clerk held out a scanning machine—one of those devices that looked like you could tap your cell phone against it.

He waved his license over it. After seeing that the device had read the info on the IC card inside it, the young woman nodded in satisfaction.

"All righty. Your name is Roberto…Roberto Catze. And you live in…th-the White House? H-hey. Wait just a minute!"

"You good over there? Smirk."

"You *changed your name, too?!* I can't believe you found an apartment called the White House! And it's even a D.C. license! You're crazy dedicated, you know that?!"

"Fine! Keep on thinking that until you're dead in the grave! Waaaah!"

With tears in his eyes, the president of the United States of America drove off. The clerk shouted her impression of his catchphrase—*We'll save the world!*—after him, adding insult to injury.

Once he got out of the rent-a-car lot, he kept one hand on the wheel and used his other to open up the attaché case he'd put in the passenger seat. Strictly speaking, it was a computer *shaped* like a suitcase. Then he took the bundled-up cables inside and started plugging them into the car's navigation device.

The imperial package.

A device that could access all cloud-based government systems on the president's authority. Everything from giving orders to different departments to preparing to launch ballistic missiles—you could do it all from here. Naturally, it required multiple forms of biometric authentication and was only operable by the sitting president.

"…Time to check what all those suddenly *suspect* people are up to."

For instance, in areas experiencing influenza outbreaks, many more people searched for the term *influenza* on search engines. But go the other way, and you could see how far the infection had spread based on the number of searches.

That was exactly what Roberto was doing.

Except instead of looking up influenza, he was making predictions about the *suspicious* people's goals.

Roberto couldn't figure out if the people doing *suspicious* things were all turning completely against him or if each of their *suspicious* acts were forced by some other hostile entity to get closer to those goals.

That said, he had to assume that anyone who had shown signs of being *suspicious* just once could do so again, even if they flipped between doing good and evil several times.

This was a clear attack—just an unseen one.

Each of these people being made into pawns had their own lives to live.

But whoever had been hijacking them was trying to access some information that only the hijacked could provide. If he could weed out what they were looking for, he could get to the bottom of things and figure out who the true mastermind was.

Using the confidential cloud-viewing service in the imperial package, he searched for spots of concentrated access to things that weren't related to the people's actual jobs.

And then he swore under his breath.

"...I knew it. They're after the detonator stored on Oahu."

A top-secret rig developed by the U.S. military.

A special device that could take the lives of tens of thousands of people, depending on how it was used.

And when he thought of how it operated and his current location—the Hawaiian archipelago—the president felt his hands tighten on the steering wheel.

[Nov. 10 / Source: Oahu, a table-mounted tablet camera in Green Café Iwamaki]

In a café specializing in Japanese tea near the airport, a game of football—which was pretty out of place given the setting—had been dragging on. The thing was, a TV station had bought out the administration rights for all the teams, so every game in the league was broadcast for free now, and the response from the patrons nearby was very positive. A piece of cardstock reading GIVE A ROUND OF

Applause to the Media Queen, Aurey Blueshake was affixed to the television.

Touma Kamijou was taking a call from Birdway, trying his best to hear her amid the clamor. He'd put his phone on speaker so Hamazura and Kuroyoru could listen, too.

Personally, Kamijou had wanted to ask what she thought would be a good souvenir to get for Index (specifically food), but everything Birdway was saying was about 700 percent shadier than usual, so he doubted he'd get the chance. Meanwhile, Kuroyoru had grown intimidated by Kamijou's sudden appearance, and Hamazura was watching her, still trembling.

"Dealing with Cendrillon let us draw another Gremlin sorcerer out of the woodwork. The new one can control other people. If they play it by the book, they won't show themselves. So it's gonna be all about how we can get them into the spotlight."

"Any ideas?" asked Kamijou.

"It's time to go fishing," said Birdway, sounding entertained over the phone. "I highly doubt a sorcerer like that would only be able to control a single person at once. The more they control, the stronger they'll get. We should assume they've already taken over random people in the area even. They'll make a big show of it to the point where they leave their own safety up to fate; chances are good they've got some kind of inferiority complex keeping them from making a more personal appearance. They're trying to make up for their perceived weakness with numbers.

"So," she continued, "first we collect samples of the poor people under Gremlin's control. Two or three should be enough. Then we analyze the spell and reverse engineer it to figure out what conditions need to be met for them to control someone and what form the connection between caster and victim takes. If we can figure that out, we should be able to trace it back to the caster…and we can even launch a direct counterattack through magical means."

"Then we'd obviously better make sure they don't realize we're snooping around, right?"

"Of course."

"What if they're not in Hawaii at all?"

"I can hide the fact that I've found them. It'll take more time, but we'll still be taking them by surprise while they're just lying around. In fact, we could even pretend to fail a bunch of times. Every time the idiot runs, they'll tell us where another hideout is. Gremlin will lose combat forces and capital each time. They might begin to suspect the idiot during the process, but if we can give them incorrect hints, we could make them think the caster is a defected spy. Then they'll just kill each other. By then, we'll have identified other Gremlin members, too, so we won't even need to trace back anyone."

"...That's pretty brutal."

Birdway's method of fighting was totally different from Kamijou's—all he did was punch people in the face to resolve the issue the same day it started.

Honestly, part of him wanted to blindly approve of her methods.

On the other hand, if someone asked him what he'd do in the meantime, he wouldn't be able to answer. "So what should I do?" he asked.

"Sit back and relax," said Birdway casually. "We have plenty of heroes. And they're better than you at operating behind the scenes."

[Nov. 10 / Source: Oahu, a tourist's video camera in front of Hotel Firefly]

Every hotel in blazing-hot Honolulu—except the really old ones—had a doorman and porter standing just outside the entrance. Completing the set was a valet responsible for bringing guests' cars to the underground parking lot.

Not only did those services always require you to tip the valet, but the hotel parking lots and garages themselves also tended to cost an arm and a leg. Thus, other cheaper paid parking garages had sprung up (on their own) near the hotels, with some places even being full of illegally parked vehicles.

Leaving your car parked outside in such a busy tourist destination was usually incredibly dangerous, but since most of the sightseers weren't from the island, they usually had rentals. A bit of cheap insurance beforehand meant a broken window wouldn't hurt one bit. And since nobody was dumb enough to leave their valuables in their cars, there wasn't much threat of thieves breaking in to steal people's belongings.

Edward Talkie slowly got out of his illegally parked car.

He was a white man whose suit was at the very least not off-the-rack, but the Hawaiian heat was quickly making him shed his usual style. He'd loosened his necktie and removed his blazer, draping it over an arm. At the rate he was going, he'd be undoing a few buttons on his shirt in another hour.

However.

Even as he was exposed to the blinding light reflecting off the hotel windows, Edward neither held up a hand to block it nor even narrowed his eyes. His pupils didn't shrink. He blinked with the precision of a stopwatch ticking.

He had come to this island not on vacation but on business.

His task was to speak with the local fishing association as the first step in building a foundation for a new venture: procuring a stable source of seawater to use in a line of new health drinks.

As he remembered, they would be negotiating prices in one of the rooms in this hotel.

As he remembered, these talks would happen in room 4911.

The hotel where he was really supposed to be having this meeting had a different name, though, and room 4911 was being occupied by another guest. But Edward, with his big-client contract and check shoved into his attaché case, would have seen this as something else had he known that Roselyne, who he didn't know, was currently in there.

Namely, he would have seen it as the theft of a great deal of money.

And in this country of guns, fleeing wasn't your only option of defending yourself. In fact, he had one such gun—a revolver with a four-inch barrel—tucked away in his pants pocket.

A single piece of information.

Its rearrangement and the long chain reaction that would occur because of it.

Unaware of the tiny bit of artificiality now wedged into his actions, Edward hummed a tune, pleased at the expectation that his business would soon be expanding.

And then an electronic message board attached to the hotel wall came crashing down on him.

The noise it made was massive.

It caught everyone else by surprise, and their shock eventually turned into cacophony. The hotel staff hesitated for a split second, wondering if they should leave their posts at the entrance, but their superior eventually came out and told them to do so. That got them to run over to where the message board had fallen.

But they didn't immediately move the busted-up board out of the way.

Electricity wouldn't be flowing through it anymore, but perhaps there was still a little saved up in its circuitry and electronic components. The message board burst into a shower of sparks as if to block the staff from approaching.

An ambulance siren blared in the distance; someone must have called it.

It was only after twenty minutes that the rescue crew moved the message board out of the way.

And…

"What?" murmured a crew member, perplexed.

The board had been hauled away. The cracks in the broken asphalt told the story of where it had hit the ground.

But that was all.

Edward Talkie, who should have been crushed, had vanished.

[Nov. 10 / Source: Oahu, a disaster water elevation observation camera in an underground sewer pipe]

* * *

"Here's number three," said Accelerator, dragging another poor victim through a manhole and into the sewer.

"That's all we need," said Birdway, sounding satisfied. "Good work."

"And the person controlling them really won't find out?"

"Probably not."

While the sewer was full of rotten water and smelled awful, Birdway didn't seem to mind it. Maybe she was used to harsh environments, despite her appearance.

"The sorcerer controlling people is probably getting information via their victim's senses. So if we just attack the victims, the sorcerer will find out…but if we make them lose consciousness naturally, they won't suspect anything."

"Can you really say for sure that the caster can't move the victim's eyeballs when they're unconscious?"

"It's not a sure thing, but I am basing that assumption on something."

"What?"

"Cendrillon. If the caster could do that, they'd have been gathering information even after I beat her to figure out how to defeat us."

But that hadn't actually happened.

"If I can analyze their spell, I won't just be able to trace the location of the sorcerer; I'll also be able to ferret out the pawns attacking us from their hiding places in the crowd and create a one hundred percent perfect plan of defense. In short, it would be checkmate."

The possibility of being attacked by an ordinary person they weren't paying attention to was a threat—and creating a situation in which those people could be immediately identified as enemies would make the threat disappear. Neither Birdway nor Accelerator were the type of person to fear guns.

"…So none of this is one hundred percent yet? You are full of confidence, but it's possible you could have attacked someone completely innocent?"

"Don't raise your eyebrows at me. I'm *still* almost certainly correct. I just want to be completely certain. Anyway…"

They'd laid the three victims in passages for workers to the left and right of the sewer pipe.

"We have what we need. Let's get analyzing. If you want to learn more about sorcery, now's your chance."

[Nov. 10 / Source: Oahu, a sorcerer's cell phone camera in a smoking area in the Coral Street shopping mall]

If there was anything odd about cell phones these days, it was that they had more camera lenses now.

The ones on the backs of phones for taking photos were normal, yes, but now there were lenses on the front for video conferences and even 3D photo lenses. Maybe one day, phones would be wrapped entirely in cameras like decorative beads.

A girl of about fifteen was busy switching her phone's camera from front to back. She had short blond hair and fair skin. She wore a turtleneck and miniskirt, both in shades of green, and thick boots that ran up above her knees. She also had on a hair band that was made of tree branches. All in all, she stood out against the jungle of glass and concrete buildings.

Wearing an expression that spoke to her frustration over her cellphone having too many features, she struggled with the delicate device until eventually speaking into it.

"Yes, right. Well, it looks like it failed. My widdle attacker, Edward, lost consciousness, and the room on the forty-ninth floor of Hotel Firefly is still untouched. Ugh. Looks like they caught wind of the message board falling and went after it. I guess attacking the assistant's group just wasn't realistic after all, huh?"

Her manner of speaking gave away the fact that she was trying to be formal but wasn't used to it.

And it also sounded like she hadn't spared a thought for the possibility of angering the person on the other end of the line or what would happen if she did. But she was skilled enough to avoid any threats that befell her, regardless.

Mainly by using other people as shields.

"Yes, yes. I'm aware. The widdle incident at the airport wasn't ideal, but the bones of the plan will start to decay if we don't boost its immune system. Anyway, we now know how many people we're up against and how serious they are, so there's a bright side to all this. No problems here."

The sorcerer wasn't so much analyzing the situation logically as trying to say whatever she could to placate the person on the other end.

"Anyway, we'll stick to the plan. We can skip taking the long way around for the bonus stages and just work on the main story—the detonator."

After giving her explanation, the sorcerer's eyebrow twitched slightly. For the first time, she seemed to show an interest in what the other caller had said.

"Ugh, yikes. I see. That figures. I knew it was probably too much of a coincidence. They're interfering, huh?"

The sorcerer didn't seem too bothered by that.

"No, no, I'm grateful. If it were me, I might have just dismissed the idea as me overthinking things. Best to make sure of stuff, y'know? Not just play widdle armchair detective—really get in there for proof. Right, yes, right. I'll handle that as well. Anyway, bye."

She hung up, rolled the phone in her hand for a moment, and then stuck it in her pocket.

It appeared promotions to decrease smokers were all the rage internationally, as nobody else was in the smoking area. On the wall was a poster of a grotesque, blown-up photo of a sperm cell, with a tagline reading YOU'LL HAVE LESS. Was this part of why the area was deserted?

The sorcerer shrugged, then turned around.

Someone was standing there. A tall Black man with a tough build and a military veteran look to him.

He was one of the people under her control. A more elaborate form of control than the others.

The sorcerer spoke.

"Well, that's that. *You're up, widdle Mr. Cheat Code.*"

[Nov. 10 / Source: Oahu, a security camera near the east entrance to the Coral Street shopping mall]

Leivinia Birdway's words were filled with confidence.

"C'mon," she chided. "We've already got the data we need to figure out their spell."

She waved her hand around—she was holding a strip of paper. It was about the size of a modest certificate but thicker, and it had a rough surface. She told him it was papyrus. A "product" used as a royal burial accessory that she'd bought from a plant-related specialist, apparently.

"Time will reveal their weak point. The automatic process will end in about an hour. In fact, it's disclosing the intel little by little right now. For example, it's revealing the nature of the connection between the victims and the caster—and where they're controlling the victims from."

Accelerator walked with the assistance of his modern-looking crutch, listening to her as they both went through the shopping mall.

"In concrete terms," she explained, "it's some Russian Catholic dropout."

"Russian?"

"They use spells named after fae spirits there. Probably Leshy, in this case. Ruler of the forests and king of all the animals who live within it. Cendrillon mentioned red and black when she gave control over to them, right?"

"Yeah. So what?"

"That'd be a roulette wheel. It's a wager. Leshy likes to gamble with the forest creatures. Naturally, the winner takes authority from the loser."

"......"

"In this case, Leshy designates its surrounding environment as its forest and the people who live in it as its creatures, allowing the caster to control them. I don't know the conditions just yet, but that's only a matter of time. The analysis spell will reveal them soon. And then it'll all be over."

"But it's *not* over yet. Aren't you a little too confident?"

"Even without knowing the spell's conditions, I can most likely ferret out the victims being controlled, at least. A surprise attack on us would have almost zero chance of success."

That was her declaration.

However…

Bang, bang, bang, bang, bang! Several dull gunshots rang out.
From behind Birdway.
From just five meters away.

[Nov. 10 / Source: Oahu, a speed limit camera on an arterial road near a beach]

At the exact moment the attack on Birdway occurred, a station wagon smashed into Roberto Catze's beat-up convertible.

The two vehicles swerved off the road and crashed into one of the evenly spaced palm trees, which sent a coconut tumbling down onto the president's head.

"Blegh… Th-that was good. Very Hawaii. I bet if I wrote this down in a picture diary, nobody would believe it."

The car was totaled, but the station wagon had struck the passenger's side, leaving the driver's seat unharmed. For a moment, he worried that the imperial package had gotten damaged, but the thing was surprisingly sturdy since it was made for emergencies. There wasn't a scratch on it.

For now, he closed the attaché case, ignored the door—which was no longer opening—and jumped out of the convertible. A frantic tourist approached, but he gestured at the man to get him to stop, then came up to the station wagon.

"You swerved straight into me," Roberto said. "Not used to driving, are we?"

Despite the crash, the front windshield of the station wagon was still intact. And it was tinted, meaning this was no respectable vehicle. Still, Roberto peered into the window of the driver's seat.

"You really hit me hard, too," he said. "What would you have done if that knocked you out, my man—or should I say, my kidnapper?"

In response, the window came down.

And a hand appeared—holding an automatic pistol.

"...But even I can kill you," the man inside said. "Anyone can be an assassin as long as they have a gun and a finger to pull the trigger."

"Whoa, give me a break," scoffed Roberto. "That gun's from War and Safety Co., the biggest firearm manufacturer in the U.S. *And one of the organizations that supports me.* Why do you have to use one of their products to kill me? That's just tragic. You're gonna get a complaint at my funeral, you know. They'll tell you off for ruining their brand image."

But then he noticed something.

There was something in the man's eyes as the airbag, still inflated, squeezed into him.

"...Oh. You're *being controlled*, aren't you, my man?"

[Nov. 10 / Source: Oahu, a sorcerer's cell phone camera in a smoking area of the Coral Street shopping mall]

As the sorcerer took out her cell phone to check the time, she heard the dull bang of a gun in the distance, followed by the screams of onlookers.

"Amateurs are scary, man. Once they decide to do something, they go hog wild."

She wasn't talking to herself, but she received no answer.

Next to the sorcerer was a Black girl of around ten. In her right hand was a flathead screwdriver. She was frozen still, the tip of the screwdriver pressed against her head.

"Gives me chills looking at her," murmured the sorcerer. "All I had to do was say I'd crunch her widdle brains up like a frozen orange, and he was completely on board."

Birdway had analyzed the sorcerer's technique.

Using the folk legend of Leshy, the caster had expanded her role as ruler of the forest creatures to gain control over people.

But if she sent people under her control at Birdway, the girl would sense them from the spell's residual mana and eliminate them before they got close.

The sorcerer's thralls couldn't get near Birdway.

That was the most important thing.

However.

There was more than one way to control a human.

For instance…

By controlling a man's daughter, I can command her father without touching his mind.

"Birdway's talented, I'll give her that. But talent always comes with vulnerabilities. In this case, I can slip straight past her, since in her mind, the only danger is the presence of my spell."

The sorcerer smirked.

Apart from the ten-year-old girl, there were several other children in the smoking area.

Each of them was a hostage she could use for a dirty trick if the situation demanded it.

The sorcerer had as many disposable pawns for pulling dirty tricks as she had hostages. For example, the criminal route of targeting Roberto Catze fell under that classification.

"And if I can slip through, that's it. It won't matter if she's a widdle sorcerer or not. Bullets tend to kill people."

Several more gunshots rang out—either the father was making sure, or the police officers who'd run to the scene were shooting the father.

Either way, it didn't matter. That first shot, delivered while the target was in a completely defenseless state, made the result all too clear.

[Nov. 10 / Source: Oahu, a security camera near the eastern entrance of the Coral Street shopping mall]

With a whole bunch of bullets now lodged in her back, Leivinia Birdway fell to the shopping mall's polished floor. The tall Black man continued to fire his gun after that.

The tourists, all taken by surprise, fled frantically and erratically from the scene.

An explosion of angry yells and screams.

Accelerator's eyes were wide as he watched the situation unfold.

The man was shaking. There were tears in his eyes. And yet he hadn't hesitated at all. He discarded the empty magazine, then put a new one in.

That was when Number One finally snapped out of his daze.

He hit the switch on his electrode choker. His power as the strongest Level Five, the power that had given him his name, activated. He was about to break the guy's neck, then crush his head in the very next move, but he heard something.

"Wow. Shit. Almost had a dramatic death there."

Birdway's head popped up.

The Black man fell onto his rear end, screaming something. Accelerator kicked him in the chest, then yelled in spite of himself.

"What the hell?!"

"Having a substitute for emergencies is as basic as it gets," she replied. "And besides, we're up against people who would say really cringe things when it comes to modern western sorcery, like saying they'll kill their old self to be reborn as their new self."

Birdway took a tarot card out of her pocket—a member of the major arcana, the Hanged Man. It depicted a man hanging upside down from a tree branch, but the card had several holes in it.

And Birdway herself hadn't shed a drop of blood.

"The symbology of Jesus's death as an age unto itself can correspond to this Crowley tarot. While this is originally not the same as the story of that execution, I can greatly improve the two concepts' compatibility, especially when it comes to stabbing wounds, by purposely stretching the interpretation… Even I'd want to wear bulletproof gear in this grand nation of guns. It's just that I'd rather not get myself all sweaty in some thick bulletproof vest.

"Anyway," she said, "I get it; your rage and sadness at my death awakened you to your true powers or whatever. Would you just get the guy with the gun out of here?"

"…Ability development's so much more direct."

"We won't get any hints about the mastermind out of him. I already have the information I need to reverse calculate the spell. Besides, he's not even under the sorcerer's control."

"What?"

"They took an indirect approach. Though I have to say, I'm a little surprised. I don't usually compliment people, so make sure to remember this."

Ignoring Accelerator's dubious look in response, Birdway approached the tall Black man with long strides. The man quickly readied his gun again. Had he remembered what he needed to do? Or had he sensed danger from the strange monster coming toward him?

"If our sorcerer sticks purely to manipulating people, then this one's an easy guess. They threatened you by controlling someone close to you, right?"

"?!"

"Unlike *some* people, I don't let the blood go to my head. No need for annoying formalities here. And no need for friendliness, either. I'll give it to you straight. Just the facts, nothing else."

Birdway stood tall and proud in front of the man, not caring about the gun that could go off at any moment as she addressed him.

"You can still make it out of this," she said, gesturing to her meager chest with her thumb. "But there won't be a next time. I don't care what your reason is or what's going on. If you pull that trigger,

I'll die. A little bit more of that trembling you're doing, and you won't be able to take it back. You'll never have a second chance. Got it? Second chances like these almost never come around."

With a sharp, terrifying glint in her eye, the victim spoke to the assailant.

In a tone that clearly implied she was intimately familiar with crossing that line.

"...Do you still want to shoot me? Do you have the guts to go through the shock you just caused yourself all over again?"

The man's shaking reached its peak.

He must have made a lot of decisions on his way here. He'd have repeated so many justifications to himself, trying to make this all seem right.

Now that he'd done the deed and failed, the house of cards had come crashing down.

Perhaps, if he was able to calmly stack them up again, he would have remembered the danger his daughter was in. And then, armed with logic, he might have shot Birdway again. But you couldn't put a house of cards back together with trembling fingers. He now knew the shock you felt when you first shot a person. He could no longer use empty platitudes to justify placing someone's life on scales of his own making.

A helpless scream rang out.

It expressed both rage at a dead-end future and atonement toward Birdway, to whom he had personally done harm.

As the man screamed, he put the gun in his mouth.

Accelerator and Birdway moved at the same time, kicking the firearm away and knocking the man out for real this time.

"A little overboard," remarked Birdway shortly before her tone changed. "Anyway, this just got hairy. I don't have any more Hanged Men."

"You just weren't being careful enough."

"Not exactly. This little stunt was the sorcerer's attempt to counter me—they know I'm analyzing their spell. But how did Gremlin figure that out? I did everything perfectly. And you did nothing wrong when you collected those people, either. And yet…"

"……"

"I'm not amused. But if we look into it, we might *find* something amusing."

[Nov. 10 / Source: Oahu, a speed limit camera on an arterial road near a beach]

After Roberto's comment, the man in the driver's seat flinched a little, even with his gun in the president's face. Maybe he was trying to nod.

Eventually, the attacker opened his mouth.

"…What does it matter?" he asked.

"Well, usually that points to a hostage situation, my man. Your lover? Or a child?"

"What does it fucking matter?!" the attacker screamed, re-aiming his gun. "It doesn't matter what the reason is! It won't change anything! So come with me. If I capture you, my family will be safe! I don't give a shit about what happens to the country!"

"…Hey, now. You seriously think that's a fair deal? You came right up to me without a shred of good faith and threatened me off the bat."

"I don't care. I don't fucking care! Even a one percent chance is good enough! If I let you go, my kid's gonna die!"

"Nice words," said the president with a grin. "But you shouldn't use them in desperation. If you're willing to believe in a one percent chance, shouldn't you have made a better choice to begin with?"

"Fuck off. Fuck off! Can't you see this gun?! Be afraid! Just follow my directions! Some lunatic kidnapped my niece. Long story, but my late wife gave her life to protect her. So I can't lose her. Anyway, things would never have gotten this bad if you police and government shits did your job!"

The man was only expressing his rage at indistinct crimes and dissatisfaction with law enforcement organizations for not being able to prevent them. Roberto doubted he knew anything about his enemy's true identity, even though he was clearly in the thick of it.

But in a way, what the man was saying cut straight to the danger the United States now faced.

They were the words of both an aggressor and a victim.

Cognizant of the irony in his would-be kidnapper's statement, the president still spoke.

"My man."

He moved slowly, completely ignoring the muzzle of the gun.

"Allow me to apologize to you and your little baby. We may be taught in this country to never say sorry, even if there's a murder, but I will lower my head and apologize. And I'll also say this. Who you saw is the true enemy I must fight. I cannot stop—I *must not* stop until I've beaten them to a pulp. After all, I'm the president of this great nation. It's my job to protect the lives and freedom of its people."

"Screw you with that shit… When have you *ever* cared about our lives?! You can drop the cool-guy act. It's not election season. I don't expect a lick of goodness from a damned politician like you!"

The muzzle quivered.

But Roberto's expression didn't change.

He placed both elbows on the frame of the driver's seat window and peered inside. The action was so casual that the man in the seat automatically drew his gun back to remeasure the distance.

Roberto ignored him and continued.

"Let me tell you a story. Something my father, rest his soul, once said to me. He loved telling me to be a strong man. The asshole was an out-of-control drunk. The only time the light in his eyes always came on was when he said that, though."

"…What …? What does this have to do with—"

"So I decided I'd seek out the greatest power I could. And that led me to becoming president of the United States."

Roberto chuckled, gazing into the gun-toting assailant's eyes.

"Let me ask you this, my man. When you think of a strong man, do you think of someone who would follow inhumane orders just to protect himself? Or someone who hides behind a facade of status and authority, then pisses himself at the mere sight of a gun? This country I'm supposed to protect is in danger. An innocent kid is being held hostage. You think one lead bullet shot is gonna scare me into tucking tail? You think my dream is to give up and live in fear?"

For just a moment, the attacker lost sight of reality.

He forgot he was holding a gun—that he was the one in control of the situation.

"I want to hear your answer, my man."

There was only the voice of Roberto Catze, president of the United States.

"How do you think my ideal strong man would react to this outrage?"

[Nov. 10 / Source: Oahu, a dashcam on a government vehicle]

The black luxury car's mini fridge was filled with bottles of perfectly chilled champagne, ready to drink, but Roselyne Crackhart didn't go for them. Well, she did actually reach for the fridge door, but then the accountant's gaze made her remember that she was on official business right now.

In the middle of the fancy leather sofa looping around the interior of the vehicle was a table that looked just as expensive. Roselyne picked up a magazine on it, but when she noticed the enormous mug shot of the president on the front cover, she tossed it aside.

The accountant scrambled to catch it, and the periodical happened to open to a certain page in the process.

"Is it true that he pushed for huge medical reforms," she said as she glanced at it, "so that nobody would have to go through the pain his father did from the cancer that killed him?"

"Of course not. That's just the usual malarkey. If you believed everything the president said, you'd think his father died eighty times over. We're thinking of throwing a party when it hits a hundred."

[Nov. 10 / Source: Oahu, a speed limit camera on an arterial road near a beach]

Face-to-face with Roberto Catze, the attacker trembled. Then he lowered the muzzle.

The president hadn't done anything. He hadn't pulled out an even stronger weapon or anything.

He'd just spoken to him.

And the words he'd used packed more than enough of a punch to open the man's eyes and whittle away at his will to fight.

"What…? What are you…?"

"If it's gonna be a one percent chance anyway, might as well bet on that, right? Let's save your kid instead of going along with some shithead criminal."

"You're lying. You're trying to get out of this with tall tales."

"Nah. We've got a chance."

The president's words instantly banished the attacker's suspicions.

"I've been wrapped up in their schemes since way back when I was on the mainland. And when I think back to the guy I met earlier today, I'm starting to see a pattern. A bit of one anyway."

Yes.

The true criminal had already reached the White House, the House of Representatives, the Senate, countless agencies, and even the military.

"It's the eyes," said the president. "Anyone suspicious is like… How should I put it? Their eyes are weird. Happened when I first caught on to all this, too. Ever since setting up that emergency financial security bill, I can sense it in their eyes."

"Their eyes?"

"It happened to the Secret Service, my second secretary, the reporter who showed up at the press conference—even the old cleaning lady. They're everywhere. And they're not all from the same group, or ethnicity, or age range, or ideologies, or religion. But they all have one thing in common: their eyes. None of them look at me for very long, but it's like I've been under constant surveillance. Their numbers grew and grew until they finally had a majority. The White House is now filled with the awful folks."

The president wasn't familiar with the occult, so he didn't know if all these enemies had sprung up organically or if someone was picking specific people to control based on the situation. Either way, the dangerous elements were continuing to increase.

And anyone who stumbled even once, even for a moment, would likely end up becoming one of them—even though they hadn't been doing anything wrong to begin with.

"…Like you can't sense what they're thinking? Like their faces are lifeless?" the man said.

"Sounds like your baby is the same way."

"With her, it was more like a, uh…a vacant expression, though."

Hearing the attacker's words, Roberto exhaled. "Since it was getting so annoying, I contacted some people outside the White House and tried to get them to investigate—and solve it if they needed to. We all know how that went. I found out it wasn't just people in the White House turning suspicious. Basically, I started noticing them in the NSA and the CIA, too. With each passing day, more and more people started acting dangerously."

And he also knew that they'd used government networks to access top secret information on the detonator.

"I have no idea what kind of tech the mastermind is using, but they can control people. And they're probably getting a ton of intel through those people's eyes."

When he checked using the imperial package, he discovered that missile research facility staff and even crew members on nuclear submarines were trying to get to the detonator. Naturally, they weren't able to use cell phones in such a special environment. Even if they got the information, they'd have to get it back to the mastermind somehow. In other words, it seemed like the mastermind wasn't gathering information via the communication devices belonging to the people under their control—they were jacking into those people's senses.

"And that's where our chance is," said Roberto. "If you were perfectly under their control, it would expose them, no matter how they tried to hide it. But that's not the case. *You're just a normal person in a hostage situation, so the mastermind has no way of getting information from you.* So there's a slim chance we can pull off a surprise attack by slipping past their senses."

[Nov. 10 / Source: Oahu, a table-mounted tablet camera in Green Café Iwamaki]

"I just hope it works."

Kamijou was listening to what Birdway had to say over the phone. They were doing their best to gain an opportunity to counterattack using the normal people being forced to fight, but…

"*You saw how easy it was for someone to shoot me. The sorcerer behind these attacks may have some way of locating us. And if they do, they might have realized the civilian messed up—and that they don't need the hostage anymore… Which is really getting this monster with me upset. God, he's such a hero.*"

"What does that even mean? The mastermind can magically control people around them, right? Couldn't they have made someone a lookout and—"

"I'd have noticed any lookouts," Birdway interrupted. "*I can sniff out the mastermind's spell already, remember? How far-reaching would their network of lookouts have to be? How would they know I was here at the shopping mall? Or are you saying they put lookouts in to cover every nook and cranny of every one of the Hawaiian Islands?*"

"...You're not saying they have some other way of getting information besides their magic, are you?"

"*They do, and it at least covers all of Oahu, if not the entire archipelago. Plus, even people on the magic side like me can't detect it...*"

"If it's not magic, then... Maybe they're using science-side tech for surveillance."

Kamijou looked around. One likely culprit was tucked away in a corner of the café, right up by the ceiling.

"...The *cameras*...?"

"*Whether or not we're right, we'll need to do something about them.*" Birdway then gave a few commands.

Kamijou frowned. "Are you sure that'll work?"

"*I should be the one asking you, but probably. To be honest, this is all science-side territory—not my wheelhouse,*" said Birdway casually.

However the cookie crumbled, they had to press on.

That's the kind of intent he sensed from her.

"...Anyway, was it okay to get those people mixed up in this?" he asked carefully. "They might have come at us with guns, but they were just normal people in hostage situations, right? Would they be able to survive a battle between sorcerers?"

"*Gremlin lurks in Hawaii, and if we want to get rid of them, we'll need to eliminate the sorcerer controlling people right now. Considering how easy it was for someone to locate and attack me, we should assume they know our faces, to an extent... And in that case, we should get help from people the enemy won't see coming.*

"*Plus,*" added Birdway, "*either way, the hostages will die unless we do something. I'd guess the string pullers trying to stay hidden will ultimately want to deal with the perpetrator actually threatening people with the hostages. Let me think. Put a gun in a hostage's hands and tell him to kill his daddy, and both will die. Two birds with one stone, right?*"

"Those bastards," spat Kamijou.

As Hamazura listened to the conversation over the speakerphone, his expression grew more severe. Kuroyoru just looked bored, though.

"...What should we do?" he asked.

"We should figure out who the people under threat are before we start fighting them at all. The more allies we have, the better. If we can get a read on how many of them there are, we can figure how many hostages we need to save."

"How should we do that?" Kamijou frowned. "Unlike you, I can't sense sorcery or mana or whatever."

"No need to worry about that," said Birdway smoothly. "They attacked me. We can assume they know your face and most of the people in our group—and more importantly, they know you're alive from the Radiosonde Castle incident. They would have put together a rock-solid plan to deal with you before even coming to Hawaii... For you personally, at least, the enemies will come to you."

Shudder.

Just then, an awful chill ran down Kamijou's spine.

With a shout, he locked eyes with a tall gun-toting man who had just kicked in the entrance door and stormed into the café.

Kamijou flung Kuroyoru's small body out of the way, then dove to the floor. A moment later, Hamazura frantically jumped over a thirty-centimeter-thick partition. As soon as he did, a series of shrill gunshots rang out.

[Nov. 10 / Source: Oahu, a sorcerer's cell phone camera in a smoking area in the Coral Street shopping mall]

Ten minutes had passed since she'd heard the gunshots.

But the pitiful berserkers worrying for their children neither contacted her on her cell phone nor came back to her.

Maybe the police in the area actually shot them dead for real, the sorcerer wondered, unconcerned.

She took her phone out of her pocket and thumbed over it as she spoke to the people nearby.

The hostages—standing stock-still.

The sorcerer was controlling four children. None of them looked any older than ten.

"Okay, everyone! Listen carefully to what I have to say now, okay?"

With the tone and cadence of a tour guide, the sorcerer drew the children's attention, then unfastened her bag and removed several automatic 9mm pistols from it.

"The adults walking around outside are really, really dangerous. Understand? But with these *police buzzers*, you'll be safe and sound. If you turn up the volume on this buzzer at the big, mean grown-ups, they'll get scared and run away. So if you see any grown-ups, *just point the buzzer at them and use it*. Got it?"

Next, she took out drawstring bags that were stuffed with bombs resembling lumps of clay. As she attached the medical electrodes extending from them to the children's wrists, she maintained her sweet smile.

"And these are *GPSes*, okay? So even if a scary, dangerous grown-up catches you, we'll know exactly where you are. *Just push the secret button*, and I'll come right away to save you. Don't ever take off those GPSes, okay?"

This was the same trick she'd used with Edward Talkie when she'd tried to have him attack the Oahu hotel.

A form of manipulation that took advantage of mismatches in information.

From an observer's point of view, her instructions were insane. But nobody was here to realize it. The children's emotions had been dampened; they simply gazed at the sorcerer with lifeless eyes, guns and bombs in their hands.

She gave a thin smile. At the very least, Leivinia Birdway was in this very shopping mall.

Ideally, she would cause a huge disturbance and slip away in the commotion, putting distance between them safely and surely.

The present issue was how they were positioned. The shopping mall had seven entrances, but if Birdway's group made it to her current location, even a commotion might not be enough to protect the sorcerer.

To mitigate that, she had contacted her "collaborator" and tried to get the enemy's position from them, but...

"...?"

With the cell phone to her ear, the sorcerer frowned. She glanced at the small screen again, tilting her head in confusion.

"Out of service?"

It happened a moment later.

Men with guns in their hands shattered the window on one side of the smoking area and dove inside.

Yes.

The very pitiful civilians she'd taken hostages for to manipulate.

[Nov. 10 / Source: Oahu, a CCD in a laptop carried by a tourist near the western entrance of the Coral Street shopping mall]

Mikoto Misaka and Misaka Worst dashed through the large shopping mall.

Pale blue sparks occasionally danced at the ends of their bangs. Having realized the enemy was likely using camera imagery to find them, they were jamming the radio waves.

"Ugh, this sucks...," grumbled Mikoto. "I finally get a call, and it's a request to be a human jammer. And he's supposed to get that cyborg's help to rescue the family of that gunner who attacked us, too... God, that idiot's got a lot of time on his hands. We came all the way here to Hawaii. This wasn't the heart-pounding event I envisioned..."

"Hmm. You seem to be gazing longingly at that swimsuit store. Which one of those are you imagining yourself in? A sling bikini? A micro bikini? Something more Brazilian? There's even one with an I-front and an O-back, you know."

"Gwaaaaaahhhhhh! Is there a rule in this county that says the less you're wearing, the better?!"

"But sling bikinis are pretty tricky, Misaka. They use your breasts to create a bridge-shaped gap. If you tried it, wouldn't it basically just be like wrapping pasted bandages on yourself?"

"One more word, and you're getting a taste of something unprecedented! Like a rail shotgun!"

"...You don't look very intimidating with that shopping bag from Cupid's Arrow in your hand."

"*Brrfft!*"

"Misaka's not answering such a sublime reaction. Misaka's a little worried about that kid's electrode choker, but it would probably be funny if it malfunctioned. Let's get jamming!"

[Nov. 10 / Source: Oahu, a security camera in a smoking area in the Coral Street shopping mall]

The sorcerer pursed her lips a little.

She'd written off these pawns as civilians, as nobodies. She'd planned on disposing of both them *and* the hostages. They were small fry, nothing more—and now they had guns pointed at her.

But then she grinned.

"Fools. Guess we're moving the schedule up!"

She snapped her fingers. The hostages who were standing totally still—the small children—began to move. Bags hanging from their shoulders and guns gripped in their hands, they advanced on their true family.

A gunshot rang out.

But no tragedy ensued.

Because just before the discharge, the ceiling of the shopping mall caved in. Someone had just built a shutter made of debris—Accelerator. And he didn't stop there. Controlling kinetic vectors, he launched toward the children at superhuman speed and kicked the bags from their shoulders, sending them careening away.

A few of the children tried to clamp their upper arms into their sides, but they didn't make it in time.

Ignition came, along with a roar of explosive flames that—outside of its immediate radius—only served to shake the building.

"...You set things up to increase casualties until those kids got shot, then blow them up as they did, eh? Yeah, we figured it out, you shithead. Got a few samples."

The sorcerer immediately searched for an exit. But then Kamijou and Hamazura darted into the two hallways connecting the smoking area with the rest of the mall.

Not good, she thought. She didn't like where this was going.

But not because of all the people who had just assembled here.

Birdway's the important one here, yet I still don't know where she is. I could cause a commotion to run away, but if she's waiting for me at the exit, things will get extremely bad...!

As she backed into a corner of the smoking area, she felt a bead of sweat trickling down her nose.

Naturally, she couldn't afford to die here. What was her next move?

She glanced at the civilians, who pointed their guns at her with zero hesitation and would pull the triggers with equally little. Just then, however, the situation changed.

Thanks to a single explosive suddenly thrown in from outside the camera frame.

[Nov. 10 / Critical error]

[F.C.E. currently under heavy load from an unknown source.]
　　[Automatically diagnosing issue... Report complete.]
　　[F.C.E. initiating reboot sequence.]

[Nov. 10 / Source: Oahu, a security camera in front of the coin lockers in the Coral Street shopping mall]

* * *

Kamijou and Accelerator burst into the space adjacent to the smoking area. Each of them had pushed the hostage children out of the way a moment before.

"What happened to Hamazura?!" cried Kamijou.

"Probably went to another exit. Along with their parents. Anyway, what the hell was that? What kind of fucking idiot would barge in like that?!"

They heard the *grshhh-grshhh-grshhh* of metal scraping against metal from the other side of the black smoke.

Kamijou tried to peer inside, but Accelerator grabbed him by the back of the neck.

A moment later, a gunshot went off.

But it wasn't from a handgun. The noise was deeper than that, and there were several. Likely an assault rifle or something.

Which meant one thing.

"That ain't anything occult...," muttered Accelerator. "That means it's my turn. You take these brats and get out of here."

"Hey...!"

"I can't respond while these kids are here. And with your power, you should be able to fix them, yeah?"

He was right. The one kid Kamijou had pushed out of the way was already acting differently than before. Just standing there in a daze—probably because of his right hand.

Accelerator didn't turn around. "This battlefield is meant for me. You get going already."

"...I'll return the favor. Don't let them kill you."

After saying that, Kamijou tapped on the hostages' heads—they were still trying to carry out their attack at the sorcerer's orders. His touch alone brought them back to their senses. He moved away from the coin lockers, bringing them all with him, while the attackers responsible for the metallic noises appeared from the curtain of smoke and made to run.

As if to challenge the assailants, Accelerator stepped out in front of them.

"Might be breaking the rules a bit here, but I'm just putting the right people to the right tasks."

[Nov. 10 / Source: Oahu, a tourist's smartphone camera on the eastern section of the first floor of the Coral Street shopping mall]

The sudden explosion and gunshots had whipped the shopping mall into a frenzy. Nobody was idiotic enough to try and get a glimpse of what was happening. Anyone with even a shred of sense ran for the exits as fast as they could, but there were just too many people. The crowds grew congested at the exits, and everyone ended up packed in like sardines.

Mark, one of the black-suits, asked Birdway, "Did it go well?"

"I still hear gunshots," she replied, "so they're still fighting it out. Anyway, our enemy sure has been taking it easy, using all these innocent people as thralls. They had to expect a counterattack at some point. What annoys me is how I can't get periodic reports directly from the ones on-site. Makes me appreciate these cell phones a lot more."

Her tone was casual as she continued.

"We got the civilians on our side to pinpoint the sorcerer's location…but who would've thought we were in the same shopping mall all along. The multipronged attack appears to be working fairly well, which means we can just do nothing and still win."

"Still, though… We have allies stationed at all the exits. With all the commotion, the sorcerer could slip away."

"We'll track the flow of mana. That way we can stop civilians from getting involved."

"What if they don't temper any mana whatsoever?"

"Impossible. This place isn't safe for them. They'll be well-defended to protect against surprise attacks. They know creating mana would put them in danger, but they'll probably still be too scared not to have some in reserve."

Birdway was operating under the hypothesis that the sorcerer in question specialized in controlling people. Her read was that they'd run away without a second thought if someone came up and attacked them.

That was why she was lying in wait at one of the exits herself, anticipating someone like that to show up. However…

"Hmm?"

She frowned at a person in the crowd.

"What's *that* celebrity doing here?"

[Nov. 10 / Source: Oahu, a security camera in front of Coral Street shopping mall coin lockers]

Five people in total, every one of them armed, had exited the smoke to face Accelerator.

They all wore special-looking silver military uniforms that covered them from the crown of their heads to the tips of their toes. Their outfits even shined like CDs. Accelerator couldn't make out their faces, but from their builds, he could just barely make out that three were men and two were women. They all sported unusual bullpup-style assault rifles, with additional recoilless guns hanging on the men's shoulders and high-tech microphones and fiber scopes suspended on the women's hips to aid in gathering information.

…*Damn it*, thought Accelerator. *Are they with Gremlin, too? That gear isn't for fighting people. It's for camouflage against sensors.*

None of the five said a word. One of the men brought his rifle up and fired it without hesitation.

Accelerator had his reflection, though. The man's bullet pierced him instead, sending him careening through the floor, but the other four didn't react with confusion or panic. They each began moving individually.

Were they just seeing what I could do?

The group had ignored individual casualties, treating the man as a necessary sacrifice for group-wide damage control. It was revolting, but it didn't change what Number One had to do.

Altering the direction of the energy in his legs, he exploded forward. The hunt had begun. No matter how his enemies responded, his reflection was perfect against bullets and explosives. Each of the attackers went down at his hand, unable to do anything about it.

However.

The last one was different.

The instant she reached her five fingers out in front of her face, fresh blood spurted from Accelerator's right arm.

"...Huh?"

There was no bullet crossing the wall of his reflection.

Nor was it a gas or a biological weapon—even unseen threats wouldn't have been able to injure him.

In other words, the destruction had begun inside his body.

The final attacker jumped to the side, and Accelerator, unable to course correct, crashed into the wall. Blood splattered onto that, too. His brain could barely register that it belonged to him.

Still up against the wall, he muttered, "Wait, then...you're..."

"All espers obey a common set of rules," stated the attacker, readying her bullpup rifle. "And when a scientifically created esper tries to use a magical spell, they face side effects."

"...You're... You're one of those sorcerers, too...?!"

He tried to yell, but blood erupted from deep in his throat.

The assailants' movements. The way they'd fled. The timing of this attack. Everything had been calculated to trick Accelerator into doing exactly what they wanted—to trick him into triggering magic.

It didn't matter what the spell itself actually did. It could be something useless, like producing a faint light at his fingertips. Actually, it could have even been something so indistinct that no one would be able to see it. The important thing was to make an esper use sorcery.

Accelerator's thoughts took him that far, but then he noticed his mind growing muddled.

He'd used something like sorcery once before, but back then, he'd known his limits perfectly and had made extremely precise adjustments. This was completely different. It was like he'd just taken a huge step into things without realizing it.

And…

The power of a scientific esper took shape via the brain and the brain alone.

With a clouded mind, he wouldn't be able to perform calculations as well—and that would affect his control over visible, macro-level physical reality.

In short…his reflection had, in essence, just been taken away.

The female attacker, her face hidden and her finger on her rifle's trigger, spoke next.

"*Gremlin* gets its name from a supernatural being that causes mechanical malfunctions. Did you never stop and think about what that could mean?"

And then.

Gunshots rang out. There was no hesitation.

Blood splattered. A human body, mowed down, falling with a thud. A pool of dark red blood, mercilessly flowing from the body on the floor.

However.

None of it was Accelerator's.

The shooter—had just been shot herself by someone from the side.

Even on the floor, she gripped her bullpup rifle. Without aiming much, she began spraying bullets in the direction the attack had come from.

But…

"You're out of the game, ma'am. Rapid-fire at random all you want; you'll never hit me. The distance isn't important—your stability is. Doesn't matter how strong your gun is. With a shitty stance, you can't even hit something ten meters away."

He heard a deep male voice.

Bang! Bang!! With a couple more light-sounding gunshots, a bloodred hole opened up in the attacker's right shoulder. This time, the rifle slid from her hand, and she groaned, out of energy to resist.

"Don't pick up a gun if you're not gonna hit for sure, idiot. You want to get yourself killed?! Nowhere on Earth is more famous for its guns than *this* land!"

"Who…are you…?" asked the blood-soaked Accelerator of whoever was flinging those insults.

"I should be saying that, Japanese boy. I came here to rescue some kids, and you took all the glory."

"…I said, *Who are you?*"

"God, does nobody even watch the morning news anymore?"

The man—probably in his forties or fifties, with a gun in his hand—gave an exasperated sigh.

"I'm the God-damned president."

[Nov. 10 / Source: Oahu, a tourist's video camera in White Beach Golf Club]

The flood of tourists poured out of the shopping mall and fled in every direction, some of them to the nearby beach. But this wasn't just an accident or a fire—they were running from a shooting, so a lot of the crowd angled toward other indoor facilities.

On any other day, the White Beach Golf Club would have been members only. Unfortunately, the security team's shouts were useless against the raging waves of people pressing in on them. They hesitated to use guns to threaten the crowd because this was an emergency and lives were already at risk.

Disguised as a member of the crowd, a Gremlin sorcerer thumbed over her cell phone.

Birdway's group was watching all the exits, but apparently, they hadn't expected her to break down a wall to get straight outside. An explosion or two could be missed in a gunfight of that magnitude.

She listened to the call tone for a few moments until it eventually went through.

Without waiting for the other person to speak first, the sorcerer flared up.

"Why did *they* show up?! They weren't supposed to show up yet!"

"Well, we wouldn't have had to deal with this setback if you'd had a better handle on things."

The voice on the other end belonged to a young woman. She continued.

"And with the enemy focused on you, I'll have an easier time acting."

"Then—"

"They've seen your face. It's only a matter of time before they track you down. We need to be faster. From this point on, we're using electronic warfare. We'll shake them off all at once—quicker than they can respond."

[Nov. 10 / Source: Oahu, a golf cart's onboard camera]

If he left the bloodied Accelerator there, he could easily be harmed when more of those villains showed up. That was why Roberto Catze dragged him onto the passenger's seat of one of those electric carts used at golf courses. Personally, he wished he could watch the reunion between the hostages and attackers for a bit longer, but he didn't have the luxury of time, either, so he set off in the cart.

Incidentally, his rental car was utterly useless now. He wondered, with more seriousness than he'd care to admit, if he could use taxpayer dollars to pay it back.

"Good thing this is a tourist hot spot. Golf carts have simpler security mechanisms than your average car. To get around the four-digit password, all you have to do is to pop the hatch and put a single code into the terminal on the circuit board, and you can create a bypass to get the power going."

A particular manufacturer's golf carts had several different models, and security measures differed for each of them, but they all used the same circuit board. Depending on the type of cart, the maker would attach whatever electronic parts were necessary to it in addition to choosing one of several input terminals. That was how they created different "personalities" for each product.

But the holes and input terminals for attaching electronic parts and soldering them were still in place, even on models that didn't need them.

Sharing a common circuit board reduced overhead, but it also meant you could send signals via pathways the machine wouldn't expect you to. You could force it to malfunction, too.

…And ever since taking an interest in that stuff, the current president started being called the highest-ranking slum-born con artist in history. Hell, if he wasn't careful, people would make a Hollywood movie out of it.

Accelerator exhaled a little, then clicked his tongue.

"…You know, if we'd captured just one of those reinforcements, we could've gotten intel from them."

"Too many things. I'm not some Hollywood star. We couldn't carry one of them, just the two of us." The president chuckled. "Anyway, mind doing something about that blood? This cart *is* borrowed property. I want it to go down in history as the luckiest golf cart in existence, ridden by the best president ever. Really don't want the story to turn into an oopsie where a passenger dies in it and stains it with their blood. Can't trouble the real owner like that, after all."

"Ugh."

"I don't have any bandages or gauze, but if you need something, use this."

The president passed him a lace handkerchief. It didn't look like something a man would carry, but maybe it was some kind of branding strategy. His face one of annoyance, he took it.

"…Wait. Why the hell do you have women's underwear with you?"

"Ha-ha. Sorry. Those must belong to that office worker I met at the bar the day before last. Guess they made it into my pocket at some point."

Accelerator discarded the pair of underwear and gave the president the side-eye. "How informed are you about what's going on?"

"I'd like to ask you the same, Japanese boy. This is *my* country. You do realize you didn't ask permission to have a barbecue in my front yard, right?"

"……"

"Some kind of occult force has overtaken the White House and Congress. Its tendrils even got to the military, the police, and the intelligence agencies. The kind of thing you just saw is happening to all our public organizations now. Even people with the authority to get other countries involved in an armed intervention are succumbing. Whoever this occult-wielding shithead is, they're manipulating every living being they see into being part of their personal army."

"…How far does this go exactly?"

"Hell if I know. Could be a few hundred people, could be a few thousand. We didn't even know back when it started. You've noticed how crazily this country's going. Not like this is some convenient test drug, so we can't pick it out. And anywhere that was safe until yesterday may not be safe today."

"Must be Gremlin."

"What's that?"

"Gremlin—a sorcerer's society that infiltrated Hawaii… A group of people using that occult stuff you mentioned. I know fuck all about it, though."

"And the person controlling people is part of 'em?"

"Yeah, probably."

"…I see. Then this Japanese hunting dog has driven the rabbit right to us, and now we're catching glimpses of this enemy of the United States in our scope."

If what Roberto said was true, there was now a chance that Gremlin's infiltration wasn't limited to the Hawaiian Islands.

And that it extended to the United States as a whole.

All of a sudden, the possibility was on the table that they could make an enemy out of U.S. military forces and its intelligence institutions.

A situation's "about" to happen, my ass. Screw you, Birdway. If you wanted to stop them, you should've done it before checkmate.

The president gripped the wheel of the golf cart and drove down the freeway. Without any windows or doors, they were exposed to the dry winds of Hawaii.

Accelerator and Roberto Catze, president of the United States, had a common enemy.

He'd realized that everything was connected.

Even so, joining forces with the president wouldn't grant him access to the great power of America. Gremlin was already devouring all of that. At most, he'd be joining forces with the man named Roberto Catze, and that was it.

Roberto spoke next.

"So these occult people in Gremlin are controlling important Americans one by one to try and hijack the core of the nation? The government, the military?"

"Probably."

"...At least, that's what it seemed like before."

"Huh?"

"What happened back there makes me doubt it. Remember? The shithead controlling people with occult stuff used kids as shields to try and make civilians attack their targets, right?"

"But then some other guys who looked like professional soldiers intervened. Their gear was weird, too. Those CD-looking uniforms, optical camouflage… High-tech colors for dealing with all kinds of sensors but not for people. But not even the U.S. military would use them—they'd hate how they looked."

"If the occult types had guys like that all along, they would have relied on them. I don't see why they'd use some civilians who could be useless to them the next moment."

"But the sorcerer *did* use civilians."

"What else is going on, then? What aren't we seeing?"

* * *

[Nov. 10 / Source: Oahu, a table-mounted tablet camera in Green Café Iwamaki]

"And there we go," said Birdway, looking at her papyrus.

It was a Soul Arm she was using to automatically analyze the sorcerer's control spell.

Kamijou, Hamazura, and Kuroyoru peered at the papyrus, but they had no idea what she'd found out.

Birdway ignored them. "Failures formerly from the Russian Catholic Church indeed. Mark, compress the data on this papyrus and send it to our contact there. Ask them if they've ever seen it—and be polite."

"...Will they give us an honest answer?"

"Russia was the main battlefield during World War III. Now it's being rebuilt with Academy City's technology and the U.S.'s resources—both of which Gremlin has already harmed. Tell them that if this goes on much longer, it'll affect the restoration process."

Taking care not to touch the Soul Arm, Kamijou asked, "Did you figure out how the spell works? What's its weak point?"

"I'm getting to it."

"We got a response back from the Russian Church. That was blazing fast. So much for bureaucracy."

"The last comment must have worked," said Birdway casually before snatching the tablet computer from Mark. "Name is Salonya A. Irivika. Fifteen years old. Born in Ekaterinburg. Proud to be a European and absolutely loathes the corner of the world known as Asia. Typical Russian."

She used her index finger to scroll the screen over.

"She was stationed at Vladivostok during World War III to stop Academy City forces from making landfall, but since the city mainly used airborne supersonic bombers during its invasion, she couldn't do much. She stole away in the commotion at the end of the war and vanished. They never found her."

Them.

Gremlin.

Those born from war who wished for it to continue.

"Salonya?" repeated Hamazura. "If she's a Russian, is she trying to overturn their defeat?"

Birdway thrust the tablet back into Mark's hands. "Could be."

"Then Gremlin wants to bring the conflict back? They're trying to redo the war…"

"Remember what I told you? They prioritize individual goals over group ideals. They might not all think that way. We can't make too many assumptions."

Just then, Kamijou's cell phone rang. He picked it up; it was Accelerator.

"Figured out what Gremlin's after," he said. *"Still don't know their final goal, but we figured out how they're gonna do it."*

"What do you mean?"

Kamijou hastily put the phone on speaker. That way, everyone could participate in the conversation. As he was doing so, Accelerator explained the core idea.

"Gremlin's tryin' to get their hands on some detonator thing."

"A detonator… I guess we can't take it too literally. Do you know if it's science or sorcery?"

"It's a device that can control active volcanoes by inducing smaller-scale eruptions. They just called it the detonator. *The U.S. military was researching it."*

"…That sounds really dangerous."

"It's literally a toy that can control the activity of a volcano. It can't stop eruptions, but it can control the damage by dispersing the energy from their explosions. Just think of it as a special explosive mixture that can stimulate underground magma and artificially induce small-scale eruptions. Those eruptions allow pressure to escape before the whole volcano blows, which would stop the worst from happening."

Apart from direct damage to the foot of the mountain, like landslides and lava flows, there had also been damage from large-scale volcanic ash blocking off air travel routes in recent years. If people could avoid the kind of economic damage such a natural disaster would cause, then it was probably worth it to them to research.

"Then are you saying that's what Gremlin's after?"

"Actually, seems like every damn person under Gremlin's control is fishing around for data on it," spat Accelerator. "But all the detonator is meant to do is stimulate underground magma. It could easily cause an eruption if misused."

Since they were after the detonator, there was little doubt they were trying to induce an eruption in an active volcano somewhere. In fact, eruptions were really the only thing the detonator was for.

But where? What volcano was Gremlin trying to set off?

"Kilauea," said Accelerator. "If they want the biggest active volcano in the Hawaiian Islands, that'll be the one."

"Kilauea, eh?" murmured Birdway. "Its main crater alone is over ten kilometers in diameter. And if I recall, there are a bunch of smaller craters within twenty or thirty kilometers of it."

"...The detonator can force volcanoes to erupt, right?" asked Kamijou.

Accelerator clicked his tongue before answering. "If Gremlin were to use it, they could cause an eruption that wouldn't be possible in nature. They could even make all the craters explode into lava at the same time."

"The Hawaiian Islands are eighty percent mountainous. The government maintains their road networks here, which have started to go even farther up the volcanic slopes. Though it definitely feels like most people are gathered in what few flatlands the islands have."

"If Kilauea erupts for real…then the lava will hit them—"

"If the volcanic activity was normal in scope," interrupted Accelerator. "If they use the detonator to force it to erupt, it'll be worse. Apparently, it can cause a chain reaction that will affect other volcanoes connected to it underground—Mauna Loa, Mauna Kea, Hualālai—and cause them to erupt, too. And if that happens…"

"They'll cover the entire island of Hawaii in lava," said Birdway, easily filling in for the dumbfounded Kamijou and Hamazura. "By my estimation, the number of resident and tourist deaths would be about five hundred thousand. Not fun to think about. But it's definitely the right kind of scale for people who come up with outrageous ideas."

CHAPTER 3
The Scorching Lava's Aim
Case_to_War.

[Nov. 10 / Source: Oahu, a public transit bus's onboard camera on a highway]

Kamijou, Mikoto, and Birdway were all on a big bus.

Hamazura, Misaka Worst, and Kuroyoru were off attending to something else. Kamijou's team and Accelerator's team were trying to stop the detonator from being taken off Oahu, but they also wanted to have some defenses near Kilauea's crater on Hawaii, too, just in case—that was what Hamazura's team was doing.

"A forced Kilauea eruption could cause five hundred thousand casualties…," muttered Kamijou to himself.

"…Hmm," groaned Mikoto.

"Have a question about it?" asked Birdway as she gazed out the window.

"I get that these terrorists are trying to do something completely outrageous, but…" Without a decent grasp on either Gremlin or sorcery, Mikoto seemed to be attempting to interpret things for herself. "Before getting their hands on it, they were collecting information. Weren't they controlling a bunch of people in the government? Like, from the House of Representatives and the Senate? I mean, I bet it's someone like our Number Five doing it, but…"

"Yes, and they can likely control a very large number of people. Why?"

"Doesn't that seem pretty roundabout? If they were strong enough to get control over more than half of Congress, they wouldn't have to resort to violence. They'd be able to change the country just fine without it."

"Maybe, if this only had to do with the U.S.," said Birdway. "But Gremlin is a bigger threat than that. If you look at places other than the States, you start to see what's in it for them."

"What's that mean, short stuff?"

"The detonator was developed in an American research facility, right? And as part of this whole thing, Gremlin is using Congress and other legislative organizations, the military, the police, and even intelligence divisions as cogs in their grand machinations. If a major terrorist attack occurs—such as the artificial eruption of Kilauea—public opinion won't just turn against the terrorists. It could turn against the U.S. government itself for letting it happen."

"......"

"On top of that, Hawaii has many times more tourists from other countries than locals. Those tourists will end up being most of the casualties—meaning it won't be just the U.S.'s problem anymore. A lot of other nations, governments, and politicians will be all over the incident, trying to find out exactly what happened leading up to the eruption. And when they find out the truth, they'll lambast the U.S. *After all, everyone in the world needs money after a war...* Naturally, the U.S. won't have the funds for all those reparations. Which will prolong the chaos."

"They're trying to hit the entire science side at once," said Kamijou bitterly. "And all they have to do is make an opportunity for it. If they can just get Kilauea to erupt, all the countries on the science side will start fighting one another. It'll drive a wedge into everything, and Gremlin won't have to lift another finger."

"...If Academy City is at the core of the world's science, the U.S. is what's keeping the science side's economy going," added Birdway. "If they suffer a crushing defeat and that grinds to a halt..."

"It'll kick-start a cycle of unemployment, poverty, and starvation," finished Kamijou. "And it won't just happen in the U.S.; these issues will erupt in developing nations around the world, too. When they realize they're getting hit even worse than the country that started it, nearby nations will get very angry. And thus, the downward spiral will be complete."

"In the worst case, terrorist groups with no connection to Gremlin could start launching attacks around the world. And then we won't even have time to track down Gremlin," said Birdway. "That's why they're using the U.S.'s strength and citizens to create a fissure here. That's their top priority. And that's why they're being so roundabout." Then she grinned. "At the same time, it puts pressure on the developed nations shouldering parts of the science side."

"Wait… What's that mean?" asked Mikoto.

"When a new enemy appears, any sane country would try to develop and distribute stronger equipment in higher quantities to counter it. But Gremlin is damaging the U.S. with its own military. Meaning…if all other nations do is strengthen their militaries, they will put themselves at greater risk. If they want to reduce it, they'll have to throw away the stuff they're using to defend themselves."

"Wait, then…"

"If Gremlin succeeds and deals major damage to the U.S., other first-world nations will be at a standstill. Politicians are just people, after all. If you saw someone fail miserably, you wouldn't try to do the same thing as them, right?"

"But without military forces, they wouldn't be able to fight!" exclaimed Mikoto.

"It makes sense in theory, but nobody wants to be the only one shouldering all the risk for having them. That's how politicians are. So nobody will act, and nothing will change. They'll stall, do nothing. A political blank. Economic activity will grind to a halt… That's probably what Gremlin's after. Or else they want to take advantage of such a messed-up world, strike out, and spread their brand of destruction further. We can't be sure what's at the end yet, but whatever it is, Gremlin hates this postwar world biased toward science. They'll probably try to change it in a way that suits them."

For Gremlin, five hundred thousand casualties and a massive strike at the U.S. were nothing more than ways to create an opportunity. That was their way of thinking.

Kamijou firmly clenched his right fist.

[Nov. 10 / Source: Oahu, a golf cart's onboard camera]

Roberto Catze kept one hand on the golf cart's steering wheel as he used his other to switch on the radio. At first, Accelerator assumed he was trying to get information from radio news programs, but instead, he heard a piece of trance music rumored to have even more to do with small animal outbreaks than moon phases did.

"...The hell are you up to?"

"Relaxing. Roselyne wouldn't let me hear the end of this, though," Roberto said. "I've gotta say, I'm feeling a whole lot more unburdened now than I thought I would. 'Cause I've got someone with me who's *definitely* not being controlled."

As the golf cart rattled and swayed, Accelerator asked, "So do you know where the detonator is or not?"

"The Marine Corps led the development since they get deployed for disaster rescue and all."

"Isn't Hawaii supposed to be the cornerstone of the U.S.'s Pacific Ocean defense? I can't even count all the bases you have here."

"Fifty-two in total if you count the Navy, Air Force, and Marine bases together. Goes up if you include proving grounds, though."

"...Is it just me, or is that even more than before?"

"There was a base-building bonanza in response to World War III," explained the president. "Which ended way sooner than we thought. Couldn't get the money back, and plenty didn't want it back anyway. Pointless construction, but that's why it's still going."

Accelerator clicked his teeth.

"A little under half of that number are under construction," said the president with a smirk. "Some of them are partially online, though, so we still need to search them."

"Then where are we going? Like, now?"

"Even I'm not reckless enough to try searching them one by one. If I get into the network with presidential permissions, I should be able to scrape some info together."

"Get to the point."

"We're going to the biggest cluster of American military bases in Hawaii—and in the Pacific region altogether. One I'm sure a Japanese person like yourself will have heard of."

"Don't make me repeat myself. Where the hell are we going?"

"Pearl Harbor."

[Nov. 10 / Source: Oahu, a traffic camera attached to a traffic light near Marine Corps Pearl Harbor Base 3]

A wire net extended for kilometers in each direction.

Near the fence, Touma Kamijou, Mikoto Misaka, and Leivinia Birdway had met up with Roberto Catze and Accelerator.

Mikoto shuddered and went white in the face when she saw Accelerator, remembering a bloody, traumatic event, but there was no time to deal with that.

"The detonator is probably inside that fence," said the president, pointing at the base with his thumb. "But as you know, this is the most well-defended base in the world and the main headquarters of the Marine Corps—if not in technology, then in raw firepower. Sometimes where there's a will, there's a way—but not this time, because if you try to cross that fence, you'll instantly be riddled with more holes than a beehive."

"...But aren't you the president?" asked Kamijou dubiously. "Can't you just order them to let us in?"

Roberto gave an exaggerated shrug. "Presidential orders aren't as useful as movies make 'em out to be. There are governmental organizations sitting between me and the people I want to give the order to. And since they're being controlled by a third party, my authority probably won't fly."

Birdway picked up for Roberto. "Salonya—the one controlling people—will be trying to get her hands on the detonator. We don't even have a guarantee that people in the base are doing what they're supposed to."

"……"

Accelerator and Mikoto exchanged silent glances.

If all the opponent had to threaten them with was a pile of normal firearms, then the two of them could have forced their way through. But...

"And busting our way in is a bad idea," added Birdway to cut them off. "The base is too big. Finding the detonator would take too long. You don't want to be fighting the whole time, because if it drags on, they'll get reinforcements. Sure, maybe you'd win, but not before turning the entire place into an ocean of flames... And if multiple explosions reduce the base to piles of rubble, *we'll never know if the detonator was inside it.*"

"Then if we want to do it safely, we have to find the detonator in person and destroy it," murmured Kamijou. "But I'm sure security's too tight for us to sneak in."

Roberto brushed off the attaché case in his hand. "There's some pointless construction going on at the base right now. A lot of construction workers and contractors going in and out. Compared to how things normally are, there's still a chance we might be able to slip inside."

"...Just a question," said Kamijou. "Is the security gap large enough to allow some Asian minors to wander around without suspicion?"

The president made a sour face.

Birdway lightly folded her arms. "We can use the white men among my subordinates, but since Salonya has her fingers everywhere, I don't want to go in with too many sorcerers. She could catch on if she's watching for mana."

"Then what do we do?"

"Well, that's not to say I have *no* ideas."

"Then you've got one? To sneak into the base?"

"No." Birdway shook her head, then said, "To go right through the front door."

[Nov. 10 / Source: Oahu, a tide-level observation camera at Diamond Marine Harbor]

Shiage Hamazura, Misaka Worst, and Umidori Kuroyoru were at a private yacht harbor on Oahu. Despite being yachts, their propulsion came from propellers rather than gasoline engines. The row of smaller vessels were more like villas in both price and furnishings—they had air-conditioned bedrooms, simple kitchens, and shower rooms.

"I can get the locks open," said Hamazura, casually removing some wire wrapped around one of the piers on the wharf, "but I don't have the first idea about piloting a boat. Can either of you do that?"

"Sure. Testament entered the information into Misaka's brain. But boy, that sounds like a pain. Anyway, we'll be fine. There's no obstacles out on the ocean, so we can be rough. Learn by failing!"

"You don't even *want* to help! At all!"

"Oh? Well, if I focused on steering, I might not be able to keep a close enough eye on little Kuroyoru here. Can the postapocalyptic emperor handle that?"

"One of these days I'm gonna rip you both to sheds!" barked Kuroyoru. "To shreds, I say! Not to pieces, not to chunks, but exactly the size of little pizza slices! Grrrr!"

"Noooooooooooooo!" Hamazura screamed. "Why do you sound like a trained military dog set on me?!"

"Could you just, like, unlock the thing so we can get into that airconditioning? Otherwise, we might be in for some bestiality here."

Trembling madly, Hamazura stuck several wires into the keyhole on the boat's hatch while looking around.

"...Locks are outside technology, so they're easy, but I'm worried someone will see. And I heard everyone here has guns."

Misaka Worst smacked Kuroyoru—who was still restrained—in the head a few times. "Come on, we'll be fine! As long as Kuroyoru here keeps watch for us."

"Wha—? Why...? Why me...?!"

"Don't you get crazy information-gathering abilities by putting on those cat-ear parts? No problem, right?"

"Blurgh?! Y-you...! How the hell do you know about that...?!"

"Heh-heh-heh. If you want to resist, then resist. But you can't even use your arms. You really think you can stop me from putting these ears on you? It's time for you to become our adorable, darling, precious, little black cat assassin!"

"Urk..."

Kuroyoru looked behind herself on reflex, but since she was at the end of the pier, she had nowhere left to run. Misaka Worst didn't seem to care about changes in Kuroyoru's appearance—she just wanted to completely ruin the girl's dark image. She brought the cat-ear parts out and fiddled with them.

"Hic...," went Kuroyoru, now backed into a corner, and then...

"Noooooooooooooooooooooooooo! What the hell?! Why am I the only one who has to go through this bullshit?!"

"Whoa!" Misaka Worst flinched a little.

Despite her Level Four Bomber Lance ability, or the fact that part of Accelerator's thought processes had been implanted in her during Project Dark May, or the fact that she was the leader of the new age darkness called the Freshmen, Kuroyoru was *also* a twelve-year-old girl at heart.

If things had been simpler between the three of them—if they had just been trying to kill one another—Kuroyoru would have been able to tough it out.

But she wasn't used to this strange humiliation. Nobody had ever done this to her. She just wasn't experienced enough with being teased to blow it off with some clever quip, so you couldn't really blame her.

Big teardrops scattered as Kuroyoru averted her eyes, and Misaka Worst looked at Hamazura for help. But he just stared back at her, as if to say *Wow, you made her cry...*

Forced to confront what she'd done, Misaka Worst thought for a moment. "Well, Misaka was only made less than a year ago. Since she's the youngest, she's allowed to be a little selfish, right?"

"I can't believe you'd go there! You're pure evil!"

Eventually, carrying a group of three wailing children, the very expensive yacht slowly left the harbor.

[Nov. 10 / Source: Oahu, a video taken by the surveillance camera at the west gate of Marine Corps Pearl Harbor Base 3]

Foreign dispatch posts were one thing, but nobody would ever waltz up to the front gates of a domestic military base and attack it. The first thing security guards learned was how to pass the time—or that was what you'd think, at least, but they *did* actually have a job to do.

Their real tasks were not, of course, to engage in fierce gunfights with dangerous elements attacking the base. They mainly warded off provocations from third-rate periodicals with nothing better to write about and from civilian groups and the like who were constantly way too wary of how their tax dollars were being used.

Here at the base, it was called crow-hunting—work considered to be on the same level as cleaning the bathrooms.

...A jet fuel–powered explosion at the airport, a firefight at a shopping mall. Why don't they just give us a damn order already? We'll shoot all the perpetrators up real good. Don't even need an assault rifle for crow-hunting. Could do it with a rubber cup from a bathroom.

With all of that, Nike Kanokus, an African American Marine—who had long since rotted in this guardroom—tossed aside his worn-out gravure magazine, took his feet off the table, and put them on the floor. The radio was saying something. Apparently, today's way to kill time had just come to the gates.

These guys were always big shots, though, so Nike could never say that to their faces. But he still slung his assault rifle—unpopular with the other soldiers here—on his shoulder and slammed open the door to the guardroom. Without his Japanese-made cooling humidifier, the goddamn sunlight scorched his dark skin.

Seeing the group of people walking over, Nike yelled at them. "Stop! Stop right there, assholes! Who the hell are you?!"

"I'm the goddamned president! Bring me the authenticator right now, or I'll cut your budget!" an awfully sturdy-looking older man yelled back with tears in his eyes.

Nike looked closer. That was a face he saw on the news all the time. The man was a legend who'd once tried to act in an erectile dysfunction commercial in nothing but a pair of swim trunks—but then the president's aide, a woman, practically blew her stack and stopped him. Once, when he was informed at a press conference that women's associations considered the things he said on variety shows horribly indecent, he'd responded by smiling and trying to introduce a new bill to expand nude beaches, only to be beaten to a pulp right then and there—again by his aide. But who were those minors behind him? Caught off guard, Nike helplessly held a tablet out to the man. He punched in his Social Security number, then slapped his hand onto the screen. The guy had to be one of those impersonators, right? But then the authenticator turned green.

Nike shook the tablet a little when the man pushed it back into his hands.

"...Is this thing broken?" he wondered aloud.

"Come on," the man said. "Would that system just so happen to malfunction in a way that just so happens to let someone pass? Just from a little dust or sand? If you think it would, then go ahead. Send a complaint to the developers—Grape Computers. They'll sue you for all you're worth within three hours."

"What? Huh... Wait. What? That would mean..."

"Yeah. I'm President Roberto Catze. You know I vanished from a press conference in Oahu two hours ago, right? The public hasn't been informed, but the military should know by now."

"Oh. Uh. Right. Sir?"

As Nike stumbled over himself, too confused to know whether to show proper reverence, the president pressed him further. "There's a terrorist plot to kidnap me. And it's still ongoing. The civilians behind me saved me. But the danger hasn't passed. We want to ask for rescue and protection. Mind letting us in?"

"Hold on. Wait. Uh, please. What do I do now? Right. Contact management. We'll get you a guest ID pass as soon as the electronic processing is done—"

"Do you really think we have time to wait? I just said the danger hasn't passed. *They're* getting closer. We can't just be inside the fence. We want to evacuate to a reinforced concrete building at *least*—they could start launching mortars at us."

"W-wait, but..."

"Hey, cowboy?" The president peered at Nike's face. "The guy who killed John F. Kennedy had his name forever engraved into history as a villain. The same goes for the people blamed for the holes in security, too. You want to go down in history like them, cowboy?"

"...Please, go right in..."

Rather overwhelmed because the authenticator *had* confirmed the president's identity, Nike Kanokus let the group in.

As he watched the civilians enter behind Roberto Catze, even Nike had to try and stop them.

"These folks saved me," repeated the president. "Their lives are in danger, too. You want to throw these national heroes back out and leave them to die?"

He had no response for that.

None of the manuals said anything about what to do when the president made an unscheduled visit. The four civilians proceeded past the dazed man, setting foot into the Marine Corps base.

* * *

[Nov. 10 / Source: Oahu, an air traffic control assistance camera at Marine Corps Pearl Harbor Base 3]

"What was that all about?" asked Kamijou, glancing back several times at the west gate they'd just gone through.

Roberto shrugged. "Don't ask me. I was sweating bullets during that whole act. You don't think this base has fallen into this Salonya person's hands, do you?"

"Oh, she's probably gotten inside," said Birdway, the only one here who looked composed. "But she hasn't reached the lower rungs yet. She probably only has the top-level executives under her control so far."

"What makes you think that?"

"The shopping mall," she replied, sounding bored. "According to the great and mighty president here, at minimum we're looking at Congress being under magical control, plus other government and military agencies. We don't know how many people Salonya can manipulate at once. But Congress has around six hundred people by itself. If she wants a majority, she'll need at least half that number. If she could control that many people at once, don't you think the shopping mall incident would have been way more tragic? For example, she could have used all the tourists to attack us like zombies, and the more we took down, the more reinforcements would pop up."

"...Now that you mention it..."

"But the only people there who were actually under her control were the four hostages," continued Birdway as they walked. "If we assume the president isn't lying, then Salonya's spell must take a significant amount of time to prepare, and there must be a limit on how many people she can control. We can assume she has her hands full taking over the U.S. government and can't devote much manpower to combat forces. She'll try to reduce costs somewhere, such as at this base."

"There are several important obstacles to gaining complete control over the country's functions," said the president with a small sigh. "To fulfill all the requirements, she'd need to have her hands all across the nation. It would make sense this Salonya person would be having a lot of trouble."

"You mean it's cheaper for her to just take over the highest officers and have them give orders on paper instead of controlling all their subordinates?" asked Mikoto, who still didn't quite have a good grasp on the concept of sorcery.

Birdway nodded. "And we should *also* assume her spell is pretty unique. Generally, anyone can cast a spell as long as they know how, but there are exceptions. This is probably one of them."

"What's your evidence for that?" asked Accelerator.

"If anyone could use it, Salonya could just control a few civilians and have *them* use the spell on others. Then her control would proliferate. But we haven't seen anything like that. The spell must be something only she can use, and on top of that, there are limits as to how far it goes."

So to conserve a degree of freedom for herself, she'd only manipulate the commanding officers at U.S. military bases... That seemed to be what Birdway was thinking.

Roberto cocked his head in thought.

"...Which means we still have a chance. A CO's orders against the president's—strictly speaking, mine would take priority, of course. But the actual soldiers probably haven't ever had to weigh one against the other. Not all of them will take my side, but everyone will be confused, at least."

"I should also explain Salonya's spell now that the papyrus has automatically analyzed it." Birdway folded her arms. "Just like we thought, her incantation is based on the Russian forest spirit Leshy. He rules over all the animals in the forest and controls them, making them respond to humans. But with regards to the spell's conditions... I just learned it uses trees."

"Wood?"

"Specifically, it needs to be a conifer growing in Russia. It can be a piece of bark or a leaf. If Salonya can make a target touch any part of such a tree, they're instantly considered a member of the forest and fall under her control."

"…I don't remember her having anything like that," replied Kamijou dubiously, thinking back to the incident at the shopping mall.

Birdway gave a thin smile. "If a tree is the only ingredient, it can be anything. Even paper or a corkboard. And they have those paper capacitor things now, too. She could easily make it look like something else and have someone hold onto it. They'd be none the wiser."

"What happens if they let go of the Soul Arm?"

"Naturally, they would regain control. But I doubt Salonya would permit that. Once she has a thrall, she'd order them never to let go of it, no matter what. Hell, she could even just tell them to eat it."

"Yuck," muttered Kamijou.

"More importantly," Roberto said, "this Salonya woman—you said she's only directly controlling the commanding officers, right, girl?"

"Yes, but why?"

"Then the biggest threat at hand would be—"

It happened right as he said that.

An off-road car drove at them from a spot close to a squarish building in the distance, with an MP behind the wheel. In the back seat was a tall, broad-shouldered man who definitely looked like someone of high rank. A military nerd might have been able to tell the man's status by observing the minor details on his uniform.

He was the commanding officer of the base.

The off-road vehicle parked in front of everyone, and the man got out.

"Mr. President."

Kamijou realized he was tensing up. The nameplate on the guy's chest said Bax Shelva.

Birdway had just been saying that Salonya would only be directly controlling the commanding officers all the way at the top in order to give herself leeway and that she would send her orders down the chain of command from there to control their subordinates.

Because of that, other soldiers might not execute an order to shoot the president, for instance. Nobody wanted to go down in U.S. history as a traitor for murdering its head of state.

But Bax Shelva was different.

Since he was under the control of Salonya's spell, he could easily assassinate the president without thinking of the consequences.

The automatic pistol at his waist really felt front and center right now.

Kamijou gulped.

If he used his right hand, he might be able to remove Salonya's control over the CO. But the man's gun made the few meters between them an absolute death zone.

As he thought about this, the CO made the first move.

"I've received the reports. I'm so happy you're safe, sir! Please allow me to muster our base's forces to protect you!"

…*Huh?* Kamijou's eye twitched. Mikoto and the others must have been imagining the same situation as him. Kamijou wondered if the CO was trying to lure them somewhere else to take them out, but then Birdway whispered something into his ear.

"She can't do it."

Before the president moved, she stepped out in front of Bax and gave him a scornful grin.

"She *could* kill the president right now. But if she did, she'd lose the chaos—her only means of indirectly controlling Pearl Harbor Base 3. So she can't. At least, not right now. Not until the detonator is brought out of the complex."

Bax Shelva twitched.

It wasn't because the CO himself was confused, though. It looked more like he'd done that at someone else's bidding.

"She doesn't want to throw away the CO like that, which actually goes to prove something. And I already said what that thing is. Have you realized?"

"...They still haven't brought out the detonator?" murmured the president before clearing his throat and switching to his public relations voice. "Commander, I'd like information on where the detonator is being stored. Where is it right now exactly?"

Bax shivered again. Someone, somewhere, was trying to figure out how to respond.

And that was when Mikoto and Accelerator slightly dropped their hips in preparation.

"...The... The detonator is..."

The commander's lips moved. Then, sweating unnaturally, he continued.

"...It's on the runway. We have permission to use a transport plane to send it to Hawaii..."

"Let's go," said Birdway. "Salonya will be sheltered in the warmest, friendliest place right now anyway. Gremlin wants to use the detonator at Kilauea, so bringing the device and its user to the same place would be most efficient."

"But there's three transport planes," said Mikoto, looking doubtfully at the runway. "Which has the detonator on—?"

Just then, there was the *bang* of a gunshot.

The group hastily turned around just as the base's CO unholstered his sidearm. The bullet didn't hit any of them, though. He'd been tackled by the MP nearby and pinned to the ground. The MP must have jumped him as he fired.

"Let's not stick around," said the president softly. "We need to take care of the root cause now and put an end to this mess."

[Nov. 10 / Source: Oahu, a maintenance camera inside the cargo space of a transport plane at Marine Corps Pearl Harbor Base 3]

Kamijou ran for one of the three transport planes. Accelerator and Birdway headed for the other two.

Fortunately, none of them had lifted off yet; in fact, they hadn't even been fully loaded. Their rear cargo doors were still open, unfolded down to the asphalt to let vehicles drive up into them.

Kamijou, Mikoto, and Roberto dashed up that slope.

"Why are you coming with me, Misaka?!"

"Because if I take my eyes off you, you're gonna disappear somewhere! Ugh! I don't want to believe in unscientific stuff, but should I just give that thing to him right now?!"

"Why isn't the president evacuating into the base?!"

"Because this is *my* country, boy."

A quick glance revealed that there seemed to be three transport planes. Accelerator and Birdway were probably each heading to one of the others.

A soldier of Indian descent was busy loading the container cubes with a military-grade forklift, but when he saw them, he quickly yelled to them.

"Hey! What are you doing?! Who the hell are you?!"

"I'm the God-damned president! And if one more person repeats the same gag, I'm gonna start my Christmas vacation early and claim it's for my mental health! Just stop what you're doing and come with us. We need that government equipment on your waist! We're canceling the launch. I repeat, we're canceling the launch!"

The forklift operator started to panic. The president could say all he wanted, but he wasn't his superior in the military chain of command, right? But wait, wasn't the president the commander in chief? But this order was going over his CO's head like a fly ball for the catcher, and he'd never had that happen before. Was he supposed to ask his superior about how to proceed?

Meanwhile, Kamijou's group ignored the soldier and charged into the cargo space. It was spacious inside—in fact, one of those big tour buses could probably fit in there. Other containers sat here and there, having already been loaded in by the forklift.

Kamijou took a look around. "Where is it? Is the detonator already on board? Or is it—?"

"Shouldn't Salonya come first?" asked Mikoto. "If we catch the mastermind, we'll stop everything from happening… Huh?!"

That was when her legs shook, and she almost fell over.

A bursting noise hit their ears. It sounded like the buzzing of a wasp, only amplified hundreds of times. It was the four turboprop engines spinning up their four propellers. The next thing Kamijou knew, they were already accelerating.

With the rear cargo door still open.

Roberto had lost his balance, and now he was rolling toward the sloped exit. The edge of the door crashed into the asphalt, sending orange sparks everywhere.

"Whoa, there!" Mikoto quickly reached out and grabbed Roberto's hand before he tumbled out of the plane.

"I'd love to thank you, missy, but that might not have been necessary."

"Quit saying weird stuff and just get in…!"

"I could have tumbled out before we accelerated and only gotten a scrape or two. But alas, if I were to tumble out now, I'd turn into a pile of Japanese autumn leaves on the ground."

"Then ditch the suitcase and grab on with your other hand!"

"Keeping this attaché case safe is a matter of national security, so I must decline. As much as I would like to do otherwise!"

In the meantime, the plane continued to accelerate.

At around three hundred kph, the floor shook again. They'd begun to ascend, with the still-open cargo door facing down, as if they were climbing up a hill.

They'd lifted off. That was the moment that *It's dangerous if you fall out* leveled up to *You're a goner if you fall out*.

Even realizing that, though, Kamijou couldn't lend Mikoto a hand.

The reason was obvious.

"Salonya…!"

A woman slowly walked out from behind one of the containers. A Gremlin sorcerer. The one with clear knowledge of how to control people by applying the Russian myth of Leshy.

Her outfit was mainly green, consisting of leather boots that went up above her knees. She had striking blond hair and fair skin. Her attire seemed a little plain for someone who was supposed rule over the "forest denizens" from her home in the woods, but the mismatch only served to make the name Leshy more suitable for her.

Nevertheless.

Inside this transport plane, enclosed in nonmetallic aircraft material, she stood out like an explosion.

If he had to give an analogy, it was as though a cutout depicting a dangerous animal had been placed there, like when protected species like alligators or scorpions showed up in Tokyo.

Now that Salonya had shown herself, Kamijou could no longer give Mikoto any assistance.

It didn't matter what sorcery she used. If he prioritized rescuing the president, he'd be shot in the back. Would it be a simple death, or would he be controlled like a zombie? He couldn't let either of those things happen.

Without turning around, he yelled at Mikoto as she held on to the president.

"Can you handle him yourself?!"

"I'll manage! Crap, did they take all the metal parts out in the latest model? There's almost no magnetic fields to latch onto...!"

The hard, sharp footsteps drew closer.

Kamijou balled his right hand into a fist.

Salonya's unique spell could control people. But there was nobody here to control. If he could prevent anyone in their group from being enthralled, then there was more than a chance his right hand would take care of things.

But then...

She snapped her fingers.

Brrrwoaaarrrrr!!!!!!

Kamijou launched to the side and crashed into the wall to his right.

He hadn't tripped and run into it—this was completely different. His feet had been in the air. He'd shot at the center of the wall like a cannonball. His breathing literally stopped for several seconds.

"Gah… Ah…?!"

For a moment, he thought Salonya had used some kind of spell on him.

But he was wrong.

Closer to the cargo door, Mikoto and the president had also been flung away. If not for Mikoto wrapping her legs around one of the thick cylinders used for opening and closing it, the two of them would have been launched into the sky.

"Right… You have…the pilot under your control, and—!"

"Even big transport planes can do acrobatics. Did you know that?"

She snapped her fingers again.

"Though nobody sane would ever try to do that."

He wasn't sure what the pilot was doing with the craft, but Kamijou whipped back to the left. He knew it was coming, but he couldn't keep his feet on the floor. It felt as though gravity was changing directions.

With one of her hands around some thick wires extending from the walls and ceiling—probably meant to hold the containers in place—Salonya used the other to reach behind her.

"Gremlin's countermeasure against your right hand is really quite simple."

She removed an item from her turtleneck—an item so ordinary that it would be right at home in a supermarket in this country of guns.

"It's a much more mundane method of killing you. One your power can't affect."

"!!"

Kamijou didn't have the ability to knock a bullet away or dodge it on sight.

But after hitting the wall and falling face-first on the floor, he swung his right leg immediately, kicking up a lever holding a container to the floor and unlocking it.

The gunshot came a moment later.

In this miniature world where a gigantic acrobatic jet seemed to be ignoring Earth's gravity, a container floated into the air and shielded him from the shot, sending orange sparks everywhere.

But this strange gravity wouldn't last.

The container, only Kamijou's ally for a moment, began plummeting toward him after that. Still on the ground, he quickly rolled out of the way to let the hunk of metal fall right next to him and break into pieces. It was of simple construction, and its joint parts must have been damaged.

Salonya aimed her gun at him again.

But Kamijou couldn't keep using the same trick. There were no other levers within kicking distance, and even if he did release a container, it wouldn't necessarily block her lethal bullet.

However, she never ended up firing.

Because an even stronger physical phenomenon suddenly shot through the transport plane. Specifically, a super-high-tension current to the tune of one billion volts.

Zzz-crash! Salonya frantically rushed behind a container, then scowled, as if concerned that the metallic object wouldn't actually protect her.

With her legs around the cylinder and one hand latched onto the president's arm, Mikoto took aim at Salonya. Despite the significant strain she was under, she grinned fearlessly.

"…If that weird right hand of yours could do something about it, then fine. But if we're up against something normal, my power is basically invincible."

Salonya was grinning, too. She was looking not at Mikoto but at the cylinder she was entangled with.

Is she gonna close the cargo door and crush Misaka in between?! thought Kamijou.

He yelled to her in spite of himself. "Forget about Salonya! Just blow up all the containers nearby!"

"?!"

The baffled sorcerer hesitated for a moment, wondering if she should aim at Kamijou or Misaka.

But a moment later, a lance of lightning shot from Misaka's bangs.

There was an incredible burst of noise and a flash of light. The nonmetallic bolts used to decrease the weight of the containers melted, and the containers fell apart. Beyond this visible destruction, the electric current had also damaged the plane's precision instruments.

They didn't know what the detonator was exactly, but they doubted it could take a high-tension current like without being damaged.

"Wha...? I...!" stammered Salonya, seeing the containers burst apart, twist around, collapse, and grow black with burns.

But *not* because the detonator had just been destroyed before her eyes. Rather...

[Nov. 10 / Source: Hawaii, a bird-watching camera in Hawaii Volcanoes National Park]

Separate from Kamijou's group, Hamazura and company had already left the posh yacht they'd stolen and landed on the island of Hawaii. Kilauea, the volcano in question, was the island's biggest tourist attraction, and the entire mountain—even up near the caldera—had been designated a national park.

There was more than one volcano here. Aside from the gigantic one at the summit, there were dozens of others midway up the mountain and closer to the foot. Even now, they could smell the odor of sulfuric gas; it was like they were near a hot spring.

Their group's goal was to steal a car, drive it up close to the caldera, and stop any members of Gremlin who tried to bring the detonator up there. Since it seemed like Kamijou's group had a chance of winning, it was possible they wouldn't need to do much at all.

However.

"What the hell is that...?"

At the edge of the huge caldera, which was over ten kilometers across, Hamazura slowly crouched down.

Someone was here.

A group of men actually, and they were far too close to the caldera to be tourists. While not as famous as the Halema'uma'u on Kilauea's caldera, there was a fissure here glowing orange that was dozens of meters long—still plenty dangerous. The men seemed to be setting up a large piece of equipment. It looked like a giant oil drum with four legs. The legs were arranged in a cross pattern. The men were driving gas- or electric-powered stakes into the ground.

"...I don't like the looks of that," said Hamazura. "Reminds me of that snowfield in Russia."

There were several oil drums. Dozens more had been set up around the giant caldera.

Now, Hamazura didn't have any real evidence for this.

But one word naturally came to mind.

"...Are those...the detonator...?"

"Seems like it," replied Misaka Worst.

"But how? Why?! I thought it hadn't been brought to Hawaii yet!"

"Only one thing I can think of." She raised her index finger. "That, uh...sorcerer? The dangerous element in Gremlin who the others are going after? Maybe she *didn't know the real plan.* The detonator was originally brought in through a different route, and the dangerous element never caught on. So Misaka and her friends chasing the detonator's storage location never found it."

"Shit. Shit, that's not good," groaned Hamazura. "...If they turn those things on, Kilauea's gonna blow. It's not just us we'd have to worry about. If the lava gets down to the tourists and residents, it could kill or harm five hundred thousand people. And if that triggers a breakdown in international relations between the U.S. and other countries, then..."

"In comes instability—and we just came out of World War III. Plenty of countries and regions aren't happy with the Academy City–led restoration efforts, too. They don't think it's enough support. Even if nobody declares war on the U.S. mainland, a lot of politicians will want to make money off whatever conflicts they can whip up."

"...Do we go? Do we stay? What do we do?" asked Kuroyoru, still unhappy—she must have still been reeling from crying in front of them.

But Hamazura shook his head. "We can't take those guys head-on.

The detonator is supposed to be triggering a bunch of different explosives in stages to stimulate the magma underground, right? But we don't know exactly how they get set off. We don't want to get them caught up in a battle if they're too delicate.

"Plus," he added, "we don't know how strong those dudes are. Anyway, they wouldn't want to get burned alive from their own eruption. There should still be time between when they leave and when the detonator goes off. Our only choice is to go after the devices once those guys leave and disable them, no matter what it takes."

[Nov. 10 / Source: Lanai airspace, a maintenance camera inside the cargo hold of a transport plane]

More of Mikoto's lightning attacks shot forth, wrecking one container in the hold after another—all to destroy the detonator that was housed in one of them.

However.

The only things coming out of the containers so far were military-grade domestic goods. Frying pans with foldable handles and small lamps lay scattered about. Kamijou didn't know much about the detonator, but he could tell that while some trickery had been used on the things here, they were really all just kitchen supplies. None of these items would be causing a controlled volcanic eruption anytime soon.

…*What's going on?*

Kamijou came up with several possibilities.

There were three transport planes, including dummies. The detonator could have been loaded onto another aircraft, but… Salonya was the one who had manipulated the base commander and decided where to put things. She'd have known which plane the detonator was in. It wouldn't do her any good to put it on another one.

And the plane had taken off before it was even done being loaded up. He couldn't deny the possibility that the detonator simply hadn't been put onto the plane yet...but then Salonya would have known the exact container it was inside, too. That was why she'd done the emergency takeoff as part of her surprise attack. And when Kamijou had unlocked the first container to protect himself, her expression hadn't changed—even though the detonator could very well have been thrown out the open cargo door, depending on how the plan shifted.

Which meant...

"You didn't know...? Wait, was the only thing they told you that *the container was in here*?"

Gremlin wasn't above manipulating even a major player like Salonya in the interest of carrying out grander plans. They'd given her false information to make her dance like a puppet.

It wasn't just Cendrillon and Salonya. Someone *else* was still involved in this incident. Someone likely buried much deeper.

"......"

Salonya stood there frozen for a few moments. She must have been trying to wrap her head around what had just happened to her.

But neither Kamijou nor Salonya had much time to think about it.

Realizing that Mikoto had swung her arm back around at her, Salonya immediately whipped around her gun. But she didn't aim at Mikoto—instead, she pointed her firearm at the front of the plane and fired all the bullets she could that way.

Roberto cried out in anguish. "The pilot?!"

Kamijou and Mikoto flinched a little at what he was implying. Salonya took the chance to grab a backpack-looking thing hanging on the wall—a parachute. The plane continued its slow ascent...and she took advantage of the fact that the rear cargo door was down a slope to roll toward the exit.

Just before she slid past Mikoto, a pale blue lightning spear fired straight through her. Salonya's entire body went limp, and her consciousness grew hazy—but she was still smiling as she jumped without hesitation from the end of the sloped cargo door.

"Ugh, damn it!" yelled Mikoto.

"No point going after her! Get the president inside!"

Kamijou made his way to the door, went up next to Mikoto, and grabbed Roberto's arm. One wrong step, and they'd all fall to their deaths, but somehow, they managed to drag the president back inside the hold.

"…God, how much do you weigh? Did you eat a few too many hamburgers or what?"

"H-hey, I'm still under two hundred pounds. And burgers are good for appealing to younger demographics. Roselyne keeps telling me to lose weight to get more votes, but I think I'm pretty slim for a guy of my height…"

After catching their breaths for a few moments, they suddenly remembered something.

"Misaka, check if there's still any parachutes."

"What about you?"

"I'll check on the pilot. If the bullets got through the wall, they might be hurt."

"I'll join you," said the president. "I doubt you'll get through to him with just Japanese."

"They might attack you at Salonya's orders, you know," warned Kamijou.

"We can only hope they still have the energy to."

Kamijou and Roberto crossed the path of wrecked containers and headed to the cockpit in front.

[Nov. 10 / Source: Lanai airspace, an aircraft recorder box on a transport plane]

As Kamijou expected, the bullets *had* made it through the thin partition separating the cockpit from the cargo space. Dozens of shots had gone through the cockpit, and there were many cracks in the canopy, to say nothing of the pilot. The only reason the pilot hadn't been blown to smithereens was because the cargo door had been open the whole time and the pressure hadn't changed.

And.

The pilot, a white man of about thirty, was slumped over their flight console, covered in blood. It wasn't clear whether he was still under Salonya's control or if she'd discarded him.

Not that it mattered.

Kamijou ran up to him, *grabbed his shoulder with his right hand*, and yelled in his ear. "Shit. Are you okay?!"

"He's still conscious," said the president. "But he's taken three shots to the back. All three rounds went clear through, but his wounds are too deep for first aid to stop the bleeding."

"The only thing I can think of is putting some cloth over them. What else can we do?"

"That's fine. You can tie arms and legs to temporarily stop a person's flow of blood, but with torso wounds like these, that would only put pressure on his internal organs."

Kamijou tried to rip off a piece of the pilot's jacket—they'd taken it off him to see the wound—but it didn't go well, perhaps because it was a military uniform. Instead, he used the knife that came with the gun at the pilot's waist to cut off several pieces to use as improvised bandages.

That was when Mikoto came in.

"Found a few parachutes!"

"…This man isn't looking good," said the president softly, gazing at the badly wounded pilot. "The impact you get when deploying a parachute is like slamming into the ground from a few meters in the air. A healthy person might just have the wind knocked out of them, but someone with potential organ damage shouldn't risk it."

"…I don't…mind…," murmured the collapsed pilot, sticky blood dripping from his lips. "You all…jump. I can at least…get the nose pointed at the sea…"

The group briefly exchanged glances. Mikoto sighed and tossed her parachute to the floor.

A trace of doubt showed in the pilot's blurred eyes. "Who are you…?"

"We're here to help. However!" said the president, putting his hand on the man's shoulder.

And he spoke clearly.

"Don't crash this thing into the ocean. Let's set our sights a little higher, eh? We'll try an emergency landing."

[Nov. 10 / Source: Hawaii, a bird-watching camera in Hawaii Volcanoes National Park]

The mysterious men finally left after twenty minutes.

Even if it was the most efficient way, sitting there watching the group set up a detonator that could affect the lives of five hundred thousand people was excruciating enough to almost give Hamazura a heart attack. He couldn't believe how unconcerned Misaka Worst and Umidori Kuroyoru had looked next to him.

After seeing the group—who were almost assuredly cooperating with Gremlin—drive away in their four-wheel-drive car, Hamazura slid down the sloped caldera and approached the edge of the central crater. He immediately felt the sulfuric gas odor intensify and the temperature rise dramatically. Were those Gremlin lackeys wearing some kind of special gear under their clothes?

"How does it look?!" he shouted.

"I think they set it up to cause powerful tremors from multiple angles at once to control the magma pressure," said Kuroyoru. "But there's no cables between them and no exchange of wireless information. The triggers are set on a timer, and the systems are all completely isolated."

"But doesn't that mean if we can destroy the central system, they'll all go down?" Hamazura looked around. "There's over twenty, just at a glance. We don't know how much time we have left. Is our only choice to run around popping lids and cutting cords one at a time, like we're in a movie?"

"…No, there's a simpler way," said Kuroyoru, pointing to one of the devices seemingly at random. "They went to the trouble of using stakes to pin the legs to the ground. I think that's to redirect the blast wind straight underground like a spear, causing a shock wave. Which also means…"

"…that we could pull out the legs or destroy them and just push the whole thing over!"

"If we're gonna do it, we'd better move fast." Misaka Worst grinned. "They might just be for controlling volcanic activity, but they're still explosives. We have no idea when they'll go off, and Misaka definitely doesn't want to be caught in one. Not the lethal blast radius from the bombs *or* an eruption from Hawaii's biggest active volcano."

[Nov. 10 / Source: Lanai airspace, an aircraft recorder box on a transport plane]

The pilot tried to carry out his mission, but he was in a state where he could barely move. Instead, Kamijou and the others followed his instructions, pressing buttons rather than helping him with the flight yoke.

"…First, we close the rear cargo hatch. That button there. As long as the plane's sealed, the air inside will act like a life preserver. We'll need that if we want to force a landing on the ocean…"

At his instructions, they pressed one button after another, but they couldn't really deduce what exactly they were doing. But they *did* understand that they were clearly descending. And not stably, either. Their footing was still shaking and swaying, and the unpleasant changes in gravity threatened to empty the contents of their stomachs.

The situation was too dangerous to just be called "air travel."

And by making them fight unnaturally against gravity, reality was making absolutely sure they knew their lives were in danger.

"…We won't get a do-over. We have one shot at this. You can still decide to give up. Once we're down too far, you won't be able to use parachutes. Are you sure about this…?"

After hearing Mikoto interpret for the man, Kamijou smirked. Ignoring the rapidly scrolling numbers on the altimeter, he said, "We're ready. Tell us how to land this thing."

"You've got guts, kid."

The bloodied pilot lifted his upper body up again.

"…But protecting the president is *my* job."

[Nov. 10 / Source: Hawaii, a bird-watching camera in Hawaii Volcanoes National Park]

Umidori Kuroyoru and Misaka Worst were the ones who actually did something useful.

A giant spear made of nitrogen directly tore apart the metal legs holding up one of the drums. Meanwhile, Misaka Worst accelerated the iron stakes, blowing them clear out of the ground and off the legs. Without any support, the Level Zero Hamazura could push the drum over just with his hands. This way, the detonator wouldn't be able to do what it was supposed to.

But there were so many. And they didn't have time.

As Misaka Worst watched, a red light near the center of the overturned drum came on. Knowing what the eerie glow probably signified, she hastily glanced around. A little under half of the detonators still needed to be dismantled. And they were all glowing with the same red light.

"Shit…," she muttered.

Then she shouted at Hamazura and Kuroyoru, who were still working.

"Not good! We won't make it! They're gonna blow!"

"There's still more left on the other side of the crater!"

"If we stay here, we die! Either from the explosion's shock wave or the volcanic lava!"

"Five hundred thousand people! You wanna leave them to die?!" yelled Hamazura.

But Kuroyoru's arms dropped to her side like someone had just turned them off. Misaka Worst had probably done it.

She managed to shrug and say, "If you want to do this alone, be our guest."

"Goddamn it…!"

Without Misaka Worst and Kuroyoru's abilities, he wouldn't be able to destroy the legs and stakes holding the drums to the ground. He'd be useless on his own.

…At least, that was what Misaka Worst had in mind.

Then came a hard *bang*, and when she realized Hamazura was kicking the hard ground as he launched into a run toward another detonator, she felt her whole face go tense.

"Hey! Misaka swears she'll leave you behind! Misaka has no obligation to go along with this!"

"No point trying to talk him down," said Kuroyoru, clicking her tongue, her unmoving arms still swaying. "Hit him with a high-tension current."

Zhhhh-chhhhh!!!!!! came the burst of electricity.

After seeing Hamazura fall to the ground, Misaka Worst gave Kuroyoru back control of her arms. She jerked her chin toward Hamazura. "Carry him. If we don't get out of here, that lava will melt us!"

"I wish you'd take our different body types into consideration."

"Well, one of Misaka's arms is *broken*."

Seeing Kuroyoru throw Hamazura over her shoulder like a bag of rice, Misaka Worst glanced at the other detonators that were still booting up.

"The detonator links over twenty units together to achieve its effects. With half destroyed, it shouldn't go as they planned!"

"I'd rather you *run* than talk. Misaka doesn't know what way the lava will flow, but this entire caldera will turn into a lake of it for sure!"

The two girls sprang into action, taking up their escape.

The center of the caldera was shaped like a crater. To get out, they'd naturally have to run all the way uphill.

And run they did.

But getting all the way past the ten-kilometer-long caldera would have been difficult even for a professional marathon runner. Kuroyoru clicked her tongue, removed her right arm from its socket, fired a nitrogen spear behind her, and launched off like a rocket. After seeing her arm fall in the distance and grab tightly onto the ground, Misaka Worst used her magnetism to launch all three of them.

"Misaka's got a name for us. What do you think of *Bad Girl Duo*?"

"You're literally gonna melt my brain if you keep that magnetic interference going!"

Kuroyoru picked up her fallen arm, then repeated the same process several times until they eventually made it to the caldera's edge.

But that was as far as they could go.

First came the deep sound of an explosion, rattling them to their cores.

But a moment later, they'd forgotten about that.

Because an enormous amount of heat and wind instantly covered everything.

[Nov. 10 / Source: Lanai waters, an onboard camera on a Marine patrol boat]

The rugged military transport plane floated on the quiet sea.

But for Arc Daniels, the man gripping the helm of the Marine patrol boat, it was more a release from boredom than a heartfelt sense of relief. He'd just come here all the way from Pearl Harbor Base 3 on Oahu. Someone from the Lanai base should have gotten this job.

"In sight! Just like the report said. Mr. Scandal and his party are standing on the roof of the craft!"

His colleague shouted enthusiastically to him from the deck. The people on the other patrol boats next to this one were probably seeing the same thing. Only the helmsmen had to shoulder the worry and anxiety.

"He's insane. Doesn't he know that emergency landings are highly likely to fail?"

"This can't be an attempt to appeal to his base, right? Hope I won't see him on TV later saying he's blessed by Lady Luck herself or something like that."

The Marines were all grumbling, but even they moderated themselves when they got within earshot of the president. About half the plane was below the water, but there were still a few meters above the ocean. That was quite different from the patrol boats, which had been remodeled from small motorboats. They'd have to attach a rope to the lightning rod unit on the roof of the plane and have the survivors descend one by one.

They'd planned to go back to Oahu after that, but the plane's pilot had been shot. Since he needed emergency transport, they would have to stop by the hospital on Lanai.

The cargo plane was now within forty meters of Lanai's shoreline. If it had gone any farther, its belly would have scraped against the ground, and the situation would be entirely different.

The pilot was in a life-threatening situation but could still be saved if they acted now. The fact that they'd safely made an emergency landing at all was cause for celebration.

However.

The people they'd rescued, including the president, didn't seem at all enthused about their miraculous landing. In fact, they didn't so much as spare a glance at the transport plane they'd just been on, nor the island they were headed for. Instead, they were looking in a single direction—with intense panic and tension on their faces.

Arc craned his head to look in the same direction. And then he noticed it.

The once-blue skies had gone black.

That dark thunderhead of a cloud—that was volcanic ash. Judging by the direction, it was coming from the island of Hawaii. The first thing that sprang to mind was Kilauea.

"An eruption... Shit! It really erupted?!"

"You've gotta be kidding me. They couldn't stop the detonator...? Aren't five hundred thousand people's lives at risk?!"

"No," responded the president; they were all speaking Japanese. "Kilauea is the type of active volcano that spews a whole lot of soft lava everywhere. If all they wanted was to cause major damage to people at its foot, they could have just brought the lava up. Something about the eruption is strange. How can it be spitting out so much ash...?"

"Maybe it means it didn't go off according to Gremlin's plans."

"I can't tell... Corporal! This vessel has an internet connection through the smart system for interunit communication, right? You kept begging for it to be funded, so you're not allowed to say no here. I want to hook the imperial package into it and get some information, mostly military..."

The president suddenly fell silent.

The reason? A long, slender strand of white smoke.

It came from the Lanai shoreline—not the near one, but rather from the edge of the other side of the island to Arc's right, over ten kilometers away. A spear of white smoke was heading directly toward them.

As it shot just above the surface of the water, Arc immediately realized what it was.

"An...anti-ship missile?!"

"Shit! Abandon ship!"

Right as someone shouted that, the missile brutally slammed into another patrol boat next to Arc's. It whipped up an explosion and a shock wave. The small vessel began falling apart as it literally flew up and over Arc's head.

Having managed to jump into the water, the soldiers poked their heads above the surface for oxygen.

If they hadn't gotten caught in the explosion, and they still had all their limbs attached, then...

"Mr. President! That was a Narwhal—the anti-ship missile we jointly developed with the EU! It's only for punching holes in the sides of ships. They kept its power and size to a minimum to cut down on the price and transportation costs. The shock wave travels straight forward like a spear, so if you get a few meters away, you can avoid it!"

"But who the hell did this? And how…?"

"Incoming! Another one! Abandon ship, Mr. President! Hurry!"

Several more strands of white smoke tore through the air right along the ocean. Their patrol boats could push to fairly high speeds, but they obviously couldn't maintain enough velocity to shake off a missile.

The president and the Asian youths under his wing (?) all jumped into the sea at the Marine's urging. He saw one of his fellow soldiers stuff the pilot into a reinforced rubber sack and close it up—being deeply wounded, the man couldn't afford to be exposed to seawater. Arc watched him dive into the water with it. It was a body bag, yes, but trivial details weren't important at the moment.

Arc Daniels hurried over and jumped overboard as well. A moment later, the anti-ship missiles struck his unmanned patrol boat, completely blowing through their means of transportation.

"Did the strikes stop…?"

Arc looked dubious. The president, however, put on his best publicity voice.

"They likely don't have sensors to detect us. Another unit will be dispatched to see if we're dead, so we shouldn't stick around. Let's thank our lucky stars we're alive and leave immediately."

"Another…unit? What the hell's even going on here, sir?!"

"I'm as confused as you, soldier."

"It's… It's another war… I don't know what country is behind this, but if people find out about the scope and how you're being targeted, they'll start demanding vengeance…!"

"As long as I'm alive, soldier, everything will be all right. And I'd never waste your lives on petty revenge."

They'd developed this model of anti-ship missile with the EU but bombing Europe just for this would be the height of folly. By the same token, even if there had been a national flag painted on the weapons, it would be weak evidence. If someone was trying to frame a different nation for the attack, the U.S. would be going after unrelated civilians.

"About these anti-ship missiles," said the president. "Narwhals, you said?"

"Y-yes, sir. What about them?"

"Do you know their specific model number? Are they D-type or R-type?"

"I'm, uh, sorry, sir. I've heard they make different sounds when launching, but I couldn't make it out for sure…"

"Since they were jointly developed, Narwhals can easily end up in other nations. Plus, the D-type is an export model meant for acquiring foreign currency. But it isn't possible for nations that aren't affiliated with the EU to sell these—the price is too high, the maintenance format is too weird, et cetera… Only grayflags—unregistered military forces—were buying them."

"…Grayflags, sir?" Arc audibly gulped. "You mean…a PMC is behind all this?"

"Could be. We can't rule out another country setting this up, but like you said, letting people start talking about vengeance is too risky. This definitely doesn't seem like something a person with a, let's say, *permanent place of residence*, would do." The president's voice was bitter as he spoke. "Whoever we're up against, they were sneaking around in the shadows before. But this attack is flashy enough to put them center stage. They won't stop here. We're looking at a huge offensive—like an avalanche."

"Y-you mean they'll declare war, sir?"

"It would have been easier if they were *that* gentlemanly, but no." Roberto pointed straight up and continued. "Even if it wasn't a full-scale eruption, Kilauea still blew its top. Ash is about to cover the sky. You know what that means, Corporal?"

"That you won't be able to launch any aircraft?" interrupted the Asian girl in English, poking her head out from behind the president.

"That's right… Which means any emergency aerial support from the mainland—fighters, bombers, and the like—will all be useless.

"And," added Roberto, "we have those anti-ship missiles. If these guys are stationed everywhere on the Hawaiian Islands and not just Lanai, I wouldn't be optimistic about ship-based bombardments or landing ship operations. Even supersonic jets have trouble avoiding antiair missiles. Boats can only go a few dozen miles. There's no way they'd be able to avoid anti-ship missiles."

"Then the Hawaiian Islands are completely isolated, sir…?"

"The perpetrators waited until Kilauea erupted to launch this obvious attack. Isolation was definitely their aim—though I don't know if it was their end goal or just a way for them to do whatever *else* they feel like."

"B-but, sir! The Hawaiian Islands have the highest concentration of military bases in the Pacific! We should have enough military power right here!"

"Oh, certainly—*if* this were just about firepower." The president's expression soured. "But I've seen the enemy, and they have powers that defy common sense. And by attacking us with anti-ship missiles, they've shown they *also* have major power that *is* plenty comprehensible: a numerical advantage, which our nation has always touted as a great strength."

The president seemed to be putting the pieces together as he spoke.

What would happen when those two powers collided? How much devastation would it cause?

He gritted his back teeth, then spoke.

"Either way, they've crossed over into a new stage of their plan—and it's very good for them."

CHAPTER 4
Collapse of Rules and Isolation
Trident.

[Nov. 10 / Source: California, a military activity–recording camera at Grand Arrow Air Force Base]

The commotion spread all the way to the largest Air Force base on the western seaboard, growing stronger as one moved inward from the ground crews doing final checks on fighter jets, to the pilots waiting for orders to launch, to those higher up in the base, and to central command.

Alfred Thirdman, the base's commanding officer, skimmed a thick sheaf of documents, then tossed it aside. Stomping on the useless scraps of paper with his boot, he raised his voice and yelled.

"You dumbass! Identifying the enemy faction can wait! The president's safety takes top priority right now! They're trying to kill everyone! Don't you understand that I'm telling you to run the calculations and tell us if we can sortie?! How far is the ash spreading?! What's its altitude? And how thick is it?!"

Something inexplicable was displayed on the satellite feed. Large numbers of troops had made landfall on the eight main islands making up the state of Hawaii. Evidently, some of the tankers and passenger boats out on the open sea had been disguised landing ships. Hovercrafts on huge air cushions were bringing in all types of personnel, including soldiers, machines of war such as ATVs and armored cars, and even anti-ship missile units. At a glance, they numbered a little under seven thousand.

However, aside from the soldiers actually fighting on the front lines, there would have to be maintenance crews and comm teams providing rear support. Add them into the mix, and that number could reach over ten thousand.

The force was large enough to cover a whole division.

And yet the military had *somehow overlooked them* until this very moment—and more to the point, they'd allowed U.S. territory to be invaded. It was enough to make the blood vessels in Alfred's temples squirm, and he knew it.

One of his subordinates gave a report. Either the man was afraid of the situation unfolding before their eyes, or he was just scared of the CO.

"S-sir, the mass of smoke is very dense and has spread over a very wide area, with Mount Kilauea at its center. We tried using satellite laser scans, but there's very little hope of them piercing the cloud. If we launch our fighters into smoke that thick, they'll almost certainly have engine trouble…"

"What about the trade winds? They might drive the spread in a certain direction. The western side—Guam, Yokosuka—might be out, but can we give them air support from the mainland here in the east?!"

"The ash is dispersing in all directions, sir. It's not quite going toward the rest of Hawaii. The, uh, the entire area two hundred miles around it is unable to be used."

Alfred clicked his teeth in annoyance, then slammed the tip of his boot into the utterly unhelpful console.

The Hawaiian Islands hosted the biggest aggregation of military power in the entire Pacific region—but considering the developing crisis, he wasn't even sure how much that would matter. There were plenty of Aegis-equipped warships moored in the military ports, and he knew they were being blown up one after the next at this very moment. In fact, he actually considered it a stroke of good luck that the *Hubble Lotus*, their nuclear-powered carrier, was on a trip to the South China Sea.

"The *president* is in there, too," Alfred said to his subordinate. "An unknown force has invaded our territory, and they're setting up anti-ship missile emplacements as we speak. Are you just going to sit here and twiddle your thumbs?"

"N-no, sir. But—"

"Our last resort is to send them seaborne support."

"Sir, if the enemy finishes setting up their anti-ship missile launchers, our technology won't be enough for our vessels to avoid them. They only fly a few yards over the water, and—"

Alfred kicked the console again, not letting the man finish.

After a moment, he spoke again. "Get me Dirty Lance in Texas. They'll be thinking the same thing as me."

"A…a ballistic missile launch base, sir?! But the president is over there, not to mention—"

"We won't load nukes onto them. And I'm not about to blow our own country to smithereens. I'm *also* not thinking about retaliation at this stage." Alfred glanced at the projector screen. "We'll explode regular warheads at a high altitude to drive away the scattered volcanic ash. Guam may have trouble sending air support, but there's relatively little volcanic ash out here on the mainland. We might be able to punch a hole through it."

"W-will that work, sir? I don't think the vice president will agree to your proposal. Also, the laws about the use of ballistic missiles within the U.S. aren't clear, and their maintenance status may not be up to snuff."

"In all likelihood, we'll crash straight into the wall known as *reality*." Alfred sighed in an almost casual way. "But the situation being what it is, we need all the cards in our hand we can get. In the slim chance we get an opportunity, we need to be ready to act swiftly."

[Nov. 10 / Source: Oahu, a soldier's camera-equipped helmet connected to the C&C cloud at Blackport Naval Base]

*   *   *

Mercenaries wearing uniforms that reflected light like the backside of CDs had already made it over the fence around the U.S. Navy's military port. One of them was Raymond Carlman. It was a miracle they'd even gotten within twenty meters of the place, to say nothing of actually stepping foot on-site. His iron-plated military boots crossed over common sense.

And they weren't just crossing over.

Pillars of dark black smoke were spouting from several frigates and Aegis-equipped warships moored in the harbor. He could hear the explosions, too. The explosives and firing charges were igniting, causing one blast after another.

"Whoa… This is fucking unreal! Those symbols of star-spangled power are tilting over. The Aegis ships are sinking!"

"Cool your head, Eater 8! This is far from over!"

Heavy cannon fire ensued. Quickly, Raymond dropped down and dove behind an overturned military-grade tractor. The U.S. Navy's counterattack was still ongoing, but it was sporadic. Their barrages were thin, and they weren't using group wave tactics or multipronged assaults. It seemed safe to assume that their chain of command had snapped. The battle was as good as won.

"Where's the carrier? That damn ship named after a president—it's supposed to be here, right?"

"Isn't it off in the South China Sea? Anyway, this all seems way too easy. Are you sure we're winning?"

Naturally, there was a very good reason things had turned out like this. Even Raymond could barely believe it. Deniers of the occult always talked about only believing what you saw with your own eyes, but this was so far beyond that. He saw, yes, but he didn't *want* to believe.

Some sort of huge, black figure was jumping from ship to ship.

Lightning strikes from accumulations of volcanic ash particles shot through the enemy soldiers behind cover with pinpoint accuracy. The explosive flames spewing from the boats changed shape and then plunged toward the durable structures as though they had a mind of their own.

This wasn't simply a case of an unknown occult phenomenon sweeping through. Raymond and the others were more or less battling the U.S. Navy with regular bullets and explosives. But that phenomenon was weaving between the gaps in their stalemate, the gunfire and obstacles, to press in on the enemy. It had created a new golden ratio. The way it dominated the battlefield was *fascinating*.

And...

"Don't go overboard now..."

Raymond heard a voice, sharp and pointed like an icicle. It belonged to a mature woman. She was wearing the same outfit as the rest of them, but one thing in particular made her stand out among the other silver-clad soldiers. She was clearly out of place here. In fact, she was the very woman who had brought this new power to the field of battle.

Gremlin.

She was one of *them*. A sorcerer.

All the suspicions he'd had about occult topics disappeared without a trace, because this woman was strong enough to dominate modern warfare.

"We don't want the U.S. to collapse," she continued. "We want to control it. If we lose any more people than necessary, it will only come back to hurt us."

"Are you telling us to have mercy? To only disable them?! Are you an idiot?! On a battlefield, anyone holding a weapon and moving their index finger is an enemy. As long as you can do that, then lives can be taken equally. That's what war is! Why the hell wouldn't we kill them when we have the chance?! Answer me!"

Raymond Carlman yelled at her, really letting her have it. The results were far beyond his expectations—or maybe the blood had gone to his head from the series of huge explosions and flashes of light.

The owner of the edged voice, however, put her hand over his gun hand, as if to gently stop him.

That was all she did.

Chhhhh-zhhhhh-shhhhhhh!!
With the noise of a sizzling wok, the flesh of Raymond's right hand and wrist disintegrated into blackened ash.

"Ah, gah… Aaaaaaaaaaaagggggggggggggggggghhhhhhhhhhhhh?! Ahhhh… Ah?"
His screams turned doubtful halfway through. His right hand had been nothing but a skeleton, but now it was like watching a video in reverse—fresh flesh and skin began to reappear over the bones. Within just ten seconds, not only his palm was back—the entire silver glove he'd been wearing was also right there again.

The pain and injury both vanished, leaving only terror in their wake.
His mind and body were telling him different things. A sense of extreme distress flooded through him.
The only thing he heard was that sharp female voice. It was quiet—but firm.
"Don't go overboard now."
The occult continued to expand its command over the battlefield.
Enemy and ally alike. It didn't discriminate.
Despite their overwhelming advantage, Raymond and the others felt intensely intimidated, like a cold blade had just been thrust into their chests.
But the strange situation wasn't done changing just yet.

"Hey. You think maybe *you're* going a little overboard with your warnings? They're laymen, you know."

The next thing Raymond knew, a man in formal attire was standing in the middle of the dock.
He honestly had no idea where the man had come from.
But a single card fluttered down like a tree leaf.
Someone with better eyesight might have been able to see what it was—the Ace of Swords, one of the minor arcana in tarot decks.

He was one of the sorcerers Leivinia Birdway had brought with her to the Hawaiian Islands.

A member of Dawn-Colored Sunlight.

Mark Space.

"......"

One of the silver-clad soldiers, the one with the sharp voice, quickly sent a question over her comm. Lanai, Hawaii... He couldn't make out the details, but apparently, *sorcerer-on-sorcerer combat was now ensuing all over the state.*

The woman simply sharpened her icicle of a voice even more.

"...Part of their infiltration team—the scattered ones collecting information."

"Essentially, yep."

Like a master magician, he flung a whole pile of cards from his right hand to his left.

If the U.S. Navy and Dawn-Colored Sunlight joined forces, they'd end up doing something pretty similar to Gremlin. Though there would be an overwhelming numerical difference when it came to sorcerers, of course.

"I doubt this will be enough to turn the tables," said the man, "but I'm sure I can buy them some time. At least enough to withdraw."

"You hand-reared sorcerer. You really think you can reach Gremlin?"

"I'll let my full set of minor arcana entertain you."

[Nov. 10 / Source: Oahu, a congressional proceedings recording camera in a government vehicle on a highway]

The government car, painted all black, rattled left and right. As one of its passengers, Roselyne Crackhart, aide to the president, shook around, she cast a sharp gaze behind her.

That military-grade ATV was closing in.

A man was sticking out of the roof, only his upper body visible, peppering her with bullets from his bullpup assault rifle. A dazzling bouquet of orange sparks continuously bloomed and scattered on her car's surface.

"...In broad daylight, with civilians around...!"

Roselyne gnashed her teeth. Everything she thought she knew an hour ago was inapplicable now—not only on Oahu but on the rest of Hawaii as well. Beside her, a uniformed police officer was simply watching the mad chase with a dazed look on his face.

This was America—but not America.

Before that thought could settle into her perception, she forced herself to stop thinking about it. She supported the leader of this nation. She couldn't afford to admit something like that.

She eyed the baffled officer and yelled, "Get the police out of here! Use my name! I don't care if you have to use a radio or a cell phone! Their bulletproof jackets won't be able to stop rifle bullets!"

"All right, but what should we do?! We're going to run out of gas at some point!"

"The closest military base is Marine Corps Pearl Harbor Base 3! Bust into it if you have to and get the men stationed there to protect us. It's our turn to show how strong the world's police really are!"

As the scenery whizzed by, she noticed several things that were clearly out of place. Several boats equipped with giant blackened air cushions had come onto the pure white beach as if to soil it. Dozens of combat personnel were climbing off—they all wore silver military uniforms—and off-road cars and even armored vehicles were alighting as well. That thing keeping its balance with legs—like a crane truck—was an anti-ship missile launcher whose payload could travel at super-low altitudes.

Are you kidding me? she thought. *This isn't just a terrorist attack. This is a whole army. This isn't an incident—it's a war...*

"Grayflags... B-but from where...?"

"Their movements lack uniformity. Those soldiers weren't trained from square one by any nation. I agree that it's highly likely they're mercenaries—members of a PMC—made up of a ragtag group of somewhat combat-experienced soldiers, but that's not the heart of the issue."

"?"

"The real question is, who the hell hired them and why?"

As Roselyne bit down, the government car shot toward the Marine base.

But even the base couldn't give them any hope.

The car screeched to a halt before it got there. No soldiers had demanded they stop—in fact, there were no soldiers around at all.

In fact.

What greeted them instead was a sea of flames.

The world's police.

The densest group of military bases, the most powerful area in not only Hawaii but in the entire Pacific, was aflame. The base's outskirts weren't a defensive line anymore. The kilometers-long fence had been torn apart by bombardments from a distance. And it was from one such opening that a group of enemy soldiers staged their assault.

This group contained five people.

The CD-like full-body armor they had on concealed their appearances, their very identities. But the person in the center was clearly different from the rest.

The U.S. Marine Corps were the strongest fighting force in contests of raw firepower against raw firepower. They would lose to Academy City and its singular technology, but when it came to standard battles, they had it all—quantity *and* quality. Out of the branches of the U.S. military, they reigned supreme, beyond a shadow of a doubt.

And yet that unstoppable fighting force was being overwhelmed.

By those five people working as a team—and by the massive avalanche of mercenaries pouring in.

The person at the heart of it all was right in the middle of that team.

They were the only one there not relying on a firearm. From their hands, flames raged, spears of ice rained down, lightning fired like living creatures, and earthen barricades rose out of the most minor of cracks in the ground.

Against this fanged phenomenon, neither the rules of physics nor chemistry applied.

The flames melted unburnable steel, and the lightning penetrated perfectly insulated concrete. While they weren't killing blows, the mercenaries followed up with their assault rifles and grenade launchers as the Marines panicked and tried to flee from behind their own barricades.

It wasn't just firepower.

Nor was it just the occult abilities.

It was a combination of the two. Something not even seen during World War III. A single result that could have resulted in world peace had they been linked together differently. The worst possible result.

As Roselyne watched the scene in dumbfounded shock, something even more inexplicable happened.

Several hundred meters away, one of the silver-uniformed soldiers looked at her. Then they jumped—farther than even the longest of baseball pitches could ever hope to go—and landed right on the hood of the government car. The silver soldier didn't say a word. They just held their palm out toward the inside of the car.

What would leap from it? Fire or ice?

Roselyne couldn't even comprehend what was happening.

Boooooom!!!!!!

All of a sudden, another individual drove a flying kick into the silver soldier, knocking them to the side.

The person's hair was white, and their eyes were red. Roselyne had no way of knowing this, but he was a certain Level Five esper, the one who held the title of *strongest in Academy City, Japan.*

"Ugh. There's no end to these gnats. Birdway! Can't you use that convenient magic of yours to blow them all away?! I'm just wasting my fucking battery here!"

"As if. Spells and physical bodies are both resources. I'm exerting myself plenty over here... That's probably why Gremlin joined up with those gun-toting jerks. To get us to expend all our energy."

"A fusion of science and sorcery..."

"It's a different setup from the Rome-Russia alliance during World War III."

A sea of flames.

Amid screams of panic from people fleeing in confusion, only these two were calm.

The short girl gave a light wave of the staff in her hand, and an even bigger white explosion went off, engulfing the wall of flames burning down the entire base plot and mowing down all the mercenaries using their armored vehicles for protection. Then more white explosions. So simply. So easily. Bright flashes lit up different areas of the base in sequence, bolstering the U.S.'s unsteady barrages.

"Ah, it's so nice and open. Don't need to worry about toning things down here. I can just go wild."

"Don't act like you're being sensible. You'll hit our allies, too, dumbass."

"Neither enemy nor ally will die. As long as they've been trained to an above-average level. I'm being considerate, here."

And then Roselyne realized something.

The U.S. Marines were still being pushed back, closed in on by the mercenaries. Gunshot wounds were all too common in their ranks. But there were no obvious corpses anywhere. They were holding back, keeping themselves just barely on the better side of life and death.

"...Looks like I've got more baggage, too. Shit," said the white monster in an absolutely fed-up tone.

"I mean, you're not gonna just *abandon* them, are you, hero?"

"Don't talk like you fucking know who I am."

"Hey, it's all good. Pretend you don't want to. That's fine. Just conserve your strength so we can turn this thing around. Buy time for the U.S. military to retreat—then we'll crush as many of those mercenary *and* sorcerer shits as we need."

*   *   *

[Nov. 10 / Source: Molokai, a security camera in Shrimp Motel]

Salonya A. Irivika was standing in front of a motel. Her back against the thin door, she drank some mineral water from a bottle. Her hair was wet, as though she'd just taken a shower. But she'd been underwater until ten or twenty minutes ago.

The sporadic sounds of explosions and gunshots were reaching her out here, too.

Just two weeks ago, during World War III, you could hear such sounds anywhere on the planet. They were noises that not only the citizens of Hawaii but people the whole world over had decided never to hear again.

The seaside motel was long, basically a row of rooms. She was the only customer here, though. Even the managers had left. *Can't blame them*, thought Salonya, casually glancing around.

The white, sandy beaches were no longer in a state to draw mobs of tourists.

Boats equipped with large military-grade air cushions for coming ashore, massive numbers of vehicles, soldiers in silver uniforms, container-shaped anti-ship missile launchers… The scattered black and moss-green coloring made her think of the stench of death. At the end of the long, spear-like smoke trail was the wreckage of a frigate that had fled the port. They weren't just setting things up. They weren't just making threats. They were following through and actually destroying things. It was none other than a second coming of World War III.

As a silver-clad mercenary walked up to her, Salonya said, "Looks like you're finally starting to get closer to our scale. Until now, well, you know. The size of the whole thing was just too small, and it was like you couldn't see much of anything at all."

"We'll be able to take control of the entire widdle island in about five hours, but we probably don't need to wait that long. We must carry out our own mission as quickly as possible."

"I saw your anti-ship missile demonstration just now. What are you doing about the submarines?"

"We're prepping low-altitude airborne torpedoes. They fly about a hundred meters, then dive down into the ocean. They were made to prevent sea infiltrations from the surface."

"Make sure you bolster your anti*human* measures, too. Frogmen, I think they were called? We can't assume specialists won't just swim here."

"...I doubt a couple of them would change the situation much. It would be like a one-on-eleven soccer match."

"I just want to be sure. Don't forget our widdle goal—the original one."

Then the silver mercenary's cell phone rang. He picked up, and after trading a few short words, he handed the phone to Salonya.

"It's from Knowledge 12," he told her.

"Who's that again?"

"The one who made the request to our company."

"Oh, her. Give it here."

Salonya switched to a more formal but still casual tone of voice.

"Hello, there. This widdle phase of the operation is going swimmingly. Any problems on your end?"

"*Actually, I'm getting anxious because I haven't found anything that stands out, and now I'm nitpicking everything.*"

"No problems, then. *What about your widdle play on the center?*"

"*It's going fine. I'm doing as much as my power lets me, at least. But it's not enough, which is why I asked you to help.*"

"It's all annoyingly indirect, in my opinion. Though I guess it's just a brief preparation period so that Gremlin can get its hands firmly on the USA. I'll just have to bear with it." Salonya's tone was incredibly indifferent as she spoke of such dramatic things. "Still, we have the widdle vice president. Can't you just have him say the president is missing and can't fulfill his duties?"

"*I would if I could,*" said the person on the other end, sounding grumpy. "*You know about Air Force One?*"

"The president's plane, right? It contains the minimum necessary facilities for him to do his job, and he's capable of taking command of the entire military from it in an emergency."

"The imperial package Roberto Catze has is the same. It has all the permissions on the intragovernmental cloud. He can issue orders no matter where he is. It's not enough that he's just absent from the White House. As long as he has the package, wherever he happens to be is his executive office."

"Well, then there's no point looking for shortcuts. We'll keep going with the plan. You can leave it to me. Before our widdle game really begins, I'll prep the last few things in a jiffy," said Salonya off-handedly, before then saying, "However."

The silver-uniformed mercenary shook a little.

Were the negative emotions emanating from her body getting to him through his electronic equipment?

"I mean, I know you did it out of consideration. If they found out where I was, I'd have a hard time fighting them off while protecting the detonator. But the next time you lie to me and use me as a diversion…*I'll take your head and the president's*, okay?"

[Nov. 10 / Source: Lanai, a security camera in Star Lounge Shot Bar]

Forcing the door of the now-empty bar open, Kamijou, Misaka, and Roberto held their breaths. After their emergency landing, right when the military was recovering them, they'd been hit by a barrage of anti-ship missiles. They'd just managed to make it to the shore somehow. Even now, off-road vehicles with machine guns on them were driving around the main roads in blatant disregard of the law.

Their clothing was sticky with seawater and sand, but they didn't even have time to complain about it.

"…I should have known."

The president sat down on the floor and put his attaché case next to him.

"Someone's out there who can use occult magic to control people.

But as soon as I was told there could be a limit on how many they can control, I..."

"What are you talking about?" asked Kamijou.

"I thought the occult phenomenon was spreading to all corners of government. The House of Representatives, the Senate, the whole thing, under the control of some strange power. But I was wrong."

"Huh? But wait, that's...," stammered Kamijou, at a loss. Wasn't that exactly what Salonya had been doing? That was why the president had sensed danger, broken away from his escorts, and begun acting on his own. It also explained how Gremlin had been controlling the military and government to search for information on the detonator, then partially used it for real on Kilauea.

However...

"*Only a handful of people were ever under her control to begin with,*" said Roberto bitterly. "Same goes for those soldiers. You don't have to use weird powers to make people do what you want."

"W-wait, then..."

"There's someone out there with the power to force others to do their bidding—but that doesn't line up with what's actually going on. Barely any occult nonsense is being used at all. *They don't have to use it. They can make people obey orders without it. Just like I do every day as president!*"

You could hear his mortification at how victim and aggressor had been reversed, at how his subordinates and combat forces had so obviously betrayed him.

But Kamijou couldn't keep up. What the hell was happening here in Hawaii? No, in all of the USA?

"Wait a second," he said. "Birdway used her autoanalysis to figure out Salonya's spell. She can definitely control a lot of people with it..."

"To be honest with you, kid, this is all outside my wheelhouse, so I'm sorry if this is a dumb question," replied the president before pausing. "But is there any guarantee the autoanalysis *didn't get tricked into giving her a fake answer?*"

"Wait a minute. That would be..."

"Both Birdway and this Salonya lady are professionals in their field. This isn't a one-sided fight between a pro and a layman. Which means they have an even chance of victory. Tricking someone when they think they have everything figured out is a classic play, isn't it?"

"But, uh, what about that package or whatever? Didn't you figure out that Salonya was controlling a lot of people to try and gather data on the detonator?! And the detonator was literally in that base at Pearl Harbor! So we couldn't have been wrong…!"

"Yeah, individuals who shouldn't have had anything to do with the detonator were definitely accessing information about it on the government hub cloud. And they must have reported the info to Salonya's group."

The president shook his head.

"But the only thing I could see was where the data was coming from and going. It's perfectly possible they were all in their right minds and still obeying Salonya's commands."

"Wait. But what about Cendrillon? Before we ran into you, we fought a sorcerer named Cendrillon at the airport! When we caught her, Salonya manipulated her into killing herself to keep her quiet!"

But as Kamijou said this, he realized that may not have necessarily been the case.

Maybe the whole thing had been an act on Cendrillon's part.

Yes, perhaps they really had heard Salonya's voice. But it could have just been a spell for communication, not the one to control people. He couldn't reject the possibility that Cendrillon had tried to kill herself of her own volition in accordance with Salonya's voice.

It would be unthinkable for any sane person. But it had worked. It had thrown their judgment wildly off.

If that was the result of them rallying every last ounce of their strength to fight back, then…they'd have to rethink everything on a fundamental level.

"I doubt *everyone* was helping Salonya of their own volition—like those kids at the shopping mall and the plane pilot," said the president. "But now we know she might not be able to control nearly as many people as we thought, and it might be simple for her to give orders to those under her control. Salonya's manipulation of other people may just be the by-product of some other attack. As in, it only looks that way—but her true intent is something else."

Yes.

"It's even possible that Salonya A. Irivika doesn't actually specialize in controlling people at all."

[Nov. 10 / Source: Oahu, an air traffic control assistance camera at Marine Corps Pearl Harbor Base 3]

Birdway put her back against the side of the transport plane, which was now tilted over thanks to the broken axle holding up the wheels, trying to hold out against the mysterious armed faction's machine-gunning. After hearing a voice over the phone, she automatically applied a magical technique to several pieces of papyrus in her hand, confirmed the information on them, and then threw them hard onto the broken asphalt.

"…Damn you, Valvina. How dare you sell me defective products!"

The woman in the black suit, who had met up with Birdway as they charged for Trident, sighed in exasperation. "I don't think we can blame her. Doesn't she only really sell the materials? You were the one who made her create the Soul Arms, too, since you said it was too annoying to do yourself, boss. I think some of the fault lies with you."

"Guess my to-do list just got even longer," said Birdway, ignoring her.

As she spoke, she waved the staff in her hand, sending an explosion of light to mow down a group of foot soldiers, who were approaching by using their slow-moving armored car as a shield.

"I have to find info on Salonya again, then analyze her spell's format, effects, and scope. I have to do *everything* I let the Soul Arm do all over again."

"That sounds like a lot. Will you manage before running into her again?"

"I'll find a way. Always do."

[Nov. 10 / Source: Lanai, a camera on a portable game device left on a counter at Star Lounge Shot Bar]

Not everyone was under the control of Salonya's spell.

While Kamijou was shocked at the president's theory, he didn't dismiss it.

Someone out there would benefit from controlling the American government. They were manipulating politicians and government workers via a bunch of different avenues. But there were some people who were too stubborn to make into pawns—people who only ever acted for the sake of the nation.

If it came to it…

"…She'll use a mundane method of control on the people who aren't particularly resistant. Then for the handful of people who can't be manipulated by normal means, she'd use sorcery to force them under her control. Is that how she's infiltrating the country from inside and out?"

"Probably."

Maybe the sorcery Salonya had mastered wasn't supposed to be for controlling people at all. But if she applied it that way, it would either have that very effect or look like it did.

This was reckless; it was like using a heat-generating motor instead of a home heater. But on a national scale. Plus, the technological aspects aside, if Salonya could take over the "world's police"— still the strongest power on the science side in terms of material resources and economics—she would be an alarming threat.

And also…

Naturally, of the people deeply involved in U.S. politics who needed to be manipulated via sorcery, there could only be a single individual who Salonya would prioritize going after at all costs.

Roberto Catze.

The current president had sniffed out the occult invasion of the government and the improper usage of the detonator, then went off on his own without any members of the Secret Service to handle things by himself—he was an unprecedented individual. For those who wanted to control the country from the shadows, there was no more troublesome foe than him.

But was the enemy's aim ultimately to control the president?

Or was it to kill him, then have his authority transferred to someone easier to manipulate?

The number one target, however, grinned fearlessly. "And this unknown occult stuff works as a threat, too. They're telling me that if I don't want to end up like that, I should obey them. Actually, it could even be an excuse. If a rebellion broke out and they demanded responsibility from me, they'd use their occult powers to manipulate public opinion. They'd make me out to be just another victim dancing to someone else's tune."

They really didn't know anything about the "occult stuff" that Gremlin was using, so they didn't have any clue as to its specific requirements. Even if Salonya could only actually control a few dozen people at once—or more, but if she went further, the control would be incomplete, and her thralls would be more like malfunctioning robots—none of this could be proven.

Say they insisted all of Congress was under the effect of an occult power.

And say they actually had a way to prove this.

When presented with visible evidence, people who only believed what their eyes told them would come to the wrong conclusions and assume everyone in the government was under the influence of the occult power.

"Wait, but it's the…uh, the occult, right? Not supernatural abilities granted by science? Even if we did have a way to prove that and we showed people that evidence, we wouldn't get anywhere, would we?"

"Maybe in a prewar world. But everyone saw all the unexplained stuff that happened during World War III. The world has begun to accept that occult concepts are real. Even if it wouldn't be used as official evidence in court, if it was someone higher than the courts—someone who was on the verge of experiencing the world's darkness firsthand, like me—they might sympathize with victims of the occult. In some cases, they might take special measures."

"You mean like a presidential pardon…?"

"I doubt sympathy is enough to go that far, but it would help some to get rid of people's preconceptions. Say they were under coercion, and that would be enough. Wouldn't have to look after them till the very end."

Roberto heaved a sigh.

"Now that I think of it, it was odd that Roselyne and I noticed something was wrong at all. We know almost nothing about the occult. We're not experts like that Birdway kid. Would we be able to distinguish between people being controlled by magic and people being controlled by other means? It wouldn't be that simple, right? I don't know crap about all this mana or spell stuff, but don't you have to be pretty smart about all that to tell those people apart?"

"Then what on earth happened…?"

"It's like an act, or insurance, or faking an illness. The people under Salonya's non-magical control would just try to make it look like they were enslaved by magic if they ever got found out. So there *was* a change in them that even a layman could notice. Of course, Birdway, being an expert, would have known they were faking it."

"…But who is it?" asked Kamijou carefully. "It's not one of Gremlin's sorcerers like Salonya. Someone has joined forces with Gremlin… Who is the other enemy?"

"If Salonya's chipping away at the government with non-magical methods, then the enemy probably brought non-magical power to the table," said Roberto, putting his attaché case on the shot bar's counter. The bar had a wireless LAN connection, so the computer inside the case was able to pick up the electric waves. "Our hint is those guys who look like CDs."

"Yeah, what country are they from?"

"I doubt they're with a single nation—they're probably mercenaries. They call the companies they work for PMCs. That label covers a lot of types of people—from bloodthirsty bodyguards to torturers who do dirty jobs in the place of real soldiers to smaller organizations serving as guides through jungle and mountain regions... But the one we're up against this time is an actual fighting force the size of a division or brigade that takes on large-scale pseudo-military operations with their own troops."

Roberto sighed again.

"At that level, they're an effective combat force but very expensive. You hear about tankers falling victim to pirates, but you never hear about those same tankers being escorted by a fleet of mercenary ships like one big daimyo procession, right? I mean, obviously escorting ships in that way would present political problems, but the issue is mainly that a single day of work from one of these PMCs would cost a fortune."

"But these guys were paid up front, right?"

"My guess is that they're from Trident, a mercenary company active in Eastern Europe. They have D-type Narwhals, optical camouflage, and can deploy in a wide scope... Plus, from how they move, it seems like a lot of their hires are former U.S. servicepeople. They're a huge business—a single company possessing all three armies."

"A huge business? How big are we talking?" demanded Misaka.

"I'd say they employ about fifty thousand, since I hear software updates have let them cut down on how many crew members they need for naval vessels."

"That's enough to fill a small town!" exclaimed Kamijou. "Trained soldiers are experts, right? How'd they even get that many people?!"

"They were all mid-career recruitments. They don't use new graduates. Every year, one hundred and fifty thousand soldiers around the world retire from service. Two out of every three don't do so because of the age limit. It's accepted opinion given totals from before World War III."

"……"

"They have many reasons for leaving. And it's not all necessarily rainbows and sunshine after retiring. The majority of soldiers who belong to Trident are former American soldiers. I've appealed for them to get great Social Security benefits postretirement, but there are some who think expanding veteran welfare would ruin us financially."

The president sighed.

"Whatever their individual circumstances, they're all former professionals. And if that was all, then they'd just be currently retired secondhand goods. But Trident uses its own training programs to get their hires back up to first-rate ability, thus making them more valuable—it's like swapping out rusty gears. NATO tried to hire Trident during World War III, but the financial negotiations actually fell through. If you had enough money to make a deal with them, the bank databases would flag the payment. No bank *wants* money flowing out of their vaults. They'd definitely give a warning."

"Did you find them like that?" asked Mikoto.

"Unfortunately, no. But that in itself is a hint. The imperial package can only look up things the U.S. has the ability to search. The mastermind must have purposely made a financial deal without getting the U.S. involved to prevent the money from being traced back."

The president pressed a few keys on the imperial package, viewing even more confidential information.

"Clearly, whoever it is, they stand to gain even more from interfering with the U.S. than what they spent. Someone with a lot of capital scattered outside the country. Someone who could build secret connections with Eastern European governments and banks. Someone able to hire Trident. Someone who can watch our every move here in the Hawaiian Islands."

"Does that narrow it down to one person?"

"Not even close. There are over thirty people in the U.S. whose total market value exceeds that of the U.S. Multinational integrated corporations sure are scary, eh? Not even national borders can break them up. Clearly, they have another way of dividing things—one based on money and economies."

The president was up-front about it.

"But several of the people with enough power to change the United States are under someone's patronage. They're essentially just subsidiaries of guys like Frack Kateman, the car king, and Douglas Hardbell, the rock star. A bunch of people like them are possible candidates, but it's unlikely all of them would have the same boss—they don't have enough in common. In which case…"

He tapped away at the keyboard, and eventually, he came to an answer.

A large photograph appeared on the imperial package's screen.

"Aurey Blueshake, queen of American media. She's the only one it can be."

[Nov. 10 / Source: Hawaii, a bird-watching camera in Hawaii Volcanoes National Park]

I'm not dead. Strange.

That was Hamazura's true, unabashed opinion.

The island of Hawaii had turned into a lava-bound hell. The gigantic caldera, over ten kilometers across, had filled up with orange magma, and the molten rock that made it over was flowing down the mountainside like spilled corn syrup.

Fortunately, the area with all the settlements was safe—probably because the detonator hadn't been able to produce its full effect. Hamazura's group hadn't been swallowed by the lava either, but the air around them was steaming like a sauna, and the odor of sulfuric gas told his brain that he was in mortal peril. Because of all the volcanic ash overhead, everything was darker, like the weak sunlight right before dawn. Tiny pieces of the stuff were falling like rain, and finger-sized cinders from the volcano made pricking sounds as they stabbed into the ground.

But something else was happening. Something that pulled his eyes away from this twisted scene of nature's threats. In fact, he almost felt *lucky* for having been so close to the lava lake in the caldera.

It was beyond the curtain of ash blocking his view like a thin mist.

Near the foot of the mountain, he could hear gunshots and explosions. Silver combatants spread out like little dots—alongside weapons like air-cushioned boats and armored vehicles.

"...Aurey Blueshake?" repeated Hamazura into his cell phone, squatting low over the mostly white ash. He had his phone on conference mode so he could talk with both Kamijou and Accelerator at the same time.

He had no idea what was happening, but he heard an explosion over the call as Birdway answered him.

"Yeah. *The queen of American media, who went over her father's head and inherited her grandfather's network. She started a news channel as a new business venture, published a national newspaper, and purchased a major cell phone company, securing her position. She also owns teams in both the MLB and NFL. Once she enters basketball, she'll have taken control over all four major league sports. She's a behemoth in the financial world.*"

Birdway's tone was casual as she went on.

"*She's also very good at getting media-related businesses involved in other fields entirely. On one hand, she's diving into construction and real estate by entering the eco–home industry—houses with computerized management of solar power and home appliance power consumption. On the other hand, she's also making headway into the automobile industry, having produced a top-class line of cars through the development of electric vehicles and automatic inter-car distance adjustment programming. A noteworthy magazine put her on a list of the one hundred most influential people in America, but her group's uninhibited expansion and talent makes her big enough to swallow up all the others on it.*"

Birdway sounded somewhat exasperated as she explained this.

Aurey had engulfed even the king of cars and king of steel as subsidiaries for her own ends. She was no longer a queen but an *empress*. A titan whom even experts in their fields and monarchs reigning over nations would obey.

Birdway offered a few opinions of this leader of an empire.

"People have been calling her all kinds of baseless things—the person closest to making life in space a reality via a completely private corporation, someone who could acquire top secret government intel about UFOs, the woman involved in thirty percent of the world's crude oil... And after recently acquiring an internet search giant that also operates a social media business, she now has complete command over all information in the U.S."

"And that was when said search giant started raising questions," came Roberto Catze's quiet voice. *"It started with an internet service called F.C.E. It stands for Free Compound Eyes. No need for any expensive plans from security companies anymore. Now anyone can set up cameras at a low cost and connect them to the internet to create their own surveillance camera network. But a group of white-hat hackers pointed out that you can actually access the video data from other people's cameras just by putting in that camera's registration number. Meaning that search giant—the hosting service—can constantly watch any camera in the United States. Naturally, the service received a citation from the Federal Trade Commission, and it should be shut down by now..."*

"...So if the mastermind knows everything we're doing, then it stands to reason the F.C.E. is still online?" asked Kamijou with a groan.

"Regular users may not be able to access it anymore, but the software behind it is probably still on their servers. And possibly with even more authority. Aurey has poured a ton of money into investments with the three major provider companies. If the same F.C.E. tool has been introduced in secret, every camera using their lines could be under their control."

"And we're not just talking about cell phone cameras here," added

Birdway. *"Any Wi-Fi-enabled device, like a video camera or a portable game device, is at risk of being accessed."*

"But what is this Aurey lady even after?" asked Hamazura in spite of himself. "Doesn't she have enough money at this point to spend the rest of her life in the lap of luxury?"

He doubted someone so fulfilled would be involved with anything urgent enough to make her go astray like this. Or did being rich come with its own set of problems?

The president's response was a bitter one. *"People have called her a third branch of Congress, separate from the House of Representatives and the Senate."*

"What's that, uh, mean?"

"It means she has just as much influence as them. Media exposure is directly tied to votes, and she owns the mass media. Even a presidential election wouldn't be able to totally escape her influence. One of her projects helped out my campaign, in fact."

"...So even before all this, getting on the media queen's bad side meant you were guaranteed to lose an election?"

"First, she restricts congresspeople," explained Birdway. *"Then, via their orders, she exerts influence over the military and governmental organizations. Information travels faster than money. And when it comes to politicians who are strong of heart and wish only to serve their country, Salonya uses her spell to control them..."*

"She's trying to take the reins of the U.S. to lead it her way—by maneuvering elections to get useful pawns into public office," said Roberto in a low voice. *"And yet the country didn't actually go the way she wanted. Actually, I guess I should say that by then, the country couldn't fall into the hands of anyone like her."*

"?"

"World War III," said the president shortly, leading to a brief but tense silence. *"I'll be honest. Things haven't gone exactly according to the U.S.'s plans. In fact, it feels like we've been left out in the cold. Maybe Aurey gave up and tried to create a system to control the country more directly."*

"And that's why she contacted Gremlin and Trident?" said

Hamazura, moaning. "If we know all that, can't the police arrest her?"

"*Nobody knows where she is. We have too many enemies. She pays her taxes like a good little citizen of Washington, D.C., but if you told me she has a base on Mars, I'd probably believe you.*"

Once the conversation ended, Hamazura hung up and put his phone in his pocket.

Misaka Worst asked, "So what do we do now?"

"What else?" he replied. "We meet up with our leader and the president. Nothing to be gained staying separate at this point."

Kuroyoru scowled. "...Are you being serious? Aren't there antiship missiles all over the islands now? You think we can just take a pleasure yacht out on the water? They'd sink us in a heartbeat."

"Then we just need one that can't sink." Hamazura pointed to one of the air-cushion military boats that had made landfall. "We gotta blend in with them somehow. There's thousands of them, right? They won't be on top of telling who's who. If we can disguise ourselves as those CD soldier guys, we can hide our faces, too. Even though we're Asian, they'll be none the wiser."

"Misaka thinks they'll find out if we kill some and steal their clothes, though."

"The U.S. is the global capital of guns. You can get pistols at supermarkets here." Hamazura wiped the sweat off his face. "You can get stuff like that at the gun shops geared toward enthusiasts. The mercenaries are supposed to be wearing a bunch of equipment from different countries, right? If they put their uniforms together from pieces that already existed rather than using bespoke outfits, then we might have a chance... We may not be able to get the exact same model, but we could just say we switched a few things up for personal preference."

"Could we? Well, that might work for you and Misaka. But a little thing like me is way too short to *not* be suspicious in a military uniform," said Kuroyoru.

"Then we can stuff her in a bag or something. She's tiny. Plus, she can take her arms off. She can get pretty compact."

"…That's a hell of a thing to say off the cuff," grumbled Kuroyoru.

"So then the issue is the F.C.E.," said Misaka Worst. "Can't do anything with them watching us, especially not change our outfits."

"Wait. How many cameras do you think there are on this island alone? We can't destroy *all* of them," pointed out Hamazura.

"Once we're done changing, they won't be able to tell the difference. Misaka will just bust up the ones we see on the way there."

Misaka Worst took a few metal nails out of her pocket. They jingled as she began to control their magnetic fields.

"Right?"

[Information]

[Camera ID 119a0e19 not responding.]
 [Searching for online cameras in the same area it was when it went offline.]

[Nov. 10 / Source: Oahu, a congressional proceedings recording camera in Marine Corps Pearl Harbor Base 3]

Right after Accelerator hung up the phone, a huge explosion went off nearby. Trident had just fired a recoilless cannon. Accelerator charged through the middle as Birdway jumped to the side to escape the aftershock, the two of them each snapping to their next targets.

That was right when it happened.

Presidential aide Roselyne Crackhart's cell phone started ringing. On the other end was a familiar female voice.

"Have I been exposed already?"

"…You've got a lot of nerve calling me to ask about something you've been spying on the whole time, Aurey Blueshake."

"Hawaii is isolated. I can make as much of a commotion here as

I want. And in just a few hours, I'll be this nation's new master. It may seem unfair, but when that happens, I'd like you all to shift gears. You're going to be my opposition party holding on to dangerous ideals, *after all."*

"You really think it'll be that easy?"

"I know so. If I can put the president under the control of this occult power, then great. If not, bullets will transfer his authority into the hands of the vice president... And you know what's become of the vice president, don't you?"

"...This is an awful lot of work to go through. And for what? How do you intend on changing this country?"

"Knowledge 12."

Aurey invoked a certain term. For Roselyne, it was a cursed one.

"The twelve occult experiments performed before World War III using UFO research funds. You've had the chance to see top secret information—you've been at the president's side. You've heard of them, haven't you?"

"...Those experiments were started without his knowledge."

"Would you happen to know who the project's biggest investor is?"

"He identified seven of the experiments and forced them to shut down before they were complete!"

"But the other five were carried out. Arts and Sciences City in the Pacific Ocean. The collection of failure reports using Uncut Gems, naturally occurring espers, in several countries. The scientists were fired up at the idea of developing their own supernatural abilities domestically, but at its deepest level, there was a different, even deeper set of rules... You experienced the war. You know what I was trying to develop, don't you?"

"......"

"The United States' defenses against the occult are horribly weak," declared Aurey in a tone filled with confidence. Either these were her true feelings, or she'd mastered the art of appealing to the masses to the point where she could do so naturally. *"And the occult was deeply involved with the war, essentially leaving the United States out in the cold. But even that was a stroke of luck. If the person who was actually* behind the war had gone after us, both our leadership and core military staff would have been helplessly massacred by curses or spells, even inside their durable shelters."

"It was all in preparation for that...?"

"Knowledge 12 didn't produce any clear results. But maybe that's because we only completed five of the experiments. If we'd done all of them, then U.S. tech might have caught up to the highest international standards."

"The president was on reasonable ethical ground to put a stop to them. And now you're saying he doesn't have the right to protect this country? You're not just demanding sacrifices from the citizenry. You want to kidnap anyone on Earth who has the attributes you're looking for and dissect them? You think that's excusable?! Don't you realize it would ruin the founding principles of this nation?!"

"*It will be*—when I remake this nation as a theocracy."

Had representatives from both the science *and* sorcery sides been around to hear that, they might have groaned in response.

The conversion of a major nation.

While it lagged behind Academy City on the technological front, the U.S. was still first in the world in proper military and economic power. It was clear what it would mean—a total defection of state.

The effects on the global power structure and the chaos it would bring were both unfathomable.

"*The president's oath of office and the opening of court proceedings involve placing one hand on the Bible and praying. In the same way, the central government itself still has roots in the Protestant tradition. Every single U.S. president in history has been Crossist. By allowing that bud to blossom, we can give this country an extremely powerful resistance against occult attacks...* And we start by welcoming Gremlin into the fold as occult countermeasure advisers."

"You used the detonator. You have already devastated our international relations."

"*Which can be reversed—by forging ahead into the occult.*"

"......"

"Why do you think I decided to tell you all this?"

Aurey had asked Roselyne a question. But before Roselyne could answer, Aurey continued.

"*First, my reasons for hiding my intentions will be gone very soon. In just a few hours, the United States of America will be reformed. Thanks to the international standard, both its citizens and people all around the world will find out about it. So I never had a reason to hide it.*"

And she went on.

"*Second, your death is already written in stone. You may take that as a threatening letter from someone intending to commit a crime.*"

"Ugh..."

"*If you've no candidates for a response to give me, then this conversation is over. I'll tell Trident to make it painless. And give whoever shoots you a bonus.*"

Then Aurey hung up.

Roselyne was quiet for a few moments. However...

"...Aurey Blueshake."

Seeing how Roselyne hung her head and muttered, her subordinate—still using the proceedings recording camera to film this—thought she was trembling in fear.

But he was wrong.

She was shaking, yes. But that was definitely a grin on her face.

"*If* you're *the mastermind, then I still have a way out of this!*"

"What do you...?"

"Everything Aurey—no, the Blueshake family—needs rests on Kauai," said Roselyne quickly, pulling a map out of the government vehicle before unrolling it on the hood. "Lindy Blueshake. Female, eight years old. The media queen cares a lot about bloodlines, and her network is passed down via legitimate heirs like a big zaibatsu. The Blueshakes have only one possible candidate for succession—this girl, Aurey's daughter. She's irreplaceable to them. Aurey has always struggled to have children, too. If we kidnap her, we'll have Aurey's very core in our grasp!"

"Wait, but... That can't be right! Why would she cause war to break out so close to where her daughter lives?!"

"Because she doesn't know," said Roselyne, smiling. "The Blueshake parents divorced because of domestic abuse, but it wasn't the husband throwing punches in this case—it was Aurey. She twisted the truth with her thorough information control and an expensive team of lawyers, though. While she ultimately won custody of Lindy, it was determined that any further investigation would be too dangerous. The government made sure the girl was taken into emergency custody. Naturally, though, Aurey used her control over the media to make sure the masses never found out about that."

"Emergency custody. Hang on… That's basically a witness protection program, so… Wait!"

"Exactly. They gave her a new name and identity, then sent her to live a second life without anyone else knowing. Aurey never found out exactly where she was. The F.C.E. uses a huge search provider—and I have a feeling the reason she even created it in the first place was to find her daughter."

Had the media queen done this to shower the girl in motherly love? Or to maintain her network, which she'd inherited from her grandfather? It seemed pretty clear which it was.

Even Aurey, who was always getting looks at the executive office and military-related facilities, had never been able to find out quite where Lindy Blueshake now lived.

"Lindy grew to resent the media because of her mother, so she might be living an off-grid lifestyle here in Hawaii."

Which was Roselyne's chance at victory.

Her *last* chance—in the tiny gap Aurey's network hadn't quite filled yet.

Roselyne instructed her subordinate to gather up all the Secret Service members and Marines who were still useful, then smiled a thin, thin smile.

One that almost…

…looked like a villain's.

"…You've strayed from the straight and narrow. Now you'll learn only devilish obstacles await you there."

* * *

[Nov. 10 / Source: Lanai, a portable game device camera left on the counter at Star Lounge Shot Bar]

"Hold on, hold on, hold on, damn it! Don't get desperate, Roselyne! You're going crazy!" the president screamed as he stared at the imperial package's screen, then pounded his palm on its hard exterior.

Kamijou and Mikoto were surprised.

"Wh-what?"

"Did your computer break?"

The president responded to their doubtful expressions with a click of his tongue. "My aide is off doing stuff without permission in an attempt to do something about all this. Aurey Blueshake's daughter is being sheltered somewhere on this island. Roselyne is scraping together every soldier she can to go kidnap her and negotiate."

As he explained the particular circumstances of Lindy and the Marine Corps in detail, Kamijou and Mikoto's faces went white.

"You've gotta be kidding...," said Kamijou. "This Lindy kid didn't do anything, right? Will the soldiers actually do this? It might be an emergency, but it's still definitely a crime!"

"The law isn't exactly functional right now," answered the president. "And the situation has the Marines seething. The enemy moved too fast, and now the Marines feel like the greatest military force on the planet is losing. They can't contain the fires of battle, and nobody can deny the possibility that things might bleed over into residential areas. If that happens, a whole lot of people could get hurt. They want to stop that from happening at all costs—*they're using righteousness to justify themselves*, burning away any guilt they felt at kidnapping the mastermind's daughter."

Depending on how you looked at things, actions driven by righteousness could have a dark side. Many people who claimed to act in the name of justice eventually lost sight of that fact.

"...How many people have answered her call exactly?" asked Mikoto.

"About two hundred. Probably the ones Roselyne personally

believes are trustworthy. It may be a small force, given Hawaii has three or four whole divisions, but we should consider them to have completely abandoned their units' commands. Frankly, *we have no idea* what *they'll do for the sake of justice*."

A military force clearly operating outside the rules.

Though their goal of taking a hostage to get the situation under control seemed to have a just cause, nobody could deny the possibility it had been inspired by hatred of the media queen Aurey Blueshake herself. That meant her daughter's safety was far from guaranteed. Lindy could be hurt during the hostage "negotiations." And even before that happened, their loathing could drive them to do something they could never take back.

Would the president's fiery aide really be able to unite her soldiers under one banner?

A reviled enemy—and her child.

Could Roselyne's soldiers say for certain there would be no violence as soon as they saw the girl?

After thinking for a few moments, Kamijou eventually got up off the bar floor.

"...Lindy Blueshake is on Kauai, right? Can you get a picture of her on that computer?"

"What's your plan?" asked the president.

"We save her," he said without any hesitation. "We get to Kauai before the Marines and escort the girl to safety. It doesn't matter where—any place works, so long as the soldiers can't find her. We need to hide her from them."

"H-hey, wait just a second!" interrupted Mikoto. "But that Lindy kid is the mastermind's daughter, right? If we fight to rescue her, wouldn't we be siding with the people trying to take over Hawaii?!"

"So what?" replied Kamijou bitterly. "Yeah, Aurey Blueshake might be the one behind all this. We'll need to settle the score with her in the end…but what the hell did that girl do?! They want to use her as a tool just because she's connected to the mastermind—is that really worth putting her life at risk over? That's wrong, isn't it?!"

His voice had all his sincerity behind it. He wasn't just letting the situation make choices for him. He was setting his own course in his own way.

"Lindy's life was already torn apart by domestic violence. But now she's finally here, living in peace and quiet, right? She's only eight, but she had to give up her name and home. She's lost so much to get this peace we take for granted. And these people want to grab her and put a gun or knife to her head in front of Aurey? Could you just let that happen? Well, I couldn't! We all want to protect the Hawaiian Islands from Gremlin, right? Well, that girl lives here. We should be protecting her, too!"

"…You're not wrong." The president sighed quietly. "The government took custody of Lindy under the emergency protection plan, so it's the government's job to protect her from Aurey. Which means I have no choice but to fight, too."

Making up one's mind was always easy.

But real, lethal bullets awaited them now—from both the Salonya-Aurey Gremlin team trying to take over the islands and from the Marine Corps force led by the president's aide trying to capture Lindy. They would need to oppose both factions at once.

On top of that, the true enemy had access to a whole lot of regular firearms to counter Kamijou's right hand, and the president was their prime target.

Normally, the two of them wouldn't have been able to even think about helping someone else like this. They should have been putting their own lives first instead of someone else's, like Lindy's.

Nevertheless…

"What about you, Misaka?" asked Kamijou. "This is our choice. We won't force you. You can hide here for your own safety if you need."

What's giving them so much determination? thought Mikoto right before realizing what it was.

Kamijou had done this very same thing when he'd rescued her, too.

Mikoto had also been saved just like this, once upon a time.

He hadn't done that so he could stand on the side of justice.

He hadn't done that while considering how it would benefit him.

He'd simply wanted to save others, so he did.

Those with no need for guilt had no need for excuses, either.

This answer was the only thing left after cutting out all the excess. And it gave them enough strength to destroy the tangled web of righteous justice that had accumulated in this whole thing.

"...Fine. I get it," said Mikoto. "To be honest, it makes me pretty mad, thinking about this Lindy girl having a gun put to her head and getting all her mental wounds reopened."

She could worry over it all she wanted, but when she put it into words, it was all so simple.

And Kamijou must have made these same simple decisions so, so many times.

"It's not her job to risk her life to take back Hawaii," she finished. "It's ours, right?"

[Nov. 10 / Source: Kahoolawe coast, UUV Carnival Shark 443]

The huge military-grade hovercraft sped through the waters near the Hawaiian Islands where the anti-ship missile network was set up. The thing was basically just a boat made of special rubber, but it was really, really big. It was as large as one of the twenty-five-meter pools in schools, probably to get military vehicles onto dry land.

With its two large propellers for propulsion, the hovercraft shot across the sea at a speed of over fifty kph. Everyone on board was wearing silver military uniforms, but they answered to neither Salonya nor Aurey.

Because it was actually Hamazura's group.

Hamazura had been experiencing a lot of things for the first time today, and this was another one: riding a hovercraft. But even though the abrupt feeling of acceleration was freaking him out, the lack of obstacles nearby and the fact that the boat was still floating wrapped him up in a strange sense of relief that had absolutely no basis in reality... That reality included the reefs and other things in the ocean, so while the sea feigned tranquility, it wasn't without its dangers. If the hovercraft bumped into any sharp boulders sticking out of the water, even its reinforced rubber hull could be torn to shreds. But sometimes, ignorance was the driving force behind reckless progress.

Hamazura had his cell phone at his ear as he groped around, trying to steer the ship.

"…Huh. So the targets they want most are putting themselves in the line of fire to rescue the mastermind's daughter?" he said, exasperated at the absurdity but smiling a little anyway.

To be frank, the whole thing about the media queen and Gremlin joining forces to take control of America was too big for him to really wrap his head around.

Finally, something he could genuinely put his life on the line for had landed in their laps.

"You'll need passage to Kauai, right?" he said. "Give us a few minutes. You're on Lanai? We'll meet up there."

In contrast to Hamazura and the others, Misaka Worst and Umidori Kuroyoru were being very indiscreet, like they usually were.

Or rather, Misaka Worst was having the time of her life.

"Little Kuro, Misaka is bored, so strike a pose—whatever pose you think is sexiest in the whole wide world."

"You—you're not taking control of me for a reason like *that* are—*gya-gya-gya-gya-gya!*"

"Hey, bad girl with the bad eyes! Don't make Kuroyoru cry again!"

"Ugh, that's the last bit I'd ever want to be part of… Graaaaahhhh!"

With control of her arms stolen, Kuroyoru lost her balance and tumbled over the deck with motions that were (forced to be) completely impractical.

And Misaka Worst and Shiage Hamazura watched her fondly.

"…Wow, Misaka's never heard someone go 'oof' like a cartoon character in real life before. Twenty-five points."

"She talks about the darkness a lot, but she's surprisingly pure, isn't she? Thirty points."

Kuroyoru ground her teeth. "How… How dare you do this to

me...!" she growled. Unfortunately, her matchup against Misaka Worst was just that bad.

The electric esper in question cast a casual glance over to Hamazura. "Think we've got 'em fooled?"

"No way in hell," spat Kuroyoru, still red in the face. She, too, looked out over the water, glaring straight at the camera's lens. "They're making us swim on purpose to guide us to the weak point."

[Nov. 10 / Source: Oahu, an air traffic control assistance camera at Marine Corps Pearl Harbor Base 3]

While most of the base had been destroyed and its functionality was in ruins, the soldiers stationed there had still completed their evacuation.

At the same time, Salonya and Aurey's PMC, Trident, must have decided any further attacks wouldn't be worth doing. They quickly turned their attention to other bases.

"...Well, shit. The aide's gone," muttered Accelerator.

"Went to personally abduct an eight-year-old girl, eh?" replied Birdway offhandedly. "These people aren't even worth saving."

The two of them had joined back up now that the battle was over. After their phone call with Kamijou and the others, they now knew the gist of what was happening.

Birdway rested her staff on her shoulder and smiled thinly. "But this is our chance."

"......"

"Don't glare at me. God, you get so much energy whenever a little girl's involved." She shrugged. "Aurey Blueshake is probably listening in on this conversation. So she'll *have* to act before our group or the Marines get to Lindy."

"Doubt we'll be able to bait the media queen herself out, though. Is the mastermind even in Hawaii to begin with?" asked Accelerator.

"If she's within our reach, then she's a huge idiot," replied Birdway before giving the staff on her shoulder a twirl. "No, she'll send Salonya, a core member, to lead a team to retrieve Lindy. They'd never focus all their forces on this. The Hawaiian Islands are home to the most concentrated military force in the Pacific, so that's where they have to hit. Salonya, though—she's leading a separate unit, and she won't necessarily act according to Aurey's wishes. And neither will Gremlin as a whole."

"...I get it."

"After all, according to Touma Kamijou's report, Salonya herself was caught in a very dangerous diversionary operation when they brought in the detonator. She won't be that trustful of Aurey—she'll want a trump card of her own to win against her at the negotiating table."

"Gremlin's plan to take over the United States will only work with both Aurey's financial power and Salonya's magical support."

"To them, the Hawaiian Islands are nothing more than prep work for a greater war—one where they take control of the U.S., create a system they can manipulate however they wish, and keep it going indefinitely. So those two will be working together for a long time. Both women would want to snag the initiative while they have the chance, even if it means braving risk," said Birdway.

"But all *we* have to do is kill one of them. Salonya and Aurey wouldn't be working together if one or the other could do it alone. If we can take out Salonya when she waltzes in..."

"...then their plans for all the U.S.—to say nothing of Hawaii—will be ruined, and we'll come out on top. You know what we have to do, right?"

"...Hmph. I'm not even in Academy City anymore, and I'm still doing the same shitty cleanup work," muttered Accelerator.

"Just be honest and call it what it is, hero: rescuing a civilian."

CHAPTER 5
What Should Your Strength Be Used For?
The_Old_Glory.

[Nov. 10 / Source: Kauai, a tide observation camera]

Touma Kamijou, Accelerator, Shiage Hamazura, Mikoto Misaka, Misaka Worst, Umidori Kuroyoru, Leivinia Birdway, and Roberto Catze. Using the hovercraft Hamazura brought them, they all landed on the island of Kauai.

"Looks like the Marines haven't gotten here yet."

"Unlike us, there's no reason they should be made to swim by Aurey's forces. They're probably trying to figure out what the hell to do about all the anti-ship missiles positioned across the islands."

"But Salonya's side is on the move already, right? They would have assigned a PMC unit to Kauai when they took it over. One radio is all it would take to make them do something."

"Neither Trident nor the woman manipulating them—Salonya—know exactly where Aurey's daughter is. They'd probably find her if they scoured the islands, but they'll also want to find hints if they can. Now that they know we're here, they're probably panicking and belting out orders, right?"

"Then the situation is fifty-fifty." Mikoto put a hand to her cheek. "We want to secure Lindy quickly before the Marines get here and complicate matters. We naturally know where she is, though, right? Where is she...?"

Birdway pressed her index finger to her lips. "Like I said before, neither faction knows where she is yet. Given how seriously they're trying to stamp out the Marines right now, they must be planning to observe our actions to find her... Of course, they probably *could* find her if they scoured the island with how many people they have.

"Which means," she finished, "what we're about to do *will expose Lindy's location*."

"......"

"If you still want to do this, then brace yourselves. To save her, we have to put her in danger. We accept the cruelty inherent in the proposition and act in spite of it. Understood?"

Birdway looked not only at Mikoto but at everyone else as well.

Seeing that nobody had any objections, she turned her gaze to the president.

Roberto was still holding the imperial package and—knowing his enemy could hear him—responded, "Lindy Blueshake is at Sunny Watcher 44-19. I've pulled the trigger. Time to start blasting these occult PMC goons."

The heroes made their move.

The person they needed to rescue: Lindy Blueshake. The person they needed to draw out: Salonya A. Irivika.

The evil plan: to make the United States into a theocracy, starting with the Hawaiian Islands before encompassing the rest of the USA and then the entire science side.

This battle would determine the fate of the nation.

[????? / Source: location unknown, camera identification number unknown, a recording provided with external video and sound]

* * *

Aurey Blueshake wore a gaudy suit, one so perfectly tailored to her body that no store could ever sell it, despite it being so expensive she could probably buy a midsize passenger jet with that money. The ten-gallon hat on her head didn't go with the outfit at all, and she completed the look with a pair of boots with spurs on the heels for horseback riding. She'd chosen her clothes not out of personal preference or practicality but to convey a specific image to the masses. No matter what anyone said, the United States still loved that good old pioneer spirit. It was a line of defense for Aurey, who was frequently criticized for being *too* cutting-edge, usually when it came to her internet business.

She was in a room that at least resembled a posh hotel suite. But it was only that the furnishings were arranged that way; perhaps it wasn't actually a suite at all. It could have been a dark basement, a military facility, a pleasure liner, or a jumbo jet. There was so little information to work with that it allowed for endless speculation.

As he poured her a glass of whiskey, her young male secretary asked, "Do you necessarily need to film yourself as well, ma'am?"

"I need to keep an objective view of the situation. When I put myself in the finder, it reminds me that I'm just another piece on the chessboard." Aurey took the glass offered to her. "You tend to forget when you're in a safe area. Pieces start thinking of themselves as players… I must not be conceited. The game board of planet Earth is always contiguous; if someone wants to chase you down, they'll reach you one day. Safety has a much lower fuel economy than I'd imagined."

The unhurried way she made her remarks was a declaration that, in contrast with her words, she was assured of her own safety and victory. Anyone in true danger would have forced themselves to be optimistic, twisting the truth until it gave them peace of mind.

The secretary was well aware of this, but he didn't point it out. "We managed to make the F.C.E. and Trident's electronic camouflage work together, too."

"It's not that effective—that's why people hate it."

"What will we do about Lindy, ma'am?"

"We bring her back." That was the only time Aurey's voice hardened. "The Blueshakes' media network began way back during the gold rush. But it only went public in my grandfather's generation. Any amount of expansion will be pointless if there isn't a Blueshake to carry on the family line."

"I doubt Salonya A. Irivika or Trident will do exactly as we requested."

"They'll come around and overextend themselves in pursuit of greater reward—because they're confident. Confident that they've taken over the Hawaiian Islands as planned. They'll start thinking about more complex, troubling matters, like taking detours to grasp as many extra opportunities as they can."

"What will we do about them, then?"

"We will make it so they *can't* think about complex, troubling matters. We will drive them into a corner, rob them of their confidence, and force them to only think of simple things. What's the basic tenet of training soldiers again? Discipline them until they are no longer able to think?" murmured Aurey, her slender fingers tapping on her laptop keyboard. "So what we need to do is have presidential aide Roselyne's volunteer Marines drive Salonya and Trident into a corner."

"Would they willingly act if we gave them information?"

"We won't just outright command them to. We'll leave a hint. Make them think they thought of it on their own, and they'll fall over themselves trying to obey."

[Nov. 10 / Source: Kauai, an onboard camera in the mountainous district of Anahola]

Shiage Hamazura, Leivinia Birdway, and Roberto Catze were heading through the eastern mountains on Kauai in an off-road car. A stolen one, of course.

Apparently, Lindy Blueshake was located on Nā Pali Coast in Kauai's northwest. Kamijou and the others, however, had landed at the southeast. Because the center of the island was so mountainous, getting to the girl would require them to do a lap around the island. Naturally, Trident had set up anti-ship missiles along the coastlines.

Because of the obstructive geography, they'd decided to split into several groups, each with different goals, and take different routes to the Nā Pali Coast. Hamazura's was heading counterclockwise around the island's perimeter.

The president was looking out the window…at the shoreline stretching beyond the mountain range and the mercenaries constructing various facilities there.

"…We've been ignored to an extent since they know we're searching for Lindy, but if they spot us on-site, guns will start blazing."

"There might be a silver lining here—that the aide and her Marines are late to the party," said Birdway from the back seat.

Hamazura, his hands on the steering wheel, frowned. "Shouldn't it be the other way around? They're definitely gonna end up fighting Gremlin and Trident for us, right? If her Marines charge onto Kauai and throw everything into chaos, they could break free of their big boss's control. Then they'd lose the power compelling them to overlook us. It'll turn into an unpredictable brawl."

"Shit," said Roberto. His eyes were still out the window. "Roselyne's gotten started. Hey, kid! Stop the car right now! We'll skid out!"

"Eh?" Hamazura followed the president's gaze, his own face dubious…and then panicked and slammed the brakes.

Krrrrr-krrrrr-krrrrr! The tires scraped against the asphalt, but a moment later, the sound was drowned out by an explosion.

The explosion of dozens of air-to-surface missiles launched from beyond the horizon.

They must have come from Oahu—twenty of the latest stealth fighters zipped across the ocean, flying only a few dozen centimeters above the surface of the water at speeds of over four hundred kph. The Kilauea eruption should have made aircraft impossible to use, but by skimming at a super-low altitude, these planes had escaped that restriction.

And the reason they were *skimming*, not flying, was evident.

They had floats in the shape of skis welded to their undersides where their wheels should have been. In exchange for sacrificing air resistance and stealth, the fighters gained the ability to grab hold of the water. They weren't just flying close to the surface—they were gently pushing their floats into it as they went along.

Trident had shored up its defenses with anti-ship missiles, but even they seemed unable to handle invaders of this level of speed. The swarm of jets wove between several anti-ship missiles, then launched their own missiles of death all across the shoreline.

A wall of orange rose out of the white beach—one that spanned twelve kilometers.

A wall born of explosions and shock waves.

Despite being more than five kilometers away, even the off-road car Hamazura had hit the brakes on was skidding sideways.

Roberto grunted in the passenger seat, the seat belt constricting his ribs and lungs. "Damn it, Roselyne...! Do you not know I'm here, too?! Or are you perfectly aware? Which is it?!"

"It's not over yet. It's clear as day that they'll do more now that the antimissile network is gone!"

Birdway was right on the mark.

Their preemptive bombing run complete, the swarm of stealth fighters turned away from the shoreline to go around the island. In their wake, a crowd of landing ships barreled toward the shore. These were ships, yes, but equipped with hydrofoils and capable of pushing out speeds of one hundred–plus kph. Like whales washing ashore, the steel vessels all slid up onto the ground.

Their rear doors opened up, releasing a flood of soldiers.

The troops were equipped differently than Trident's. These ones were all wearing the same thing—the U.S.'s official military uniform. The group of over one hundred and fifty charged onto Kauai.

"This is what we've been waiting for," muttered Hamazura,

turning the engine key to get the car running again. "An uncontrollable battlefield. A three-way deathmatch over Lindy Blueshake."

[Nov. 10 / Source: Kauai, a backup camera on an abandoned sedan at a Blue Energy gas station]

He hadn't escaped in time.

Weck Lunasand was hiding in an empty gas station, squatting near the vending machines near the corner of the shop. He exhaled heavily.

Several sets of footsteps passed right behind the vending machines—not seventy centimeters from where he was. The crunch of feet on the white sand. If they found him, he would be out of luck. He wasn't holding a hand to his chest, but that thought still made him hear his heart in his ears.

The employee ID hanging around his neck showed that he was a children's surf instructor.

Clearly, he'd gone overboard with his work ethic this time, though. He'd messed up for life.

Right after the commotion started, Weck had put as many students in his SUV as he could, heading to an abandoned building in Chinatown. The place had nothing but dust and cockroaches, but he knew it was a civilian nuclear shelter. It was only twelve square meters at most, but it was enough to hide out in. Nobody would bother forcing their way into a desolate ruin—it wasn't some sparkling resort hotel filled with gold decorations. At that point, all they had to do was shut the thick doors and wait for the whole thing to blow over.

But that was when one of his students had said something.

One of the students was missing.

"...I should have just abandoned him. Damn it. This is above my pay grade. I only get paid two thousand a month."

Despite bursting out of safety, he'd never actually found the child.

Shining soldiers who looked like CDs were everywhere, equipped with assault rifles that resembled hacksaws, like you'd see in movies. They were making it very difficult for Weck to get anywhere. They didn't look like the U.S. soldiers at the bar or public training. *But if those weren't U.S. soldiers, then what the hell were they?* In any case, he knew things would take a turn for the worse if they found him. They hadn't yet, but it was only a matter of time. They'd blocked off all his escape routes.

"……"

He recalled the heavy sensation in his right hand.

It was a 38mm revolver that had been in the glove compartment of a sedan that someone escaping had left behind at a gas station. He doubted it would change his situation, though. If anyone heard a gunshot, the entire squad would be on him like hunting dogs who had just found out exactly where the meat was. He doubted he'd even be able to hit his first shot anyway, and this was a gas station. If the gasoline evaporated and floated around, it could cause an enormous explosion as soon as he discharged the gun.

It was just for self-defense.

Something to prevent him from panicking and doing something really, really stupid.

"…First, I've gotta get out of here alive. Emergency evacuation. That's right—there's gasoline here. If I put some in a container and blow that up, it'll distract everyone. It's okay to break the law if the alternative's dying, right…?"

He was saying it out loud to himself, perhaps trying to warm himself up to the idea. Even here, Weck was as soft at heart as ever.

And then came another trial for the softhearted man.

A little boy screamed.

Weck scowled, rested his back against the vending machine, and unconsciously covered his face.

"Shit! Is that Steve…?!"

It was the student who'd gotten separated from the others. Weck dropped to his hands and knees on the concrete—which reeked of oil—then peered out from the shadow of the vending machines to see a dozen or so men and women being made to walk along the white beach. Four or five silver-clad soldiers were guiding them along with their rifles.

Among them was a ten-year-old boy.

The difficulty of his task had just skyrocketed.

The same choice flashed through his mind as before—should he leave them, or do something about it?

"But what could I even do…?"

His breathing quickened. A sickening feeling built in the pit of his stomach. But not just because of the threat to his life. It was also from his clear attempt to abandon someone else to their fate.

"I've done enough. More than enough. Rescuing seven people while on the clock at my $2K-a-month job would win me an award, sure. But why be greedy? Come on," he murmured to himself before realizing he was speaking out loud and catching his breath.

A ritual to convince himself of a viewpoint he didn't actually have.

And that was enough for him to realize he'd *never* be satisfied with that.

"…You'll die an early death…"

After muttering that final thing *that wasn't convincing him*, Weck looked around. This was a gas station—with a crap ton of gasoline. He could put it into several containers. Scatter it along the beach so the evaporated gas would be carried on the wind. Depending on how he did it, he might even be able to get the silver soldiers at his mercy, if only for a short time.

But just as he was trying to put together a concrete plan in his head, he heard a small, metallic *ga-chak*.

One of the silver soldiers had approached without him realizing it, and their gun was now pressed against the back of his head.

He'd messed up, leaning out like that.

And to make matters worse, he was carrying a gun for self-defense.

"Goddamn it. I'm too young to die…!" he shouted.

But the soldier didn't care whether he'd convinced himself of it or not.

Weck's eyes shut tight—when it happened.

Ga-boom!
The man holding the assault rifle to his head suddenly flew several meters to the side.

At first, he thought a dump truck had hit the guy.

Because it certainly didn't seem possible to do that with a reckless kick with such slender legs. Even turning around and seeing it for himself, he couldn't believe it.

After the silver soldier crashed into a vending machine, destroying it, everyone else's attention immediately shifted over to the person responsible. But he didn't seem to care.

White hair. Red eyes.

A shadow that looked more like a wild animal than a human being.

"…What a fucking pain."

There were two girls with him. Both had the same face, but their eyes and expressions couldn't have been more different. The one who looked like she was in middle school or so still looked normal, but the older one had a face fit for a mug shot.

"We should handle this first," said the middle school–aged girl to the white shadow. "If I can hack into Trident's C&C cloud, I can tear down the anti-ship missiles' security network. If we do that, Hawaii will be open to naval support from elsewhere. There are *so* many things I want to say to your face, but this isn't the time to obsess."

"I may be trying to make things right for the clones, but *you* don't get any apologies, Original. You didn't conveniently forget you were on the wrong side of those experiments, too, did you?"

"Sure, I'll atone for it. Naturally. But it makes me a tiny bit *pissed off* that you're making me out to be the big baddie there."

With the tension growing by the second, the two of them slowly headed toward the beach. The reason went without saying. They were going to rescue the tourists who'd been taken hostage by the rifle-toting soldiers.

As Weck looked on in confusion, the girl with the evil eyes shut

one and said, "Look, they're just tsunderes. What they meant to say is that everything'll be fine now."

With an explosion, the two monsters took control of the injustice on the battlefield.

Number One and Number Three.

The Level Fives who had fought in World War III *separately* and still survived began to whip up a tempest of pure destruction.

[Nov. 10 / Source: Kauai waters, a soldier's camera-equipped helmet connected to the C&C cloud]

Salonya A. Irivika was on a landing hovercraft. The steepest spots on Nā Pali Coast, where Lindy was speculated to be, were very difficult to cross in a regular car. It was faster to take the aquatic approach.

Trident had been instructed by their client to assemble a team to search for Lindy, but Salonya's participation was an irregular action in opposition to that request.

The Trident member helming the hovercraft addressed her. "We'll focus on slowing down the other factions. Can we leave capturing the target up to you?"

"Yes, probably best that way. You little guys are too good at killing. You might spill her blood when you only mean to threaten her."

"…The client will do the killing. I have no clue who will be hired."

"Aurey Blueshake? I couldn't care less about her," said Salonya with an incredible air of nonchalance, feeling the sea breeze. But she didn't stop there. "And I couldn't care less about Gremlin, either. Or Trident, of course. This whole idea of making the U.S. into a theocracy and ruining the balance of the sorcery side and science side? I literally could not care less about any of it."

"Y-you know the F.C.E. is watching this…"

"Yeah, probably! I bet they are! But you're no different, are you? Trident has its own goal here, and you have yours. No matter what you focus on or how, what's important is whether you as an individual can profit in the end," said Salonya.

She took a plastic pill case from her pocket. Inside its several partitions were seeds from trees.

"The country I used to live in is a wreck now. All because of World War III."

"……"

"And a bunch of countries and territories split up the profits from that war—the main ones being Academy City and the USA. And now they're trying to change my home country however they like by controlling the flow of money while insisting they're just paying reparations for war damages."

"I, um, heard they're mainly working on infrastructure…"

"Well, winter's coming. They requisitioned our little natural gas pipelines under the guise of repairing them, but *our* businesses are having trouble reopening because of their clearly unnecessary construction. They *know* heaters are a lifeline for us and now they're trying to make us swear loyalty. It's unforgivable."

Salonya smiled thinly.

There were no thorns in her timbre—it was even sweet, as though she were changing it intentionally because she was speaking to a man. Yet that didn't stop the veteran member of Trident from quietly trembling.

"So let's have it all put back to normal, shall we?"

Placing her palm over the pill case containing the tree seeds, Salonya rolled them around, taking in their scents and biting down onto them with her back teeth.

Then her eyes lit up as though she'd just remembered something, and she continued talking.

"Of *course*, widdle Academy City and the widdle United States would give us money. Of *course* that's really, truly for little Russia's benefit. If they're not going to improve our infrastructure, then I'll just do it myself. We made so much in that war, after all. They used us as a springboard, so a little payment from them seems like a fair deal, right?"

Normally, Trident considered its client's position. The man probably should have stopped Salonya by force.

But he couldn't.

He was afraid of Salonya and the strange magic she so freely wielded. Even the mercenaries, accustomed to dealing with death, were petrified.

"Isn't that right, widdle Aurey Blueshake? You know, you're on the list of people who made some awfully big money from the war."

Salonya had never planned to obey Aurey.

All sorcerers put the individual above the group. It was in their nature. And Salonya's nature was readily apparent.

As she made her way toward Lindy Blueshake, her ferocious intentions were clear on her face.

[Nov. 10 / Source: Kauai, a camera attached to UAV Ginyanma 300 at Nā Pali Coast]

The Nā Pali Coast was registered as a state park, but the dangerous spot at its deepest reaches was a kilometers-long row of sheer cliffs like saw teeth, too difficult for any normal vehicle to enter. In the center of the danger zone sat a log cabin.

Standing at over two meters tall, a man named Harzack Lauras was busy maintaining the stairway-like gardens near the cabin. The gardens were originally supposed to be for growing food, but then the cabin's original owner had started planting decorative flowers and the like, so now it was completely disorganized. Harzack wasn't growing plants for food, either. Despite his large frame, he moved delicately as he took small buds from a planter and transferred them to the vegetable garden.

As he was doing that, the cabin door opened. Harzack straightened up, responding without turning to the girl who had turned the knob with both hands.

"If you aren't swimming, you don't need to wear a swimsuit."

"It's too hot. I can't run the air conditioner all day because we only have a power generator and solar panels. It's going to be another tropical night anyway, so we have to conserve batteries. Also, I'm going to catch some fish again come evening."

They had this conversation every time. Harzack never really tried to cure the girl of this habit. He quickly changed the subject. "There's a textbook in the mail for you."

"You brought it all the way here anyway, Mr. Harzack. You don't need to put it in the mail."

"This house belongs to you, Lindy. I'm only here to help out. You should get the textbook and check to make sure nothing's missing. I wouldn't be able to bear going back and forth on that road over and over."

"…I don't like this textbook."

"Not many people would say they like studying."

"I like listening to your stories better, Mr. Harzack."

"Unfortunately, I can't help you much there," he replied, redoing the soil next to the small buds he'd just put in. "Either you learn like a citizen of the United States or you learn like a native Hawaiian. Both ways of learning are useful, but I can't fill either set of shoes for you. My name should have clued you in on that. My parents didn't make much of an effort to be naturalized, so I don't know the native language or culture very well. But I also can't get used to modern life in the United States."

"Mgh." The girl he'd called Lindy puffed out her cheeks. "But your stories are still more fun."

After saying that, the girl grabbed the shrink-wrapped textbook from the mailbox and went back into the cabin. *She's so purehearted*, thought Harzack. *She can't let a half-wit like me drag her down.*

He'd heard that the true king of Hawaii still breathed, but he'd never even caught a glimpse of him. He didn't know if the man was in an unexplored area or blending in with the people in town, either. Once, he'd wanted to find the king and become a member of his kingdom, but he'd lost his backbone by now. He'd run out of energy halfway up the mountain, and now he dreaded the climb back down.

Harzack got up once he was done tending to the vegetable garden. He wiped the sweat off his face with his arm, then cast his eyes up to the blue skies, which were covered in a light layer of volcanic ash.

It was rare for ash to get all the way to Kauai. If this went on for too long, he might need to cover the vegetable garden in vinyl.

And then he spotted something odd.

It looked like a dragonfly but much larger—twenty or thirty centimeters long.

But it was different.

You wouldn't call a vehicle with a polycarbonate body, ABS resin wings, a motor to move around, a transceiver, and a camera lens a dragonfly.

"...A lens... A camera...," murmured Harzack.

Then he remembered. Remembered the reason why Lindy Blueshake was living way out here. That which was so thoroughly despised. The reason the government worker had invited the girl to this unexplored land absent of any and all media.

"Not good... Lindy! Lin—"

Harzack turned around on reflex and tried to shout for her, only to find that someone had reached around him from behind and clamped his mouth shut.

From where? How? When did they get close?

Unable to make sense of things, Harzack was thrown to the ground by the vegetable garden, as if by some sleight of hand. The reflected light obscured his attacker's face, but he could make out the silhouette of a person holding a gun in their hand.

He was going to be shot.

Pain flooded him—it was like his heart was being constricted by a kite string—and he waited and waited, but the gunshot never came.

He couldn't comprehend what was happening.

Gradually, though, he caught on to three things. First, the attacker straddling him was trembling. Second, what seemed to be a transparent spear was pressed up against the attacker's neck. Third, the owner of the spear had come up behind his assailant without a sound.

There were two Asians behind the attacker, one boy and one girl.

The boy had strikingly spiky hair, and the girl—even younger than him—had a disobedient look in her eyes that would put even Lindy's to shame.

They both spoke in Japanese.

"...Must be Trident." Then without waiting for a response, "A nitrogen spear or a regular fist. One hit with either. Your choice."

For just a moment, the assailant glanced at the gun he was pressing to Harzack, then whipped it around behind him.

But before he could actually counterattack, the girl lopped off the tip of his gun and the front of his helmet with her lance, sending him flying, and the boy slammed his fist right into his face.

As the attacker in the silver uniform collapsed backward, the boy said, once again in Japanese, "Hope you're grateful. I am sort of the guy who saved your life."

"I did most of the work, though. Including knocking those other guys out."

"You get way too into this stuff, Kuroyoru. You'd have cut off their heads if I hadn't stopped you."

"Where are the others? Are we the first to arrive?"

Harzack didn't understand them, but he looked where the boy was pointing and saw four more silver uniforms lying on the ground that way.

As he lay there petrified, the boy glanced at the ocean past the cliffs and said something. It was in Japanese, so Harzack couldn't make it out, but then something strange happened.

The evil-looking girl's right hand.

It was like her five fingers were typing on a keyboard but were going as fast as a sewing machine. They made a series of taps against the fence of the vegetable garden, and the way the sounds combined and melded into one another created words—English words, pronounced correctly, as if through a speech-to-text program.

"The team Aurey Blueshake hired is trying to take Lindy back. Since you're her guardian, you must know why. Don't give her to Aurey. Take her and run away as fast as you can!"

"Wha...? What...?"

Harzack was utterly confused, but the girl didn't look like she would answer any questions.

"Just go! They're coming up from the ocean! There's no time!"

His eyes automatically darted in that direction, where he saw a large hovercraft pull onto the shore at the foot of the sawtooth precipice.

But he didn't have time to watch the show.

Just then, several silver-uniformed people who had gotten to the top of the cliff pointed bullpup assault rifles at them. Driven back by their shrill gunshots, the boy and girl dropped themselves to the ground. Harzack frantically dove toward the log cabin.

"What's the plan now?" asked the girl.

"We get Lindy and her guardian out of here, at least. We have to fight until we take care of Salonya anyway."

"Pretty confident despite all the assault rifles, Japanese."

"...To be honest, I'd be shaking in my boots if they had regular guns. But those things are so crazy-looking that they barely feel real."

The two of them heard the sounds of Harzack and Lindy escaping out the back of the cabin. Once they were sure the pair was gone, Kuroyoru and Kamijou went back there themselves, trying to use its outer walls as cover.

But suddenly, they smelled flowers.

And then it happened.

Clunk!

The boy's left arm abruptly *dropped*.

Straight down. Dangling. The joint was still connected, but the arm was completely limp; from the way it was dangling, it had indeed "dropped." Every part of it was immobilized, finger and shoulder included. He felt no pain, or heat, or cold in his arm—it was absent of all sensation. Even the left side of his face had gone numb; he couldn't imagine the expression he was making right now.

"Ugh!"

He quickly grabbed his left arm with his right hand, but nothing happened. Evidently, this wouldn't be a quick fix for Imagine Breaker.

"My left arm…"

"What happened? I didn't detect any chemical weapons."

Likely imagining it from the way the skin on his face quivered, the girl *moved her hand like she was holding onto something*. But the boy vaguely understood that it wasn't a chemical weapon that had done this to him.

It was sorcery.

A spell from someone who knew exactly how to make him, specifically, suffer the most.

Cradling his unnaturally behaving left arm, the boy took a look around the cabin's outer wall toward the precipice, then spotted a familiar face among the silver uniforms.

"Salonya A. Irivika!"

[*Nov. 10 / Source: Kauai, a camera attached to UAV Ginyanma 210 in the restricted northern area of Nā Pali Coast*]

The deepest area of Nā Pali Coast consisted of a series of jagged, sawtooth-like precipices, a path which was impossible for any normal vehicle to get through.

But as with everything, there were exceptions.

Monster trucks, for example.

If you grew up in Japan, the remote-controlled toy version of these vehicles would probably be more familiar to you than the real things. They were the ultimate in off-road vehicles, featuring four gigantic tires and a suspension as thick as a pillar. Thanks to their four-wheel drive, they could easily launch into the air when driven over a ramp—*monster* was the perfect way of describing these trucks.

Naturally, they'd stolen this one.

Its owners, a group of tourists, had run away in the middle of a barbecue party and abandoned it, so they'd borrowed it and left the off-road vehicle behind.

"Found her! There she is! The girl in the picture! Why isn't she at the log cabin like she's supposed to be?!"

Vrooom! Shiage Hamazura gripped the wheel of the stolen truck as they jumped over the steep incline with a roar. The actual president, sitting in the passenger's seat, was pale, like he was about to vomit at any moment. Meanwhile, Birdway was in the back seat without a seat belt on, her hands folded all cool-like as she fully embraced the gravity-defying shaking.

None of this mattered—things were easy now that they'd located the target.

Hamazura tried to bring the monster truck over to Lindy and the tall man holding her hand as they ran up another steep incline.

But then something else happened.

Their vision went white, accompanied by a massive *bang*.

No, that wasn't right.

"The windshield…?!"

A soft shell, like the kind with balls in it used for dispersing rioters, had been fired at them from a grenade launcher. One that wouldn't cause the shock wave to penetrate—one that spread across the entire surface.

Blinded, Hamazura immediately hit the brakes but then noticed something a moment later.

That was exactly what the attacker was after—taking away their mode of transportation.

"Shit… Shit! Get out, Hamazura! You won't make it even if you floor it! Not with this thing's top speed!"

Roberto dove out of the passenger seat in a roll. Hamazura turned the key first, then followed suit. First, the windshield shattered under a hail of gunfire, and then a barrage of bullets came after them, mainly the president. Roberto rolled behind a protruding piece of rock on the precipice, giving himself some makeshift cover.

The person in the silver uniform must have been concerned about hitting the wrong person, because he rammed his bullpup assault rifle's stock into the tall man next to Lindy instead of firing at him, taking him out of the picture. Then the mercenary grabbed the girl's arm and threw her in the back seat of the monster truck before climbing into the driver's seat and turning the key that Hamazura had left in there.

A moment later...

Kkk-chreeeeee! With a bursting noise, the silver mercenary fell backward.

"That's what happens when you mess with the ignition and the ground," said Hamazura, slowly returning to the driver's seat and opening the door. "Doesn't matter how ripped you are—you'll never win in a fight with a three hundred–volt high-amperage current."

Grrrk-snap-crack! Several sounds of primitive violence ensued.

With the silver-clad mercenary now completely unable to move, Hamazura took his gun and assault rifle and threw them out the door. After removing the little trick he'd put on the vehicle, he turned the key again, as though he were its owner.

The president, who had arrived a few moments later, suddenly looked behind him, and his face froze.

"Miss Birdway!" he exclaimed. "You didn't get out of the truck?!"

"There was no reason to run," said Birdway, waggling a dagger at him—who knew where she'd gotten it. Lindy Blueshake, who had been thrown into the seat next to her, grabbed the driver's seat headrest and leaned forward, despite being scared of the blade.

"Um, umm, Mr. President!"

"Whoa-hoh! A-at last! Someone who knows *and* believes I'm actually the president at first sight..."

"D-don't start tearing up like that, please! I have something to tell you, umm...!"

"Huh? But I thought you hated the media. You don't read newspapers or watch TV. I'm surprised you recognized the president—"

Roberto moved over and covered Hamazura's mouth, then stuck out his chest in pride for some reason.

"It happened during the investigation of the F.C.E. Aurey Blueshake had gotten the help of an army of pain-in-the-ass lawyers to just barely avoid legal culpability, but then information regarding Lindy and her home environment got out. It was basically a gifted education program for crazy folks. A form of love where the parent is convinced their child is going to live up to their wildest expectations, and whenever something goes even slightly wrong, they yell and scream about how they've been betrayed and blame the kid for everything. It was too hard for Roselyne to intervene, and everyone else was muttering about how they couldn't spin the PR well enough for it even if they took on a lot of risk. But I didn't give a damn about the implications, so I stepped in and saved her. I feel like that deserves praise."

"Wait, so then you've met before!" retorted Hamazura. "Of course she'd know you were the president right away."

"Please let me get to the point!" exclaimed the girl. "Please! What should we do about Mr. Harzack?! This is terrible... He's getting smaller and smaller...!"

"I understand how you feel, little missy, but they're after you and me, not him." The president took her by the shoulders and nudged her back into her seat. "I'll get you back to him, I promise. But for now, staying away will keep him safe."

"......"

Her energy gone, Lindy Blueshake sat back down and made herself small. It wasn't that she was confused by everything that had happened. No, her face implied something different—that the worst-case scenario they'd already envisioned had come to pass.

"...Is Mom already this close?"

"That's right."

The president was honest.

"And so is the moment we overcome her."

[Nov. 10 / Source: Kauai, a camera attached to UAV Ginyanma 300 at Nā Pali Coast]

*　*　*

His left arm now unusable, Kamijou was hiding behind the log cabin with Kuroyoru. Even now, the mixed PMC-Gremlin force was continuing to come ashore. The soldiers in silver uniforms alighted from their hovercrafts below the precipices, then easily traversed the perilous terrain, aiming the muzzles of their bullpup assault rifles at the pair.

Bam! Bam! Bam! A series of explosions tore at the log walls of the cabin.

"What the hell is Number One doing?!" snapped Kuroyoru. "He hasn't drawn any of them away! What do we do? They'll surround us if we stay here!"

"A big army with regular old firepower," said Kamijou, conscious of his unmoving left hand. "They're gunning for psychics—and it's not just me. It'd take more than a couple bullets to overwhelm Birdway and Misaka. But they're only human, too. To deal with a full barrage, *they'd have to expend some of their power.* It would slow them down and mess them up. Then Salonya and Gremlin's sorcerers could go around and deal a fatal blow."

"Gee, thanks for the explanation. So what the hell do we *do*?! Your right hand and both of mine are the only weapons we've got. How do we solve this?!"

"…They think we're too scared of getting shot to charge at them. And the true sorcerers will naturally cut off our escape route."

"Yeah, so?"

"If we do it—if we charge at them—then we can mess up the two groups' coordination."

"Are you for real right now? Who cares if we take 'em by surprise?! We've got nothing to finish the job with!"

"I need to ask you. You're a cyborg, and you can create as many nitrogen spears as you have arms, right?"

"Yeah, but so what?! You Academy City fuckers took them all away from me! I only have two right now!"

"If you don't have enough, then we just need to get you some more."

"...Are you serious?"

"Technology doesn't have to be pretty—it just needs to work. Since we're not in Academy City, we won't be able to scrape together extra limbs that look like a human's, but *if we just focus on how they need to be able to shoot spears*, then we might be able to create some more limbs for you to use with the materials we have access to."

"Pfeh. You mean if we can hide how many we're making, our surprise attack will be that much more successful?"

"Do you have blueprints for them? Honestly, I don't know a thing about engineering. You'll have to do everything."

"...I can manage, I guess. But what about you?"

"The enemy has more weapons than just regular guns." Kamijou took out his cell phone. "I have to think about how to deal with Salonya," he said, dialing up Leivinia Birdway, who was in a separate team right now.

"Birdway!" he shouted into the phone. "Salonya's spell! Uh, Leshy or whatever! Did you analyze it all the way?!"

"*Everything my papyrus autoanalyzed was fake. I sent Mark and the other black-suits all over Hawaii to support the Marines under attack by Trident and to gather information, but they haven't gotten me any good news so far.*"

"That papyrus—can't you use it the other way around?"

"?"

"Salonya planted the false information, right? That means she wants us to believe that info is correct... If it were me, *I'd plant data that had as little to do with my own weaknesses as possible*. Like saying Imagine Breaker is a projectile weapon. I don't know anything about psychological analysis, but can't you use the fake stuff to figure out something out that she's trying to hide?"

First, the plan to replenish Kuroyoru's mechanical arms, and now this reverse usage of the papyrus. The boy's quick wit was practically abnormal. Was this the measure of their difference in experience?

"*I see what you're saying,*" replied Birdway. "*That could be a fun little puzzle to solve. I'll pass it along to my team.*"

After hanging up, Kuroyoru—starting to panic from the hammering of assault rifles—shouted at him. "Hey, you, Mr. Hero Who Doesn't Do Anything Himself! I need to break down these home appliance transformers and this water heater. Give me a hand!"

"...Wait, you're trying to make cyborgs out of *what*?"

Partly exasperated, Kamijou nevertheless got to work.

Whatever anyone else said, they simply had no time left.

[Nov. 10 / Source: Kauai, a camera attached to UAV Ginyanma 210 in the restricted northern area of Nā Pali Coast]

Leaving the unconscious man who had tried to protect Lindy behind, the monster truck started off again.

"So, uh, Mr. President? We're bringing her somewhere safe, right? Where the hell could we take her that the F.C.E. wouldn't see?!"

"No idea, honestly! But with this monster truck's mobility, we'd better get to the mountainous terrain in the island's center! Once we erase our tracks, we'll be able to find a way off the island!"

Yes. There was no guarantee. On anything.

There were emergency underground command centers in the Hawaiian Islands in case of a massive state of emergency, but even those shelters weren't guaranteed to be safe.

Immobile, already-registered facilities were worthless to them. Better to stay on the move, flowing from one location to the next, to reduce the risk of being attacked. Even that wasn't guaranteed to protect them; they were walking a dangerous tightrope. But with Trident and Gremlin hot on their tails, all they could do was keep running.

Then Roberto saw something on the imperial package's screen that made him groan. "That's actually incredible..."

"What's the problem?"

"Warnings are going out everywhere across the Marines' network. Two kids from Academy City—Level Fives, you called them? They've been going around disabling everyone they can find, Marine or Trident."

"Must be Number One and Number Three. Can't believe they write 'student' in the occupation field on forms," said Birdway, evidently amused.

Even now, the map showed red X marks appearing one after the next. Broadly, they were taking two routes, dozens more of the marks immediately showing up along their paths.

A great deal of untouched nature remained on Nā Pali Coast, with some of its terrain so wild as to be impossible for regular vehicles to drive through. The relatively flat places, however, also served as tourist spots. Tourists who would have been left behind, for instance, in areas like where the two Level Fives were scattering red X marks all over the place.

"They're monsters. What, do they want someone to make a Hollywood movie about them?"

"Here they come. Look—a fantastic girl is flying right overhead!"

"What?" said Hamazura, immediately looking upward.

A moment later, there was a dull *crunch* on the monster truck's roof—like someone had just fallen out of the sky and onto it.

The person pulled open the roof, then poked her head into the truck upside down.

"Everyone here safe?!" exclaimed Mikoto.

"I thought you were with Accelerator and Misaka Worst stirring up the two enemy factions!" replied Hamazura.

"We're doing what we need to… Is that girl with you—Lindy?"

"Yeah," said the president. "We're just barely edging this out at the moment, missy."

"Good to hear… That idiot's not with you? Great. I really needed to ask about the whole 'tag ring from Cupid's Arrow' thing, too."

Mikoto's casual remarks earned a puzzled look from Lindy and a question in English. "Are you looking for a boy you have a crush on?" she asked.

"*Hrk?!*" Mikoto started sputtering and coughing. "Please don't just hit a bull's-eye on your first shot like that!"

"Hmm… Boys are pushovers, though. You just have to throw your bra at them, and then while they're surprised, you hug them without a top on. From there it's just like two dogs in heat, right?"

"Do you even know what that means?! I really hope you don't actually know what that means!"

And you're probably not even wearing a bra to begin with! she added to herself.

"The president said that once before," explained Lindy. "So it must be right."

"That's right, missy," said Roberto. "If you want a guy's attention, just put on an exposing swimsuit and snuggle up to him with a beer in your hand. Get your chest right in there and get those bikini straps undone. It'll be even easier to understand if you're in a motel on the beach."

"Hey, uh, Mr. President?!" exclaimed Mikoto. "I'm skipping straight past slaps and just punching you at this point! If you call that your national character, then you're basically humiliating everyone who lives in America!"

"No need to worry about that, missy. My approval rate went up a little when I put a bit of extra funding into string swimsuit R&D. After all, slowly but surely, the population of the United States is aging and is on the way to running into social spending issues. We need drastic countermeasures to increase childbirth rates."

"That can't be what America is about! What the hell is wrong with the 'guys' you mentioned?!"

"Yeah, Roselyne was on her last straw about it, too. Not sure why. It's all so simple—what's there even to think about?"

That was when it happened.

Snap, snap, snap, snap! With a series of noises that sounded like someone stepping on foliage, a hunk of metal came sliding toward them. It was a khaki-colored tank covered in tons of explosive reactive armor that resembled phone books. The treads of the massive object spun noisily as they shaved down the surface of the rocks. The tank was moving surprisingly fast. Over eighty kph, in fact. And now it was practically on top of their monster truck.

Exasperated, the president called out, "Ah, it's the bargain tank from Northern Europe! They built that thing when they tried to launch into the tank industry because of how much they love Germany! I wondered where it disappeared to after it lost that competition in the EU—never thought its hard times had led it out here!"

"Is it Trident's?"

"Yup. I doubt it's gonna fire its main cannon at us, but a spray from that light machine gun would go straight through us!"

"Birdway!" exclaimed Hamazura. "Can't you do anything with that sorcery of yours?!"

"I could, but we're too close. I'd blow up this monster truck with it."

"Then I'll handle it."

Mikoto pulled her head back up to the roof, and a moment later, there was a loud bang. Hamazura checked the rearview mirror and saw Mikoto land cleanly on a sharp, sawtooth-like rock.

She'd offset all the crazy momentum from the monster truck—that alone made her superhuman.

And then she stood directly in front of the tank barreling at her at over eighty kph, after which *something* happened, and the tank *crashed into an invisible wall*—what did *that* make her exactly?

Hamazura watched with a spooked expression as the girl disappeared from view.

"…She's a monster. I can't think of a better word."

But that wasn't the end of their issues. A new crisis was soon upon them.

It started with a sound.

Boom! Like the snap of a firework going off overhead—and then a moment later, there came a shrill, flutelike noise from up above, drowning out the first sound. Again and again, from ten to thirty times.

When the president figured out what was making the sound, his face went white.

"Get down and curl up! Here it comes!"

Hamazura didn't even have time to ask what.

Explosions.

Hundreds of thousands of blades came raining down from the heavens.

They were called jointed cutters, and they were a type of bearing submunition: blades wrapped around the inside of artillery shells like springs or coils to enhance the antipersonnel killing power of 180mm cannons. The blades were intentionally easy to break, like hobby knives. Once the artillery shell exploded, the shock wave would split them up into countless tiny fragments, the force causing a torrential downpour of the things.

One shot had a lethal radius of about seventy meters.

And now they were up against anywhere from ten to thirty shots, a blast that covered a wide range with sharp metal fragments, leaving no safe spots. The cannons themselves were all a specific mass-produced type, but the rounds' ballistic courses diverged thanks to tiny factors: temperature, humidity, wind direction, and how the cannons evacuated their combustion gas. And the shots had been sprayed with remarkable evenness, as if to cover a whole wall in paint without missing any spots. The artillery strike spoke to considerable skill on the part of the gunners.

Every last branch and bough on the trees in the mountainous area was torn away, and showers of orange sparks flew on the monster truck's roof and hood. The blades ripped the truck's tires to shreds, too, sending the massive four-wheel-drive vehicle into a sideways skid.

"Agh! Was that Trident again?!"

"No, those were 180mms. I signed off on their adoption. So unless they've been captured…"

"That means it's that group of Marines!"

There was no time to discuss countermeasures.

Several people approached without a sound, attacking the truck's driver's seat and passenger seat simultaneously. They didn't open the doors; instead, they dragged Hamazura and Roberto out through the broken windows. Another man, looking into the back seat, saw Birdway and Lindy there. Birdway had her arms folded and a dagger in her hand, but *strangely enough, the man didn't see the weapon.*

He spoke into his radio next. *"Three-one. Lindy Blueshake spotted. I'll take her back with me. Prepare for negotiations."*

"W-wait...," the president managed, completely out of breath from his back having hit the ground when he was dragged from the vehicle. "I will not...condone these methods. As president...of the United States, I... I order you to..."

"Quit barking. You lost," spat the Marine. "Who would bow to a president who doesn't care to come up with ways to defend this country? You have an *obligation* to your voters, but you neglect it. Don't you *dare* keep calling yourself the president."

The muzzle of the man's gun rose.

"We're only doing what you should have done all along. And if you're still gonna get in our way, then there's just no saving you... Fortunately, we only reported Lindy Blueshake. We didn't say we found *you*. Nobody will be confused if we fail to bring you back."

Without hesitation, the Marine put the current president's face in his sights, then grinned.

"Are you some kind of idiot?"

[Nov. 10 / Source: Kauai, a camera attached to UAV Ginyanma 113]

Somewhere on the island, a gunshot rang out.

[Nov. 10 / Source: Kauai, a camera attached to UAV Ginyanma 210 in the restricted northern area of Nā Pali Coast]

Roberto Catze never shut his eyes.

Time stopped as the powder smoke began to billow. And in that strange tranquility, Lindy, still in the half-destroyed monster truck, was shaking badly. The nearby gunshot had just put her in a state of shock.

But something was missing from the scene.
The scent of blood.
And the reason for this was clear.
The president hadn't been shot.

A gun had been fired, yes.
But it belonged to a different Marine, one who had discharged a warning shot at the feet of his colleague aiming at the president.

The next thing anyone knew, another group of male Marines—all in the same uniform—surrounded the tiny band of soldiers going after the president. A member of the new group spoke, his tone filled with resentment.

"You're the idiot here," he said.

"Are… Are you insane? We're both Marines!"

"Doesn't matter. Drop your weapon. Now!"

The smaller group threw down their weapons at once, then let the others bind their hands behind their backs. As the traitors were apprehended and cables were wrapped around their wrists, the Marine who'd fired the shot turned to the president and saluted.

"Please forgive all the rudeness, Mr. President. We were unable to ascertain their identities until now. We decided this would be the fastest way to get to you."

"And… Can I ask who I'm speaking to…?"

"Corporal Martin Flowers, sir." The Marine quickly gestured to his chest with his thumb, then pointed it over his shoulder behind him. "From the right, we have Sergeant Elute Rax, PFC Shaolong Harvard, and…"

"Then I assume I can trust you all?"

"It would do us great honor if you considered us trustworthy, sir."

"Thank you for the help," replied Roberto genuinely. He switched his tone to the PR one. "But I hope you're prepared. At this point, siding with me is going against the grain. You may even be fired on by fellow U.S. soldiers."

"…It is true that idea of the United States being the world's police force is tempting, sir. And with the way they're doing things, the Marines under presidential aide Roselyne Crackhart's command are on the shortest route to that destination."

Even after saying all that, Martin Flowers looked the president straight in the eye.

"But those things do *not* involve capturing a child struggling with abuse and using her as a sacrifice, sir. A powerful United States, the world's police—we're the ones who should be *protecting* people like her. And you, sir, have made that clearer than anyone. We want to help you accomplish that."

Roberto gave a thin smile. "...Looks like neither of us is taking the easy way out, eh?"

"Perhaps, sir. But mark my words—*we* will have the last laugh."

The United States had acted.

Acted in this critical situation, supported by those who hadn't lost sight of the order in the chaos—those with willpower forged from steel.

[Nov. 10 / Source: Kauai, a camera attached to UAV Ginyanma 300 at Nā Pali Coast]

Behind the log cabin, Kamijou was hard at work wrapping duct tape around several reassembled pieces of home appliance transformers and a water heater into the shapes Kuroyoru had specified when his phone went off.

"That you, Birdway?" asked Kuroyoru.

"I'm still investigating the thing you told me to. I'll be honest—I haven't grasped the entirety of Salonya's spell yet."

"We could use any hints we can get. If she was any closer, she'd be on top of us!"

"Good," said Birdway, sounding satisfied, before getting to the point. *"The fake analysis from the papyrus said she needed to use a*

plant specifically from Russia. Seems like that was one of the things meant to throw us off the trail. In other words, her magic can make use of plants from anywhere."

"Then she can basically do anything...?" asked Kamijou dubiously, looking around. There were plants everywhere. Naturally. They supported the bottom of the food chain. If she could use them as a basis for her sorcery and render his left arm useless, he got the feeling he'd have to run to somewhere like a desert or the South Pole to win this.

"I'm not finished," said Birdway, cutting off his concerns. "To be specific, Leshy is a spell for taking control of a small forest in Russia. But it has a way of creating exceptions—enclaves."

"Enclaves?"

"When creatures go back and forth between places at regular intervals—think migratory birds—they can apparently make those places their enclaves. And these areas create a phenomenon, an effect like when you bring a pet onto a passenger plane. But more importantly, migrating creatures have a magical link to the local plant life."

"...You're gonna need to spell this out for me. What do you mean, magical link?"

"Leshy controls the denizens of the forest. Through some kind of exchange between the forest and its creatures, it acknowledges them as members of its society. If she wants to make the plant life in Hawaii an enclave, then she would have brought animals from Russia, which would give her something from the local vegetation."

"Like how some animals eat berries, and how some hairy plants drop seeds on the ground?"

"I'm thinking it's even simpler than that. Pretty much every animal on the planet is dependent on something. The role of plant life isn't just to support the food chain. It's what gives planet Earth its most important characteristic."

"......" Kamijou thought for a moment. "The exchange of oxygen and carbon dioxide...?"

"Must be. Apparently, Salonya's been seen in conifer forests quite *often in the past. They wouldn't provide food. So if the animals are going to depend on the plant life there for anything, it would be the air itself."*

"Any animal that's part of the cycle of oxygen and carbon dioxide in Leshy's forest becomes a denizen of that forest. When a denizen goes to another land, as long as they can recreate that cycle using local plant life, it'll get registered as one of Leshy's enclaves," said Kamijou, listing the conditions for himself. "But if she can take control of every living creature in one of those enclaves, wouldn't she also have taken control of us a long time ago?!"

"I said I didn't know the exact details, remember? We don't even know if Salonya's spell is actually for controlling people. If it were that convenient, I think Gremlin would have worked it into their plans for World War III."

"...So what, then?"

"Maybe Salonya can control creatures with simple brain structures, like insects and reptiles. Don't you think she might be replicating the ruler of the forest itself—the spirit Leshy? It has a large cerebrum like humans. Maybe she can't control the more complicated creatures, but she can secretly switch around simple perceptions and make them more susceptible to suggestion."

"Is that all a guess, too?"

"We can use the people she captured on Oahu and the kids she took hostage at the shopping mall as samples. They were acting like zombies, right? Gremlin's goal is to manipulate things to get a majority in Congress. If they can get enough people on their side using election-related information suppression, they'd be able to take control of even the congresspeople with strong wills—who would be unable to speak and would be treated as absent."

"But the people in her effective range would still become weak-willed, right? Then why hasn't Hawaii turned into one big zombie theme park?"

"Again, there's a lot of details here I'm not seeing yet. But if I had to take a stab at it, I'd say it takes time to create that cycle of oxygen and carbon dioxide. Three or four days at the longest. One week would match the amount of time God took to create the world, but it's *probably not that long. If it was, the sorcerer wouldn't have come here to begin with. That's why the effects haven't manifested in us yet—we just got here today."*

"And if the target leaves the enclave during that three- or four-day period, the spell will be incomplete... Which means the enclaves she can create at one time must be pretty small. Like the size of a neighborhood park."

"Salonya just needs to figure out her target's schedule. Then I think she could create a small enclave at their destination and stall for time."

Maybe that was directly connected to the mechanism she used to control animals and humans.

"But," said Kamijou, looking at his limp left arm, "if Salonya knew those conditions, I doubt she would have come to the front lines to begin with. She wouldn't be able to stall for three or four days in this situation... *She would have prepared a spell she could use whenever she needed.*"

"I agree, but I don't know what that could be."

"I see." He rubbed his paralyzed arm. "Then we'll just have to ask her personally."

"Finished!"

Kuroyoru connected her "limb," wrapped in duct tape, to a joint on her right flank. It wasn't an arm so much as several metal pipes bundled together, though. Needless to say, it didn't have five fingers.

Kamijou was dumbstruck for a few moments as he watched her arm writhe mechanically but eventually snapped out of it. "You only made one? Doesn't that mean you can only shoot three nitrogen spears at once?!"

The mixed Trident-Gremlin forces were inching their way toward them at this very moment.

The troops were focusing on shooting more bullets than necessary to stop them from moving anywhere, probably because Kuroyoru and Kamijou were from Academy City. They were wary of any hidden tricks. They'd advance with a hail of gunfire, force their hands, and then press in for victory when all was safe.

Kamijou, meanwhile, would clash with Salonya directly to find out more about her spell, then try and figure out a way past it.

Information was a lifeline for anyone who relied on supernatural abilities.

They were probably more concerned about Kuroyoru than Kamijou, but he had no idea how long that would continue for. If they took his lack of action as an eerie silence, all the better—but if they just decided their target wasn't doing anything, the soldiers and sorcerers would come down on them like an avalanche.

The situation was desperate.

"...I was never trying to rely on Bomber Lance in the first place," said Kuroyoru.

"What?"

"The arms Academy City made could move around by themselves. I used them as a hoard of unmanned weapons. But a limb thrown together on the fly doesn't have the specs for that. When I realized our initial plan wasn't going to work, I changed course." She grinned. "I was there when you were all sitting through that sorcery lecture back in the city, remember? One of the explanations stood out to me in particular: that sorcery is a technique for those without talent, and aside from a few exceptions, it doesn't demand any special capacity from the user."

"W-wait. You can't do that, dumbass. I don't know much about sorcery, either, but I know that's not how it works! It doesn't function like it does in dreams. Unless you have a crap ton of talent, you can't just start improvising everything and expect it to work. And do you have any idea how bad the side effects are when espers like us use sorcery—?"

"That's fine," interrupted Kuroyoru. "It doesn't matter what the spell is. Doesn't even need to be powerful enough to break anything. And I'm not dumb enough to think I can pull it off perfectly after only having heard about this stuff. It'd be like doing open-heart surgery right after watching someone else do it. I'd fuck it up. And it wouldn't be a problem. *As long as that failure leads to success, there's no problem at all.*"

"...What are you...even saying...?"

"This. I'm gonna cause those side effects or rejection responses or whatever *on purpose*."

With a heavy *thunk*, Kuroyoru dropped the duct tape–wrapped arm to the ground. And then...

"I'm a cyborg. The limits of my body are extremely vague. It's a shot in the dark, but if I can perfectly perceive an object connected to my body as my own flesh, then..."

He heard the sharp *kreeee* of something hard creaking. At first, he thought it was coming from her arm, but it wasn't.

"...then don't you think I can transfer the side effects onto any target I want and destroy it?"

The ground.
One of the cliffs lining the jagged terrain.
Esper Umidori Kuroyoru had triggered something like sorcery, the price of which was a rejection response—which traveled through her improvised limb and rippled into the ground...
And as a result, the entire cliff collapsed.
Everything beneath the log cabin, separated from the structure by a very thin line, fell. The silver mercenaries and sorcerers who'd been trying to walk along this path also plummeted and were engulfed in chunks of earth as they were carried to the seawater below.
It was such a smooth slide down that it could have easily been a roller coaster, too.
Unfortunately, this attraction wasn't obeying any safety standards.

"Gah...?!"

"Kuroyoru!"

At that short cry, Kamijou took his eyes off the scene below the cliff and saw that Kuroyoru was trembling. Her makeshift arm wrapped in duct tape had fallen apart completely, and the skin on her two slender arms had ripped up from the inside, exposing her artificial interior.

"Damn it... Couldn't avoid all the feedback. Guess it really isn't that easy."

"Are you insane?! You clearly didn't cut off all the pain, did you?!"

"...Ah. So this is insanity, then. Well, unfortunately, I've got all of Number One's more aggressive thought processes embedded artificially in my brain. There's a mismatch between that and my own instincts. I do feel danger at minor pain, but I'm basically unafraid of lethal wounds. Apparently, that's a common tendency for people who aren't accustomed to crowd psychology."

Kamijou was no doctor, so he couldn't tell if the damage had stopped at her mechanical parts or not. But from the way she was still shaking, he knew it would be cruel to force her to fight any longer.

Kuroyoru didn't give him any time to think about it, though.

"...More importantly, keep your eyes on the prize. The enemy boss is here."

"?!"

Below the precipice.

Evidently having jumped back as the ground gave out from under her, Salonya A. Irivika stood alone on the jagged cliff. When she realized the entire PMC had fallen into the sea, she barked an order over her radio.

"Requesting support to the west Nā Pali Coast. Repeat, requesting support to the west Nā Pali Coast! Damn it. Their entire C&C cloud's been destroyed..."

Clicking her tongue in anger, Salonya threw the radio to the ground, then set her gaze on Kamijou and smiled.

A brief, empty moment.

One-on-one, like the eye of a typhoon.

If Kamijou could take Salonya down here, then it would crush Gremlin and Aurey Blueshake's plans.

"Okay, okay! Pizza should be here in a bit. I hereby grant you, widdle boy, the right to play with me until then!"

"Sorry, but the only thing *you're* gonna be tasting is a mouthful of sand!"

* * *

[Nov. 10 / Source: Kauai, a congressional proceedings recording camera in the Waimea Canyon]

Waimea Canyon was a giant canyon nestled in the mountains of Kauai. With a long line of cliffs towering at several dozen meters, the canyon was prized as a tourist attraction, but it was far from convenient to move through. It was one of the routes to Nā Pali Coast where Lindy Blueshake was thought to be, but the naturally dangerous terrain limited the ways one could pass through it; a single defensive encampment there would make traversal extremely difficult.

At the moment, presidential aide Roselyne Crackhart was held up there herself.

The small road through the mountains had been closed off by several armored vehicles brought in by Trident. Fortunately, the enemy forces had already been eliminated by anti-tank missiles and the mercenaries had withdrawn, but there were still scattered pieces of armored vehicles littered about. Unless she could move those, she wouldn't be getting any farther.

Roselyne clicked her teeth in annoyance, then noticed the video camera recording her. "You're still recording?"

"I, uh, I feel like I'll pass out unless I focus on my job..."

"I hope that camera's not connected to the internet."

"I switched it off manually, ma'am. Every part of this thing that can connect to the internet should be offline."

"Are you sure?"

"Yes, ma'am. See? It all says *off* right here."

"Hmm. Fine, then."

When Roselyne took her attention away from the video camera, another employee called out to her.

"Ma'am! Uhhh..."

"What?"

"There's a call for you."

She accepted the phone he held out. When she saw caller ID displayed on the screen, however, she scowled. She picked up and heard the voice of a man she was well acquainted with.

"Yo, hey there, Roselyne! Figured it was high time I had a chat with you."

"I should be saying the same…!"

Roberto is a genius at riling people up, she thought, clenching her back teeth. "You won over some of my Marines, splitting them into two groups. What's the meaning of this?! We're already at a disadvantage against Trident. How much have you lowered our chance of success by tearing us apart from the inside…?!"

"Figured you'd say that. Which is why I've come to you with a deal, my dear Roselyne."

"A deal, you bastard?!"

"I'm not resisting to try and get the Marines to shoot at each other. They came to me wanting to help—that was pure coincidence. But I figured I'd milk that cow as dry as I could."

"This doesn't sound like one of your bluffs. How do you intend to beat Trident?"

"Oh, that's *impossible*."

He said this so readily the Roselyne's mind went blank for a moment.

Eventually, she snapped out of it. "Wha…? Hey! You idiot… That's… What?!?!?!"

"You know, I've always thought you'd fit right in with those Japanese tsunderes. Normally, you handle everything perfectly, but you always get flustered when I throw out random comments off the cuff."

"Don't be a total moron! Isn't that just sexual harassment?!"

"I must not have used enough words. I don't even have to split the Marines in two. If they run into the Trident squad searching for Lindy, they'll sink right into the swamp. And I'm the president, right? It's my job to keep my people from losing their lives for no good reason. What do you think, my dear Roselyne?"

"…Then you split my forces just to meddle with my plans?"

"That force belongs to the United States," said Roberto Catze, immediately correcting her. "I have two issues to deal with here on Kauai. The first is the Trident team looking for Lindy, and the second is you, Roselyne. I'm solving them one by one. It gets too complicated if I try to tackle them both at once."

"Are you trying to tell me that if you take command of my volunteer Marines, you'll be able to worm your way out of this?"

"I mean, hey. Even I think about stuff before I act."

"I'm sorry, Mr. President. You seem awfully suspicious all of a sudden, so I'm hanging up now."

"Am I just a total loser to you?! My referendums have gotten me the highest level of trust in the country...sort of!"

"Really? I'm supposed to have faith in the man the *Washington Stream* called 'the most unrealistic politician in the world, but one whose off-the-wall ideas might be helpful enough to kick-start the stalling American economy?'"

"Come on, just listen to me. There's a way to deal with Trident."

"Besides getting Lindy Blueshake?"

"Besides getting Lindy Blueshake."

Roselyne sighed a little. She'd finally hardened her conscience with determination, but now she could feel it crumbling down.

She clenched her teeth and gave the armored vehicle a kick in the tire, then urged Roberto to continue. "Fine. What do we do? I can at least hear you out and look into things, but I can't promise anything more than that."

"Thanks, my little tsundere. First off, Aurey Blueshake is the one financing them. Our grand scheme (heh) is to take a VIP named Salonya A. Irivika captive. If we topple her, the whole house of cards will come crashing down. Which brings us to a problem. You know what it is, right, Roselyne?"

"...Trident won't necessarily stop if their boss gives up. They're fighting under the assumption that Aurey will get enough political power to have their slates wiped clean in the United States. If she pulls out, they won't just be committing treason—they'll have committed the unprecedented crime of bringing war to the United

States. This year will then see the most death penalties in U.S. history."

"They know that wherever they run, the world's police will follow. Most of Trident's soldiers are former U.S. soldiers, after all. So they won't stop. And we'll need to do something about them. But if we can settle things right now, they're done. Gremlin is among the PMC, and they probably won't continue fighting on their own. So we'll start by going after them alone. Which is why we need a countermeasure against Trident."

"What did you have in mind?"

"Something that doesn't involve using Lindy as a human shield, at least. That's the trump card against Aurey. She won't help at all if the PMC she hired starts going crazy."

"Yes, so what did you have in mind?"

"I gave you the answer already. Trident's biggest impetus, the thing that has their backs to the wall, is that they'll be put to death if they retreat. I don't know if these former soldiers wanted to show the U.S. or if the pay was just too attractive to pass up, but this is the only way to break their spirit."

"…If you're not going to answer me, I'm actually going to hang up."

"First up is Trident's commander. Or maybe company president?" The president ignored her and continued. "Anyway, they're on Kauai. Just like Salonya, they'll either try to use Lindy as a safeguard against Aurey betraying them or get Aurey indebted to them by creating a situation in which they personally save her. I don't know which. But both scenarios have pretty massive benefits… They're using a C&C cloud. It's a service that uses soldiers, radars, and even civilian satellites to provide high-speed, multilateral information support on the battlefield. Their HQ's server is probably outside the country, but they're using United States networks to exchange data right now. We can use Aurey's F.C.E. network to spy on them, and I can use the imperial package to meddle with their plans."

"Are you saying you know where the commander is right now?!"

"That's the first problem we need to solve, Roselyne. Even if we unite all the Marines under our command, we wouldn't be able to get rid of Trident on Kauai, much less the entirety of Hawaii. But what about a small team escorting their commander?"

[Nov. 10 / Source: Kauai, a camera attached to UAV Ginyanma 300 at Nā Pali Coast]

Kamijou kicked off the rough earth and sprinted for Salonya. His greatest weapon was his right fist. To get things started, he needed to create an environment in which he could use it effectively.

However.

Wh-what? I'm... I'm falling...?!

"Okay, okay. Can't control your own weight now, can you?" Salonya smirked. "Your arms help balance your body weight. And your widdle left arm is taking a widdle coffee break right now. Amputees learn to adapt eventually, but since your arm got put out of commission abruptly, you won't be able to control yourself any time soon."

"Ugh!"

"And your weight is directly linked to how strong your punches are."

Then there was a dull *whoooom!*

Salonya had just shot her foot out at Kamijou's chest. He barely managed to block her kick with his right arm but tilted backward in the process. He only avoided falling over by staggering back a few steps.

She certainly seemed well trained, but Salonya was still a small girl when it came down to it.

And yet she'd knocked Kamijou back. His lack of control over his weight really was throwing him off.

"Ugh...," he grunted as Salonya hummed to herself and kicked again.

This time, it was a roundhouse aiming at his left flank.

And his left arm wouldn't move.

Her sharp kick connected exactly at the gap in his defenses.

"Gah...ahhhhhhhhhhhh?!"

"Gremlin has been very eager to counter your widdle Imagine Breaker, you know. Why do you think we messed with the ley lines and put that fortress in the sky to make sure you were safe?" Salonya smiled thinly, estimating the damage from what she'd felt from the kick. "That's why an indoor sort like me has been sweating her ass off at the gym three times a week. Oh, my wonderful legs have beautiful muscle on them now!"

"Shit!"

"Yep. I figured you'd try and get away at first."

As Kamijou tried to back off, clenching his left side with his right arm, Salonya's slender arm brutally grabbed his collar.

As she pulled him in, she swung her head like a blunt weapon.

With a dull *wham*, Kamijou careened backward.

...*None of* this makes sense for someone who controls other people...!

Now at the mercy of another one of Salonya's kicks aimed at his left side, he squeezed the next words from deep in his throat.

"(...But she's not using her special spell—is she showing how wary she is around Imagine Breaker, just like with Radiosonde Castle?)"

"That's about right."

By aiming for his left side, she was preventing him from grabbing her by the leg. She continued kicking away at him.

"But everything has its use. Even if we can't directly bind your widdle Imagine Breaker, binding your *left* arm reduces the power of your punches."

Knocking Kamijou, who was unable to fully support his own weight, to the ground with a flurry of kicks, Salonya used her right thumb to make a flicking motion directly upward.

...*Here it comes!*

On the ground, he brought up his right arm, but contrary to his expectations, nothing happened.

Several empty seconds passed.

Unable to grasp what had happened, he rolled to the side to try and get away from Salonya. But the sole of her shoe followed him.

There was no real reason she had to use a feint in that situation. Which meant...

"It misfired?!" he exclaimed.

"Seems like it." Like someone kicking a soccer ball up with all their strength, her kick connected.

It hit with a *wha-gam*, and Kamijou had to suppress the urge to vomit as his breathing grew ragged.

"...What...are you...doing...?" he managed.

"Huh?"

"The war's finally over... Everyone's starting new lives for themselves, but you..."

"We're stirring the pot, and you want to know why, huh?"

A smile broke out on Salonya's lips, but a sharp light appeared in her eyes to contradict it—it was as if Kamijou had just mentioned something he never should have.

"Sure, the war's over. You played a pretty important role in it. Now that the chaos is over, countries around the world have started trying to put things back together. But," she quickly added, "*our* country is being used as a springboard for that."

"......"

"Sucks, doesn't it? It really blows. Kids who should never have to starve are going hungry. Old people who shouldn't have to experience the cold are shivering. And it's because all these big countries are strangling the flow of materials and money. They cancel only what they need and call themselves good widdle heroes. Makes me feel like justice has been whored out."

Kamijou couldn't determine what exactly was going on there or if Salonya was even telling the truth to begin with.

But he needed to try to figure things out himself and take her at her word.

Even as they spoke, something was progressing.

The shadows of the devourers were flitting in and out of sight.

He was no prophet, and there was no way he could foresee the results of every one of his deeds. But the things he'd done were definitely related to how *this* was turning out.

"Salonya…"

"The only saving grace was that *you* didn't get a big pile of gold rolling into your pockets."

The sorcerer in green smiled.

The spirit.

The leader of the forest.

The girl who brought death to those who wandered inside—she smiled a ghostly smile, like someone sharing the winnings of an off-handed gamble.

"But that doesn't change the fact that there's still enough reason to kill you."

"……"

No matter what he did from here on out, no matter how he confronted the consequences of World War III, he couldn't do anything if he died here.

He needed to see Salonya's attacks and her spell for what they really were. What was the logic behind them? What steps did she need to take to use them? What could he erase and what couldn't he erase? He needed specifics.

…What do I need to destroy to get my left arm back? That's the first thing to figure out!

"Let's start this for real, shall we?"

Salonya loosely put her hands together, then thrust them in front of her.

"It's time for a gamble with the spirit Leshy, the leader of the forest!"

And then, as if to launch something directly overhead, she flicked both her thumbs.

[Nov. 10 / Source: Kauai, a tide observation camera at Nawiliwili Port]

At a private port in the west of Kauai, Trident's commander, Kinesic Evers, put his hands in the air. He was wearing an outdated, albeit popular, French officer's uniform that he'd acquired from who knows where. Even after leaving the military and going private, men who were getting on in years never seemed to lose their lust for power.

The reason he had his hands up was simple. The United States Marines had deployed all over the docks and mercilessly blown up an armored vehicle covered in C&C antennas, and they were now pointing their rifles at him.

In the middle of all this.

Roberto Catze approached, pushing his Marine escorts aside with a cheerful smile on his face.

"Yo! Hey there. I thought these tactics looked awfully familiar. It's the former French Navy staff officer who fell from his position after being blamed for a poor response to the British Halloween. You never could have climbed the ranks in such a short amount of time. So what? Did you hijack management during the chaos of the war or something?"

"…Why would you need to know?"

"Just wanted to get my facts straight. Anyway, what's all this? Are you going to tell me the EU is supporting you? I know they're having financial difficulties of their own. They also didn't get much out of the war—the only thing they earned was exhaustion, huh?"

"You have no evidence to back up your accusation. There is nothing to prove that we have a connection to the EU."

"Right, which is why I said I just wanted to get my facts straight. I think I know everything at this point, though, since you covered for the EU and not Trident. Now that I think of it, the fact that Trident is mainly active in nonmember nations in Eastern Europe reeks of politics. You must have had connections there before you took over. Anyway, none of that really matters," said the president casually. "Honestly, this problem is quite the pickle, ain't it?"

"Are problems like these ever easy to solve?"

"Suppose not. But things are different this time around. I'll be frank. The crime of engaging in war against the United States is unprecedented. I have no idea what kind of legislation is in place for it. So while I could just arrest you all right now, my chances of actually throwing you into prison are an unknown."

"……"

"Which puts me in a bind, you see." Roberto shrugged. "If existing law can't judge you, then we might have to deal with you as we would foreign invaders. See, *if the law can't judge you, then it can't protect you, either.* I'm throwing the word *war* around quite a bit here, but in essence, you're literally executing people without trial."

"…You're too late. If Aurey Blueshake and Salonya A. Irivika can take over the central government, they'll turn everything on its head."

"Unfortunately for you, that isn't happening," said the president with another shrug. "You know Salonya isn't using regular firepower or regular troops, right? They use *that technology*—the stuff that mega-sadistic tsundere-hopeful princess of England showed us so much of during the British Halloween and the stuff that vexed us so much during World War III. I may be president, but I'm a high school dropout. I don't get any of this crazy sorcery stuff, so I decided to leave that to an expert."

"An expert…? No… You can't mean…!"

"Yes—one of the people you probably hate the most. But you gotta leave these jobs to the ones with experience. My plan is already in motion. Salonya will be taken out soon. And when that happens, your defeat is assured—yours and Aurey's both… But if you still don't get it, then maybe I need to spell it out for you."

Roberto stared Kinesic right in the eyes to stress his authority, then spoke slowly.

"…This isn't a negotiation to decide who wins and who compromises. You and Trident have already lost. This is a negotiation about how much you can lighten your sentence. So you'd better shape up. Trident is effectively liable for committing a massacre. You'll be treated as enemy combatants. You may have removed our advantage by making Kilauea erupt, but if the issue drags on, and both forces clash again… Well, you may have fifty thousand soldiers at your disposal, but the combined military personnel of the United States clocks in at five million people. And that's not including all the armies of our allies. You don't really think you can win, do you? I know this is rough on you, since it's like a slaughter without a trial... But hey, *there's no legislation covering this.* You'd better get thinking. How can you subtract from your crimes to keep yourself alive?"

"Are you telling me to abandon our agreement with Aurey and withdraw our forces at once?"

"If that's your choice, then so be it. We'll have full say over everything in that case, though. That includes your time, by the way. So be careful."

"......"

One of the Marines next to Roberto handed him a military-grade radio, and the president pressed it to Kinesic's chest.

He took it in his hand, then thought for a few moments before heaving a sigh.

After setting the frequency, he brought the radio to his mouth.

And then he spoke, his tone one of defeat.

"Attention all personnel currently deployed throughout the Hawaiian Islands. I don't care about all the other regions. And I don't care how much the American forces push back. Everyone is to immediately support the actions of Salonya A. Irivika, who is currently active on the Nā Pali Coast."

Roselyne Crackhart's face went white when she heard that.

Roberto, his expression as firm as a stone, asked, "Are you sure about that, shithead?"

"I am indeed."

"You do realize this decision will affect the futures of your fifty thousand subordinates, including the ones who aren't even part of this?"

"If you want to shoot me, then do it," said Kinesic, tossing the radio aside. "But if we can link up with Salonya, we can turn the tables. This is where our target is. And Lindy Blueshake, the girl we need to make a deal with our client, has shown up as well. It's our sorcerer against your anti-occult operative—the winner will determine once and for all who should withdraw."

[*Nov. 10 / Source: Kauai, a camera attached to UAV Ginyanma 300 at the Nā Pali Coast*]

Salonya's spell was named after the Russian spirit Leshy, said to be the ruler of the forest.

Something unknown yet very real had paralyzed Kamijou's left arm and some of his left flank as well.

Salonya put both her hands in front of her, then flicked her thumbs upward as Kamijou tried to roll sideways across the ground to get away.

However.

"Wait... Nothing again? Another misfire?!"

"Well, shit. I just can't seem to hit the mark today!"

Unfazed by her spell not working, Salonya resorted to a more surefire method of attacking her opponent—kicking Kamijou while he was down. However, she was a moment too late. In that time, he had gotten an appropriate distance away from her and had managed to stand up.

As her foot came down like a hammer, he stopped it with his right arm, then gave her his best guess.

"Is your magic more like a land mine or a trap...? You're not aiming and firing like you do with a gun. You're waiting for me to step on a trap to attack, aren't you...?!"

"Guess it wasn't hard to figure out. But as long as you're in range for me to *throw* my widdle land mines at you, they take on a different property—they become hand grenades."

Kamijou watched Salonya fiddle with something in her hand. Each of the objects she held was only about a millimeter long. They were like grains of sand. But they were actually...

"Seeds?!"

He immediately twisted to try and avoid the hail of seeds shooting at him like a buckshot.

"Oh, too bad."

Salonya smiled.

"Even plant *pollen* will work."

Suddenly, Kamijou fell straight down.

Unable to support his own body weight, he collapsed to the ground.

It had been like a magic trick. Salonya had grabbed a few plant seeds—easy to understand—and then used her other hand to undo the tie on a small bag.

"Gah... Gah..."

"Looks like that one got your left half for real. Man, you really tried, though! Anyone else would have breathed it all in and experienced multiple organ failure."

Her very first strike—when Kamijou and Kuroyoru had been hiding behind the log cabin—had been that pollen on the wind.

"It's kinda like a biochemical weapon. Pretty nasty. But once the secret's out, it's a pain for sure. You have to figure out where the wind's coming from and even create a gust yourself. There are two places I can use this. As a first strike when I clearly don't have time to analyze my opponent and as a surprise attack for when I really need it... You, however, got to taste it twice. Not many people can say that."

Plant seeds.

And pollen.

The spirit Leshy, on which Salonya based her spell, was called the ruler of the forest. It dominated all creatures within its area of influence and performed exchanges through gambling. That was what Birdway said, wasn't it?

Which meant...

"Then it's...a penalty for whoever damages a possession within the zone...?"

"I'm not exactly about to give you the answers here," said Salonya, clenching more plant seeds in her palm.

But she might as well have told him the answer just then. It was a punishment for anyone who obstructed plant growth. That was the root of Salonya's spell. It could be stepping on a seed or getting in the way of drifting pollen.

That said…

…*I still can't figure out what she routes her attack through after I step on a seed… How does it work? How is the damage getting to me…?*

Just then, an image flashed through Kamijou's mind like a revolving lantern.

Unable to rise from the ground, he spoke.

"The ruler of the forest, then."

"It ain't just forestcore fashion."

"If you could make the bigger animals attack me, this would have been a lot quicker."

"…Well, nobody's ever omnipotent in *every* widdle situation."

Salonya had tried to answer him fluidly, but there was a tiny bit of hesitation in her response.

I knew it, thought Kamijou. If she was going to call herself the ruler of the forest, then only being linked to plants would make her too weak. She could probably interfere with nearby animals and insects, too. Birdway had also suggested that even if she couldn't get to humans directly, she probably had control over creatures with simpler brain structures like insects and reptiles.

Then had Kamijou been attacked by a poisonous insect or something?

No, that wasn't right. His arm would have stung if that were the case.

If he had any hint at all, it was…

…*The pollen she used right at the beginning hit me but not Kuroyoru?*

Was it because she was a cyborg? Did it not work on her cyborg arms?

No.

Kamijou was the only one whose left arm had been exposed to the pollen. Kuroyoru had been standing next to him, so the pollen would have gotten on another part of her body. And yet it hadn't affected her at all. Aside from a portion of her upper body—her arms mostly—she was a regular flesh-and-blood human.

The issue wasn't that she was a cyborg.

This was based on a different unique trait.

They'd artificially implanted part of Number One's thought processes in her brain.

Her instincts were at odds with that. She was resistant to the whims of crowds.

Still on the ground, Kamijou looked at his unmoving left arm again. He'd thought this was a hardware issue, but it wasn't. Salonya was interfering with the software responsible for issuing movement commands to the hardware.

But that didn't mean he was under her direct control, either. If she could do that, things would have been much worse. This was a penalty for trampling over some plants. She was doing this only by manipulating groups of insects and other small animals.

Kamijou thought for a moment.

"Ah!"

Immediately, he pulled his cell phone out with his right hand and hit a few buttons.

"I told you, I'm not gonna let you check your answers!"

Whoom! Salonya sent a flurry of kicks at him.

Her first went for the wrist of his right hand holding the phone, and the second connected with his side, where he'd let go.

"Guh... Gah...!"

"Trying to call widdle Birdway from Dawn-Colored Sunlight, were we? Would you stop trying to get all the answers you need just by talking things out? This age of search engines really *has* emptied our brains."

Kamijou glanced at his phone—it had bounced a long way off—then turned his gaze back to Salonya.

"...Elimination from the 'forest' you created as your zone. Combine insects, reptiles, and other creatures together, and that means *you're* the one who controls a majority of the living things inside it. You'll always win any majority decision. Which makes it like crowd psychology. The denizens of the forest are forced to connect, and if you focus their hostility and enmity on a single point, this is what happens. *You can mess with a person's mind from outside their body.*"

The penalty: the act of eliminating irregular elements to maintain societal stability. The suppression of the minority by the majority. Salonya was replicating that in an offensive way. She sounded fed up when she spoke next.

"Right. No wonder you rely on that widdle cell phone of yours so much. Crowd psychology only works with humans, idiot. You were on the right track with the whole expulsion-by-the-forest denizens' bit, though."

She grinned at him.

"My technique, on the other hand, first recalibrates the minds of all creatures within the zone to be equal. They can be widdle humans, or widdle beetles, or whatever. Doesn't matter. The only difference is whether they're inside the zone or outside of it. Only then can you start to apply crowd psychology."

She'd just revealed the workings of her spell.

He'd gotten the information he needed to beat her.

However...

"So? Did you figure out my weakness?" asked Salonya, still smiling as she approached. "But what are you gonna do about it when the left side of your body's completely paralyzed, hmm? Like I said, your weight directly factors into the strength of your blows. You can't even dig your heels in. To knock someone down in the state you're in, you'd have to be as strong as a grizzly bear."

"...Not true."

"?"

Salonya didn't even have time to ask what he meant.

Bang!

A moment later, Kamijou suddenly got up off the ground—an act which should have been impossible for any human. Using his heel as an axis for movement, he'd shot to his feet with the force of a basement trapdoor bursting open.

"What…?!"

Salonya was shocked, but then noticed something.

The spindly girl's arms were wrapped around his waist. Spears of air had fired from their palms, forcing Kamijou off the ground.

Salonya watched as the limbs wrapped themselves around Kamijou's left leg, holding it in place like a plaster cast.

No, that wasn't it.

Like a powered suit reinforcing his physical power with mechanical power.

"Mechanical arms? Wait, then that phone call before—"

"Who said I called Birdway? Who said I was even calling *anyone* in the first place?!"

Makeshift though the arrangement was, there was no problem as long as his left foot could move.

And now that Salonya had waltzed right into his striking distance, he stepped right up to her and slammed his right fist into her with all his might.

It was the attack Gremlin dreaded the most.

A right-hand punch with Imagine Breaker behind it.

Whuuuuump!

Salonya A. Irivika's small body bent over backward.

But that was all.

She held herself up. The edges of her lips split, and red blood dripped from them. But she held herself in place.

"Like I said…," she spat, grasping another handful of seeds in her right hand. "Your left arm's still paralyzed. Just because you can use your foot doesn't mean you can control your goddamn body weight!"

She threw the seeds right in his face, as if scattering salt.

Hit directly by her projectiles, Kamijou fell to the ground. His body spasmed. He had no idea how he looked right now, but he could feel his blood vessels pulsating eerily. Of his four limbs, only his right hand and forearm could move.

"...Shit. How are your organs still online? Maybe I should have washed the pollen straight down your throat."

"...Guh... Kah, hah..."

Kamijou couldn't even breathe unless he fully concentrated on it.

Using his right hand, the last thing that could move, to drag himself along the hard ground, he slowly squirmed forward.

"You were the one who ended the war. I was looking forward to having a chat about it if we ever met."

He knew how Salonya's Leshy spell worked now.

But he still had one doubt.

She'd created numerous enclaves of a little Russian forest to use her sorcery in. Birdway had predicted that setting them up took a few days or so.

But Salonya would have only learned about Lindy Blueshake being here twenty or thirty minutes ago.

She wouldn't have had the time to create an enclave.

"I wanted to ask you why the hell you ended the war *the way you did*. You know how all the places exhausted by the war are undergoing redevelopment, first and foremost my widdle Russia, right? What do you think that looks like?"

"Academy City...and America are..."

"Are fooling around, making a mess of other countries for their own benefit."

Salonya grinned, but there was no joy in her smile.

"Instead of just giving us a whole bunch of money, they've been talking about political measures. They're taking over our electric and water infrastructure, unilaterally choosing who gets to be saved and who doesn't. Even though *they* were one of the sides that kicked off the war. They split people up like oranges in boxes, and any boxes they don't like the taste of, they just throw out."

"......"

"My little forest has already been cleared away, replaced with asphalt. If I hadn't met Gremlin, I wouldn't have been able to transfer the power that made me a sorcerer in the first place."

Then had Salonya made the entirety of Hawaii, or maybe just all of Kauai, into one big enclave? No, that wasn't right, either. If she could do that, Lindy would have already been in a "mentally absent" state before Gremlin even tried to kidnap her. Even against amateurs, she would have eliminated any possibility of escape or resistance.

"And look, I get it. The old world's gone now, and there's nothing we can do about that. But we're still trying to live. That's why we want to create a foundation. One that isn't subject to unilateral bullying from Academy City and the USA."

There must have been a reason for that.

A hidden trick that would let her make this place into an enclave as an exception, without the several-day restriction.

"The rest of Gremlin and widdle Aurey are trying to remake the United States as a theocracy to ruin the balance between science and sorcery, but even that is just trivial to me. I don't care what happens as long as Russia and the European region can push back against the people *trying to flout justice for their own benefit.*"

"...We..."

Keeping his breathing from stopping, Kamijou managed to get out a few words.

"We didn't stop that war...for something like that. I... We..."

"But that's how it ended up."

"Then...it's my job to fight...the people flouting justice...who are making you all suffer. There's no need...for the rest of the...world... to criticize you."

"You're naive. You were only able to stop the war because of the arrangements everyone else made for you. They gave you the opportunity. You're just a pawn. And you think you can do something about it?"

Salonya needed two things for her Leshy spell: plants and animals. They were linked by the cycle of oxygen and carbon dioxide, and by combining them, Salonya designated a particular area as a forest. Then by ruling over that twisted zone, that twisted community, imposing twisted penalties based on twisted rules. That was how she was getting the better of Kamijou.

"And you're weak, too. Together, Gremlin is taking on the people who won the world, see? You're just some loser who can't even beat *one* of us. Accomplishing a feat that grand is beyond you."

Did that mean she couldn't replenish her plants?

It wasn't that she was using the cycle of oxygen and carbon dioxide to integrate the plant life into her enclave across several days. *She'd brought the original plants from her forest and had planted them directly into the soil.* That would nullify the need for a several-day waiting period. If she unleashed the insects and small animals under those plants' control, it would give her control over the majority of the forest denizens.

There'd been signs of this. In fact, he'd seen the very person who had brought the plants here.

"Anyway, it's time for me to stop that widdle heart of yours."

"Salonya…!"

"If you're going to talk big, you'd better have the strength to back it up. Of course, in *the previous war*, that was why we were trampled over."

Harzack Lauras.

The tall man acting as Lindy Blueshake's guardian. Just before the attack, he'd been planting buds. He wasn't one of Salonya's lackeys, but maybe she'd taken control of all the flower shops and unattended sales places where he would go to buy the seedlings. Then she'd just have to swap them out for her own, and he'd do her job for her.

It was even possible that Trident had waited to strike until all the buds were planted.

That was the origin of her spell.

The place those buds were planted.

The little vegetable garden next to the log cabin!

"…Eh?"

Salonya made a confused noise. She'd scattered countless seeds on Kamijou, yet his breathing still hadn't stopped.

And then she figured it out.

He'd been dragging himself along the ground with his right hand—and before she knew it, he'd reached the vegetable garden. With the only part of his body that could still move, he began ripping the buds out of the soft soil.

The origin of the spell named after the forest-ruling spirit.

Normally, there would have been countless plants within her zone, but this one was hastily improvised—the plants in the garden were the only things supporting her spell.

With his right hand that nullified any and all sorcery, he plucked every last plant from the garden.

"No… You…"

"……"

Kamijou slowly rose to his feet.

Nothing was there to constrain him anymore. His arms and legs regained their movement. He could once again unleash punches with his full weight behind them.

Kamijou rotated his right shoulder to get a feel for it, while Salonya watched him from a short distance away, unable to go on the offensive now that she'd lost her game-winning card. Even her vaunted kicks had only worked because he had been unable to control his body weight.

They'd switched places.

One of them had gotten his game-winning card back, and the other had lost hers.

"…Sorry about this, Salonya."

"Uh, wait—"

"I've caught up to where you are. I can see the things you see now. But if everything you said was true, then you're not the one I should be risking my life to fight."

"Oooooooooooooooooooooooooooaaaaaaaaaaaaaaaaaaaaaaaa aaaaaaaaaaaahhhhhhhhhhhhhhhhhhhhhhhhhhhhhhhhhhhhhh hhhhhhhhhhh?!"

* * *

A moment later came a series of noises made by the most primitive form of violence.

Bam, wham, boom, wham, crack, bam, crack, crash, crush!!!!!!

[*Nov. 10 / Source: Kauai, a tide observation camera at Nawiliwili Port*]

After receiving the notification, President Roberto Catze pointed to the radio that Trident's commander, Kinesic Evers, had thrown to the ground.

And then he spoke.

"Pick it up, shithead."

"So Irivika has fallen."

"Your dreams have been crushed, and it's time for you to face an empty reality."

Kinesic had the option of rallying his forces to recover Salonya, but they could easily use her as a hostage, and then that would be that. And even if they could recover her, they would kill her as soon as they realized the threat. Then the plan to control the United States that she and Aurey had spearheaded would fall to pieces.

The members of Trident had lost any hope of wiping their slates clean; fighting any further would be akin to strangling themselves. Hawaii's isolation from the Kilauea eruption wouldn't last forever.

"…What are your terms?" he asked.

"We'll start with three hundred years' imprisonment in an unofficial penitentiary in Alaska—specifically the Arctic Circle—without trial. Withdraw your forces immediately, put an end to the chaos, and give us all the names and information you have on Gremlin, which you made a deal with. That will be factored into how much we lighten your sentences… Basically, I'm telling you to disarm all your forces and cough up everything you know."

EPILOGUE
The Ever-Reliable Birdway
Queen_Period.

[Nov. 10 / Source: Oahu, a security camera in the lounge of an international hotel in Honolulu]

It had been a few hours since they'd taken the Hawaiian Islands back from the fierce attack of the PMC Trident and the sorcerer's society Gremlin. Kamijou and the others had assembled at a hotel used frequently for the president's press conferences and scandals alike.

Among their number was Lindy Blueshake.

Conscious of the young girl, Roberto faced Kamijou's group and said, "We just got confirmation that Trident has disarmed and surrendered. We can assume the problems plaguing Hawaii have been put to rest for the moment."

"...You don't look so happy about it, though."

"Because we only found Trident." The president heaved a sigh. "They were being helped by people with occult powers. And a lot of them, too. They had blended in with the others by wearing the same silver uniforms. If there was one in every single group, down to the smallest of squads, there would have been several hundred. But we've been investigating every single Trident member we've arrested and haven't turned up a single one.

They had taken down a few sorcerers among the soldiers before Trident had even made its big move, but even those had vanished.

Had they taken advantage of the commotion on the islands to escape?

Considering their numbers and connections, a massive amount of Gremlin sorcerers had been aiding Trident. They would have had far less protection than Cendrillon or Salonya—nevertheless, they were clearly quite skilled. Their vanishing act even threatened to overshadow the impact of Cendrillon and Salonya, the actual big shots in this affair.

That was who Kamijou and the others were up against.

They weren't just some random assortment of people. Each individual was on the extreme end of idiosyncrasy, and now they'd also shown off how strong they were as an organized group.

"Gremlin…"

"Our only leads are Salonya, who had her own tight security detail, and that Cendrillon girl. But the rest of them might move to stamp out any hints that couldn't be covered up right away."

To where had Gremlin vanished after their withdrawal?

The sorcery side supposedly had its own theories and official stances, but they'd shown such finesse that one could be forgiven for forgetting about such things.

Kamijou gave a bitter scowl. "And the final mastermind is still untouched."

"Aurey Blueshake," said Roberto, exhaling in annoyance.

Hamazura knotted his brows. "But nobody knows where she is, right? You might have to search beyond the USA to find her… Can you really pin her down in a day or two?"

"She's a lady with many enemies," said the president. "In all honesty, I'd be surprised if we saw her at all for the next decade. That said, we *can* use her unexplained absence against her."

"?"

Kamijou and the others looked at the president with dubious looks on their faces.

Ignoring them, Roberto pointed at Lindy with his thumb. "Finding Aurey would be too tough. But with the little missy's help, we *can* snatch away the power Aurey prizes so much."

[????? / *Source: location unknown, camera identification number unknown, a recording provided with external video and sound*]

"Trident has failed."

Hearing the words of her aide, Aurey Blueshake sighed. "And Gremlin?"

"Our hotline to them has been severed. They've likely terminated our cooperative agreement, ma'am."

"...We've been forsaken," said Aurey. "The fool. My financial power can easily survive a failed operation or two. For now, let's wait. They'll come crying back soon enough."

"Is there an alternative plan for taking control of the United States, ma'am?"

"Now that Salonya's control has been broken, the situation in Congress will have partially collapsed. But we still have plenty of pieces ready to control the information war during the next elections. We may not be able to acquire a majority, but we can still throw our opponents into disarray. First, I'll create a political vacuum for myself and buy time, during which we can contact Gremlin or even another organization and prepare for our return."

Then it happened.

Aurey glanced at the TV they'd left on.

Even when she was overseas, almost all news traced back to her, so she didn't generally watch TV. It was like reviewing information that she herself had made.

But this time, things were different.

The female newscaster on the screen said, *"Breaking news."*

"?"

* * *

"The American Bar Association has made an announcement regarding Miss Aurey Blueshake, also known as the media queen. In accordance with the intentions of her lifetime inheritance, her management group has officially conferred all her assets and economic infrastructure to her only child, Lindy Blueshake."

Aurey's thoughts completely stopped for a moment.
"I haven't heard about this… I've said nothing about this!"
A moment later, her laptop was open, and she was checking her internet banking account.
But she never completed the process.
When she entered her ID and password, she received only one simple sentence:
"*You do not have permission to view this page. Your password may be incorrect.*"
"It's *my* account!" she screamed as the emotionless newscaster continued her explanation.
"*As Miss Lindy Blueshake is eight years old, her guardian, a Mr. Harzack Lauras, is regarded as the most likely recipient of the fortune. However, we've also gotten word that Miss Aurey was intimately involved with today's incident in Hawaii. Some speculate that if this is true, then most of her assets will be spent on patching up the situation and on reparations…*"
It was disappearing.
Her wealth. Her economic infrastructure. Her network. Her *power*.
The power she'd used to hire a PMC, contact a sorcerer's society, and gain control over the United States' information networks.
And that wasn't all. If she lost her power, she would also lose all the people supporting her. Her opportunities would disappear, too.
"Damn it! Call up the team of lawyers at holdings! Like hell I'll let them take away my power with this…this farce!"
"We can't…"
"Do it anyway! Even at this very second, we—!"

"This was never aboveboard to begin with, ma'am! It's like bugs have eaten away at the holes in your plan! But they're doing all of this legally! The president must be behind this. A trial won't solve this problem!"

"*...Matters such as bankruptcy are already being sorted out for her child companies and equities, but apparently this is only a measure to minimize stockholder losses. The market value of Blueshake's group is plummeting, and it's not clear how much trust her organization will have once the new system is in place...*"

"It just never ends..."

Her throne.

Her empire.

Everything she'd worked so hard to build was crumbling before her very eyes.

Aurey clenched her teeth, then grabbed the coat hanging on the wall.

"M-ma'am, where are you going?!"

"Out. The proxy is twisting my words however they want. If I make an appearance at the government—"

"If word of where you are gets out, you'll be assassinated!"

"Ugh!"

"You've made too many enemies, ma'am. There's no guarantee you'll get back the assets you need to protect yourself. And even if they don't kill you, judging by this breaking news, they're *already* hunting you as a major culprit in this case. If you go out there, they'll arrest you!"

"I know it's risky! But if I can just get my money back! My power—"

"You'd probably get back what Miss Lindy has. But if you create a new company and transfer all those assets there, it might look like all the money you got from her just vanished! They'll set it up that way for sure—all to whittle away at your power!"

"Then... Then... What should I do...?"

Her aide couldn't answer right away.

Now that she'd lost all her financial connections, he didn't have any reason to stay by her side. This room would cease belonging to her in the near future.

There was no way for her to know what would become of her after that.

She'd lost her money, but her enemies remained.

No. If they knew Aurey's assets were all gone, the factions she'd been keeping control over would *also* explode into rage. The chances were by no means low that the fire of wrath would be lit in the people supporting her backroom business once she stopped paying them. Perhaps certain factions would even take into account how Aurey had abused Lindy and bring her daughter gifts in the hopes of roping her to their side.

"I, um, I have an idea, ma'am."

The last resort for someone who had lost everything.

The most reasonable choice available to her—that was what the aide, as commanded, told her.

"...W-wouldn't you best defend yourself by coming out of hiding and allowing yourself to get arrested, ma'am?"

"When I'm penniless...?"

"Yes, ma'am."

"Me? Go to j-j-jail...?"

"Yes, ma'am! It won't be long before someone lets it slip that we're here. If you're going to act, now is your only chance!"

[Information]

[Manual%> Confirmed disconnection from Knowledge 12.]
   [Manual%> Confirmed connection to Unknown.]
   [F.C.E. rebooting...]
   [F.C.E. surveillance network reconstruction completed by username Unknown.]

* * *

[Nov. 10 / Source: Oahu, a security camera in the lounge of an international hotel in Honolulu]

Kamijou and the others were watching the breaking news on the lounge's big TV.
This one wasn't about Lindy Blueshake's inheritance, though.
A different news story came on directly after it.
"…Twenty-seven organizations in partnerships with Academy City have issued a joint statement."
The voice was cool and calm.
"'We are greatly concerned by mounting evidence that citizens of Academy City have intervened in today's incident in Hawaii. We do not wish to give them the power to sway the future of national governments, much less the future of the great nation that some call the world's police. Everything we've done has been in service of building partnerships with other nations to increase mutual benefit, but this is rooted first and foremost in other nations. If Academy City can dispatch personnel to alter the course of another nation's history, that cannot be called a partnership. We are neither subordinate to nor slaves of Academy City.'"
After a brief pause, the newscaster continued reading the statement.

"'Therefore, these twenty-seven chief organizations will hereby unilaterally break off all partnerships with Academy City. This is a necessary step to protect our country.'"

Kamijou paled.
His efforts to save someone had produced unintended consequences.
Perhaps…
Perhaps *this* was why Gremlin had started the crisis.
"…Aurey Blueshake wasn't the only one peeping through the F.C.E.," he said. "Were those partner organizations interfering in the network…?"
And then he recalled something.

Who was it who had told him that Gremlin was here in Hawaii and encouraged him to foil their plans?

Her.

She, too, was a sorcerer.

And unlike those in the English Puritan Church, she didn't belong to the side of peace, law, and justice.

"Birdway..."

He looked around. She'd disappeared. When had that happened?

"Birdway!"

He glanced at the hotel lobby from the lounge exit, but he didn't see her or any of her subordinates out there. He took out his cell phone. Even though he knew she might not pick up, he called her anyway, and surprisingly, he got a response.

"*Can't put two and two together without asking, eh?*"

"Did you make us come here because you knew this would happen?"

"*Twenty-seven was a little more than I thought, though. Decisions take time to make, and all those corporations are too specialized to run themselves in isolation. I expect they'll merge into three or four bigger groups in the near future.*"

"Answer my question, Birdway. Are you...? Were you...?"

The severance of twenty-seven major partners from Academy City. Internal strife on the science side.

It was the perfect avenue for Gremlin to gain a huge amount of power.

"Were you with Gremlin all along?!"

He was terrified of learning the answer to that question.

Birdway's response, however, was quite simple.

"*...I'll leave it to your imagination.*"

That was all.

She hung up.

As Kamijou tightened his grip on his phone, the breaking news announcement continued to play.

"*...While the partners responsible for this statement lack the technology to compete with Academy City, they did lend many* cutting-edge unmanned weapons to them for World War III, which are confirmed to still be in use in postwar peacekeeping efforts. If Academy City doesn't return these weapons, they may be looking at a large-scale conflict between its own military forces and..."

[Nov. 10 / Source: Oahu, a customer's cell phone camera in the lobby of an international hotel in Honolulu]

"Were you with Gremlin all along?!"

As Kamijou went into the lobby upon noticing something was wrong, Mikoto followed him and heard those words.

She wasn't able to hear the rest of his conversation, and the person on the other end of the line seemed to hang up rather quickly.

Kamijou stared at the small screen of his phone for a few moments. He was confused. The look of hopelessness on his face didn't suit him one bit.

That's not good, thought Mikoto, partly out of instinct.

She'd seen that look before. Once, she'd been wrapped up in a major incident involving cloned humans. It drove her body and mind beyond their limits until eventually, she'd tried to get rid of the mastermind herself, even though she knew it was suicide. At the time, she'd made that exact face. The very face he was making now.

What had he just found out?

And where was he about to go?

Mikoto didn't know the exact details, but there was one thing she felt safe assuming. Anyone with that look on their face wasn't headed toward the finish line. Even if their road went on and branched out for decades, centuries, their ultimate fate would be destruction—a pit to hell itself.

Kamijou was standing at a crossroads.

She clearly knew that one mistake would drive him off the path entirely.

But...

...I'm here now.

Mikoto faced forward, stifling the oppressive feeling in her heart.

She took a single step.

A step straight toward him.

...I'm not just here to watch. I'm not just going to learn what happened after it's all over this time. I'm here right now. I have the power to change reality before me!

How had it been for him?

When he'd confronted her as she embarked on a suicidal mission to solve the clone issue, when he'd felt pressure so intense it could distort the air around them, what had his determination felt like?

No, it didn't matter if they felt exactly the same way or not.

Not if she could bring him back.

...I took his hand and came here with him for a reason.

She could reach.

She would *make* it reach.

...All because I wanted a chance to bring him back to where he belongs!

And then.

The boy finally turned off his phone and muttered something to himself.

"...I was wrong."

A quiet voice. A very hoarse voice. A voice with no enunciation, a voice hard to even make out. But Mikoto felt like those three words had nailed her feet to the floor. His admission of defeat stabbed through the gaps between the gears of her mind like a strange curse.

"I was wrong! Birdway was manipulating me from the very start! Why? I had plenty of chances to figure it out. Dawn-Covered Sunlight gave me all the information on Gremlin. I should have realized it could have meant she had an ulterior motive!"

"Dawn-Covered Sunlight...?"

"I'm talking about Birdway. Leivinia Birdway. She and her lackeys took advantage of what happened today in Hawaii. She pit Academy City and its partners against each other and tried to do massive damage to the science side! ...And there's no guarantee the former partners will abide by the science side's rules, either. If Gremlin wants the science side's power and technology, they're the perfect people to strike a deal with!"

The balance between science and sorcery would utterly collapse.

Gremlin would throw everything into disarray.

"…Misaka, I'm not going back to Academy City."

He was clear.

Clear in his intent to set foot into a strange new world.

"I have to make up for this failure. I can't go home until I do. I have to solve everything that results from my mistake. I don't have the right to go back until I do!"

"…A failure."

Her near-paralyzed mind trembled.

And in those tiny shakes, she gained strength.

"It wasn't a failure."

She'd be clear, too, this time.

She spoke.

She was *able* to speak.

No matter how overwhelmed she felt, there was one thing she needed to set him straight on.

"I don't care who took advantage of what. We—you—protected the people of Hawaii from Gremlin! I won't let you deny that. I won't let you get it in your head that you failed by saving those people."

"Birdway worked the fact that people would be saved into her plans. If the conflict between Academy City and its ex-partners gets worse, the folks we saved will think other people are getting hurt because they were rescued! I can't let them carry that burden. Dawn-Colored Sunlight rescued me from the Arctic Ocean. They used me. I have to carry this alone!" Kamijou retorted.

There was a difference between someone who chose freely and someone who was only mixed up in things.

This time, Kamijou had decided to fight right from the beginning. He'd chosen, and he'd clearly chosen incorrectly. So now he was trying to shoulder everything on his own—he thought that doing otherwise would turn the people without the chance to choose into scapegoats. He didn't want people to blame the civilians he'd saved in Hawaii for all this.

And maybe that line of thought was correct.

Maybe Mikoto couldn't tear it down with hastily made counterarguments.

In which case, her only option was…

"…Then I'll help you carry it."

"…Misaka?"

"If we chose incorrectly in Hawaii, then, well… I was one of the people who messed up, too! If I'd chosen differently, maybe things would have turned out differently. If I'd ever had the chance to talk to Birdway, maybe I could have figured out what she was up to before all this happened! But I missed it. So I'm not letting you carry this burden by yourself. Just because you say you messed something up doesn't mean you need to carry it all on your own!"

After saying all that, Mikoto felt just a little bit better.

Maybe part of that was how dumbfounded the boy looked.

As if to deal the finishing blow, she added one thing.

"We're walking the same path. Don't ever forget that."

[Nov. 10 / Source: Oahu, the camera of a portable game device forgotten on a lobby sofa in a Honolulu hotel]

However, Misaka had forgotten one thing in particular.

At last, she remembered what the hard sensation in her palm was all about—but then closed her grip over it more tightly, hiding it in her hand.

Two rings.

The tag rings from Cupid's Arrow.

A one-of-the-kind pattern had been etched into them by electrolysis. The technique used to create this kind of jewelry gave rise to stories—ones not based in science—that tag rings were charms that could prevent adultery.

Generally, Mikoto didn't believe in phenomena that weren't based on science.

But then World War III had broken out, followed by the crisis in Hawaii. Even when such strange things had taken place right before her eyes, even though she knew they *seemed* to defy the laws of reality, she hadn't been able to just throw her hands up and chalk everything up to the occult.

And then.

Precisely because of that…

…she couldn't give him the ring. What did that mean? Had something happened to prevent her from being able to? She slipped them both back into her pocket, unable to see the truth of the matter.

[Nov. 10 / Source: Oahu, a camera on a food-order tablet in the lounge of an international hotel in Honolulu]

Kamijou let Mikoto drag him through the airport.

He was genuinely grateful for what she'd said to him.

But at the same time, he thought this:

I can't let someone willing to say all that to me stay involved in this. I'll have to settle things on my own after all.

With only a dozen or so centimeters between them.

With that one small action that didn't come to pass.

The future nevertheless clearly changed.

Perhaps not for the better.

[Nov. 10 / Source: Oahu, a storefront product camera at a cell phone store on Diamond Beach]

* * *

Acquiring a cell phone was much simpler in the United States than it was in Japan, as the market was flooded with prepaid phones. Several such samples sat on a stall in an open-air shop, where a girl tapped away at a smartphone.

Sample cell phones were usually dummied-up versions of the real thing, but the biggest selling point for smartphones in particular was how they felt to use. You might be able to explain their appeal in words, but it could be hard to visualize.

The girl had silver hair in braids and brown skin. The only things she was wearing were a pair of glasses and some overalls that sat right against her skin.

"These are pretty cool. But I'm not sure I should buy a second phone just because it's cool…"

"Think of it as a small device for hooking into networks instead of a cell phone. Lugging around a laptop's such a pain, right?"

"I feel like the laptop is small enough, though."

"It's just like air conditioners, regular cell phones, and convenience stores. We were all fine before we knew they existed, but now that we've found out about them, we'll never escape them. Smartphones are every bit as convenient."

"…You sound like a 'just say no to drugs' commercial. Like it's a bad thing that we found out about them."

The brown-skinned girl and the salesclerk went through the same basic script that usually happened.

She swiped the screen to the side, shifting her attention to the pre-loaded apps.

"Oh, hey. You can call up a map, too?"

"You can do just about anything with these. If you get lost with one of these babies on you, then you have fundamental brain issues."

"So strange to think this little device is connected to satellites in space."

She scrolled all over the map.

And then something strange happened.

The map screen suddenly seemed to blur out, and then she

got a whole bunch of messages that even the clerk, who did the maintenance on the phones, didn't recognize. It wasn't just a malfunction—it was clearly being overwritten by some sort of different programming code.

"All right," she said. "If the tech is this advanced, I might be able to link it up to my Soul Arm. Gold is used in the chip, after all."

"What the—?"

"Prepare for impaaact," she said sluggishly.

Boooooooom!!!!!!
A stream of pure white light fell from the sky into the ocean.

It had happened several kilometers away, and yet the shock wave reached them like the aftermath of a lightning bolt. Stall roofs were blown away, crashing into creaking and swaying palm trees. The clerk ended up upside down. His expression was more confused than terrified.

"I'll be taking this."

"What? …I'm sorry, what?"

"This thing here. Hmm… I won't need a contract or anything. I changed the settings so I can use it without one."

Then something else happened.

Kreesh-kreesh. There was a shrill sound like crystals hitting each other.

The brown-skinned girl glanced in the direction of the noise to find something unnatural approaching. Something that looked like an oil drum, except made out of black stone.

Nobody else would have realized that this it was a human who had altered themselves to the extreme.

The girl, however, spoke to it with the kind of tone one might use with a childhood friend.

"Oh? Whatcha need, you little spoiled kid? Keep clinging like that and your *tired* dvergr *older sister* is gonna sit on you."

The girl plopped herself right down on the oil drum, without asking it for permission.

She put her index finger to the screen of the smartphone she'd just acquired, messing around with it, a happy look on her face. If you looked at that part by itself, she would look like she was doing what *everyone* did when they touched a device like this for the first time.

However.

The conversation she was having was clearly abnormal.

"*Heya. Salonya A. Irivika failed. As we expected her to. They're probably relieved now that they've saved the United States. Nobody would believe that all we were after here was* the eruption of Mount Kilauea."

The brown-skinned girl gave a thin smile, then whispered something, as if she were talking to someone other than the person on the phone.

"…Nah, they'll think it's strange. The detonator is for stimulating artificial eruptions at Kilauea. It can't change the properties of the magma. Normally all that thick magma would have come bursting out, but for some reason, it was only some dry, old volcanic dust getting kicked up. *It'd be normal to assume there was another weird trick at play.*"

"*How is the output looking?*"

"Within acceptable range, I guess. As a natural reactor core, it's better than Iceland. Now that we've extracted the energy we need and solidified it, we can blow this popsicle stand. Phase one complete."

"*That was a long phase one.*"

"They called me here, remember? It wouldn't end that easily. More importantly, what about the blueprint?"

"*Brunhild Eichtbel, was it? The natural-born Valkyrie. I have an interesting report from her. It's only a piece of the spear, but if you can use it, then we're all good.*"

"I see. Then let's do this thing." The brown-skinned girl grinned. "Your path to the Gungnir is secure now, Odin—or should I say, Othinus."

"*It is indeed, little dark one—or should I say,* dvergr."

The girl used her index finger to end the call as the black cylinder she was sitting on wobbled around.

"Hey, quit that. That's rude—I'm not that heavy. Next, we have to think about what to do with Academy City's ex-partners... Huh?"

She abruptly looked up just as a sorcerer covered in wounds approached her.

"Uhhh. Who were you again?"

"...Cendrillon..."

"Hmm...? Oh! Right, I remember you! Yeah, you were the French sorcerer who got knocked out in round one right at the airport, right? How've you been since then, girl? Thought they pounded your head to a pulp."

"I escaped while everyone was preoccupied by the Kilauea eruption and Trident's invasion. More importantly..." She spat out some blood. "What was that just now?"

"What was what?"

"You said you expected the plan to fail, and also mentioned Kilauea being a reactor core, and also said the word Gungnir!"

"Sorry, not sure what you're talking about. Never said any of that."

"I thought the whole reason we used the PMC Trident to try and take down the United States was so we could make it into a theocracy and wreck the balance between the science side and the sorcery side!"

"What? Of course not. To begin with..."

The dark-skinned girl remained seated atop the cylinder.

"Gremlin isn't some group of losers who got crushed in the war, you know."

"......"

For a few moments, Cendrillon's thoughts completely stopped.

The dark-skinned girl continued in the meantime.

"Sure, I won't deny we sprung up because of the war, but our goals don't have anything to do with it. Besides, we only hired most of you as temp workers. We didn't want to waste our official members on this. But some sacrifices have to be made for things to work out. Once you fulfilled the requirements, we just said whatever to get you on our team. And man, did you all do a good job. Trident, Salonya, and you. Your score's been recorded as a contribution to the group, just so you know. You can be proud of it."

"That's… Don't give me that…!"

Impulsively, Cendrillon cast a spell to use an incredibly fast martial arts move in an attempt to grab the dark-skinned girl.

But then the girl fell backward over the cylinder and landed on the ground, and as she did, a shower of pale blue sparks exploded from the front of the cylinder.

"Gyah?!"

They quickly shot through Cendrillon's entire body, disabling her.

Moving herself into a sitting position from off the ground, the dark-skinned girl said, "No, don't do that. First thing you gotta do against projectile weapons is find cover. Mjölnir is my pride and joy—you'll never even come close to getting past it. It's powerful enough to roast the snake encircling the world whole. I'm not gonna sit here and say that sorcery is all about brains, but if you're having this much trouble making calculations, you probably shouldn't be on the front lines."

Grinning, she stuck her hand into the open side of her overalls and came out with several tools.

A hammer, a screwdriver, a saw, a hand drill, a file, a plane, and several others.

Aside from the fact they were made of gold, the objects were all things you could easily find in a home improvement store.

"Now then. Marianne Sringeneier, one of the world's precious few remaining *dvergr*, has a question for you, Miss Cendrillon, former French elite and now just a loser and a grumbling annoyance."

The tools certainly didn't seem like things one could alter someone's form with, but she lined them up on the cylindrical "person" as she continued.

"…I'm gonna make a few alterations to you. A table or a wardrobe… Which would you prefer to live as from now on?"

*   *   *

[Nov. 10 / Source: Oahu, surveillance camera at an immigration gate at New Honolulu International Airport]

Leivinia Birdway was at the airport.

One of the many men in black suits serving her, Mark Space, softly spoke to her.

"Are you sure that was the right thing to do?"

"I mean, what I'm doing is certainly subject to criticism."

"I was referring to simply revealing the truth to the boy."

"And where would that get me?" Birdway smiled sardonically. "Even if we chase down Salonya A. Irivika, we won't get a full picture of their organization. We need to force the sorcerers at the core of Gremlin to get more publicly involved in the world. Are you suggesting I split up the science side and leave the partner groups hanging there as bait?"

"It would probably be quite effective. There are signs that Gremlin tries to purposely work foreign objects from the science side into their spell construction. Until now, it was the PMC Trident, led by the U.S. media queen, but they won't have an easy time finding any large organizations to replace them. On top of that, *the group of partner organizations even possesses hoards of Academy City unmanned weapons.* We don't know Gremlin's ultimate goal, but if they need the power of science to get there, I can't think of more attractive bait."

"There's no guarantee. A little caution could dash that hope."

"Even so, we'll at least see them exercising that caution. Gremlin wants to pit themselves against Academy City. They don't want the group of partner organizations to meddle and ruin the balance of power. Whether they cooperate or oppose one another, Gremlin's next move will have to be based on those partners. In other words, *the bait will work no matter what they do.*"

"And so this is an act of justice? How naive of you," said Birdway without skipping a beat. "It doesn't matter what my goals are. The fact is that I separated twenty-seven partner organizations from

Academy City, removing them from their position among the world's defenders."

"……"

"Perhaps I had these intentions all along, but I'm the one who decided to act on them. They'll be criticized for ruining peace in the world, and if there's a direct clash, people will be hurt. And maybe even more. And *that* is not exactly something someone standing on the side of justice would do."

Birdway paused for a moment then, as if to confirm her own position.

"And I don't remember ever telling you I was on the side of justice, young man."

AFTERWORD

For those of you who have been reading one book at a time, it's good to see you again. For those who bought all the books at once, it's a pleasure to meet you.

I'm Kazuma Kamachi.

New Testament has reached its third volume! This time, the story is set on the Hawaiian Islands. I placed a little bit of a limitation on how things were shown to the reader, which should remind you of a certain gimmick.

The key occult concept here was the spell for controlling people.

But just as the characters pointed out in the story, there's never been an occult concept that took so much investigation. Even if a caster could make people act on their command, I think it's pretty vague whether that's actually because of something magical or if it was a trick all along, planned out in advance. It's sort of like claiming a dog can do mental math.

In terms of remnants of World War III, we have Russia first and foremost. The Russian Catholic Church links to fairies and spirits, but I wasn't sure if going for something like Lorelei, for example, would be too on the nose. After some research, I came across Leshy. Like other fae, Leshy is terrifying in one way—he wouldn't hesitate to kill a person—but oddly charming in another.

Besides that, Cendrillon is just casually part of the same system as Vasilisa in the Russian Church. Maybe that's worth checking out, too.

I also threw in some real effective countermeasures to Imagine Breaker.

The people who showed up at the very end are obviously of a different type from the Russians, which I think was clear enough to you, the reader.

I'd like to thank the illustrator, Haimura, and the editor, Miki. I know this must have been an annoying story with the sheer number of characters involved. Thank you so much for sticking with me for this long.

I'd also like to thank all my readers. I can only write such annoying stories because you all give us your energy and allow me to do so. Thank you all so much.

> *Now then, as you close the pages,*
> *and as I pray you will open the pages again next time,*
> *here and now, I lay down my pen.*

Oh, hey. A magic god's name finally showed up.

Kazuma Kamachi